Birds of Darkness

Ben Zeller

Strategic Book Publishing and Rights Co.

Strategic Book Publishing and Rights Co., LLC
USA I Singapore

For information about special discounts for bulk purchases, please contact Strategic Book Publishing and Rights Co. Special Sales, at bookorder@sbpra.net.

ISBN: 978-1-68181-410-0

Book Design: Suzanne Kelly

This book of fiction was inspired by the known and unknown sexually molested women of the Armed Services and by the known and unknown men who perpetrated the hellish crimes against them.

Acknowledgments

Many authors include a list of thank-yous to acquaintances, friends, and family, including detractors, cynics, and supporters. *Birds of Darkness* has had its share of each.

This novel was inspired, in part, by the work Kirsten Gillibrand of New York. A leader in the Senate, her Military Justice Improvement Act would create a professional, non-biased, and independent military justice system so survivors of sexual assault can get the justice they deserve.

If only behind the scenes, women are and always have been the true leaders in all societies. Men in charge cringe at the thought and attempt to relegate the female sex to the position of kitchen help, wet nurse, and sexual slagheap. Let there be change.

I thank all, male and female, kind enough to have listened to me read pages from the *Darkness* and those dedicated enough to read one of the early drafts. The book has definitely benefitted. My daughter Shannon may be my toughest adversary. Sierra Fourwinds is another. Lori Utley of La Veta plowed through a final draft correcting my dyslexic spelling—a monumental task.

In *Darkness*, the character of Hap, a man to listen to, the bartender for many years in the Big I, was in real time and life a close friend. Hap and his work behind the bar and on the many stages of Fairbanks will always be remembered in Alaska with love, pathos, and laughter.

Gene Earnest and Larry Irving are two master Alaskan raconteurs I have listened to for years. While researching and hacking out the first draft of *Darkness*, I moved into Larry and Kathy's Fairbanks home for months. Skip Lipscomb, an Alaskan bush pilot living on the family homestead on Chena Ridge, suggested the Helio Courier as the most versatile and safe bush plane Adriana could pilot. Skip has flown thousands of miles in that aircraft. The Helio, developed in the late forties, remains a favorite among bush pilots in Canada and Alaska. Reed White, a retired bush pilot from La Veta, Colorado, and the wilderness state of Montana, added his doubts and expertise to an early draft of my narrative. And thanks to Tom Cade with whom I have paddled miles and miles of the Colville River. Thanks to all for their input. It has made this a better book. Furthermore, I wish to sincerely thank Suzanne Kelly Print Manager at SBPRA for the direct simplicity and strength of her presentation of this novel.

Ben.

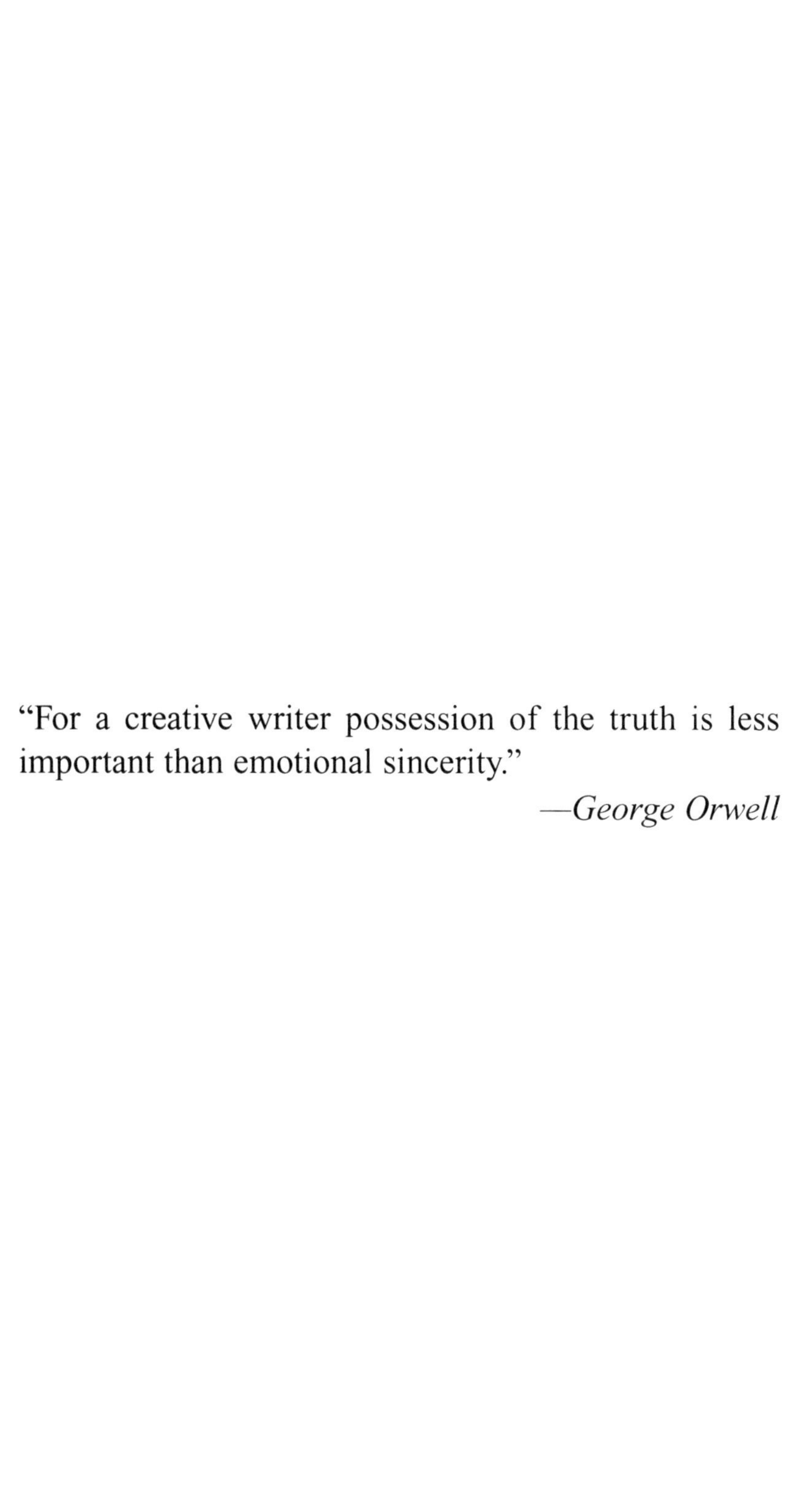

"For a creative writer possession of the truth is less important than emotional sincerity."

—*George Orwell*

CHAPTER 1

Midnight Poison

From a dead sleep, Jack Kerns snapped to a sitting position. In the chill air he was suddenly wide-awake and listening. It was darker still. The moon had followed the sun down over Antigun Summit miles above the Alaskan Arctic Circle. The sound of a plane diminished in the distance. There was nothing else to hear. *Nothing disturbs nature*, Kerns thought, *so what the hell woke me up?* The engine of the plane ceased throbbing all together. Nature was now silent as death, a troubling thought. He smiled at that assumption. *Mother Nature isn't this silent*, Kerns reasoned. *She always has a reason: a breath of air at least. Some foreign noise besides that plane was loud enough to wake me: a sudden noise—a crashing noise.* He relived it now, his sleeping mind remembering the unusual. Whatever it was, that noise had silenced Nature.

Kerns was not frightened, but he definitely was curious—and careful. He slid out of his sleeping bag and pulled on his britches. He took the time to lace his boots. If he had to move quickly he didn't want the laces tripping him up. He slipped his Smith & Wesson into the holster on his belt and gripped his unlit flashlight. Kerns could be as quiet as nature's shadow. He was that quiet now. The only sound he made was silence.

Moving in slow circles, like a wolf searching for spoor on padded feet, he felt for spruce branches and tested each step before placing any weight on it. His eyes, now accustomed to the starlit dark, picked the path. The mossy ground was damp and quiet beneath his feet. He was in the swamp now, sinking deeper into the tundra with each step.

He spotted something, half in and out of the murky water of the small pond he had seen when he made camp. It was a lighter color than the green around it. It didn't move. Kerns didn't blink for thirty seconds. The chalk-white shadow in the mud suddenly gave vent to perhaps a human sigh, or moan. Kerns flipped on his light.

A naked body lay half buried in the moss and mucky water. Kerns holstered the pistol he had drawn and stepped quickly forward. The person's hands were lashed behind his back. The head was twisted into the mud. Kerns turned the body face up. It was a man—a man terribly bruised and broken, but miraculously, maybe, still alive. Kerns studied the ground for signs of someone having dragged the body in. Nothing. It was clean. "Somebody was really pissed off at you, man." Kerns spoke his thoughts quietly.

Then he looked up. Limbs of the thick black spruce stand above him were freshly broken; the bark was stripped clean, the white of the coniferous under layer bright in the new light that struck it, white as the body in the dark mud. Kerns looked up again, recalling the sound of the plane. "You came from the air, man," he spoke aloud. "What you do to them to make them tie your hands behind your back and shove you naked out into the night? It was a long way down. You maybe dropped ten thousand feet. There is nowhere else you could have come from." Kerns studied the area again. "Where else could you come from?" Kerns spoke in a whisper, not expecting an answer. He was talking to a dead man.

***

Jack Kerns, a freelance journalist and photographer, was returning from a month and a day above in the headwaters of the great Colville River. He was photographing gyrfalcons on the western rocky crags of Alaska's Brooks Range. His friend, Curtis—Dr. Curtis as in PhD—had been on the North Slopes of the Brooks Range studying habits of the gyrfalcon a month before him. Curtis was writing an article on the great bird's present health and population. The gyrfalcon was the largest of the falcon family and one of the fastest killers in the air. Curtis's article would be much more academic than the one Kerns hoped to sell to a hunting and fishing magazine, or *High Country News*, but Curtis would use Kerns' photographs. That was a plus. Kerns tentatively named his article "Birds of Darkness." Curtis's scholarly paper, *The Gyrfalcon Today*, among other things, would trace the effect the severe Arctic climate change will have on the bird's survival.

Kerns left his friend in the darkening northern latitude where Curtis chose to remain as long as the weather permitted. It was an iffy permission. Mother Nature controlled the weather and Mother Nature moved at her own will and speed.

Kerns had hired a bush pilot to fly him, his camera, and his equipment from the shores of a grassy, unnamed slip of water in the wilderness to the bleak town of Deadhorse, outside of Prudhoe Bay. He'd parked his camper at Deadhorse a month earlier where she'd picked him up and flown him in to find his friend. Heading back today, their takeoff was on the sharp edge of life's experience. Adriana O'Donovan—a beautiful name for a beautiful lady, Kerns thought—if not very talkative, was one hell of a pilot. As she pushed the throttle full forward Kerns held his breath, clutching the seat. The pontoons whipped through nothing but wet grass as they rose from the opposite shore of the lake. At this point Kerns started once again to breathe. Beneath them, during the remainder of the flight, was a beautiful palette of pastels and bright fall colors. Above the Arctic Circle, Alaska, as Kerns knew it, was a land of infinite beauty, danger, and untamed mystery. It hadn't disappointed him this time.

Adriana brought her Helio Courier down smoothly at the north end of the Alaskan pipeline. The controversial oil pipeline was bordered by the rough, frost-heaved, sparsely paved Dalton Highway. From Deadhorse, Kerns drove his pickup and camper south toward Fairbanks, a rough frontier town he had called home in years past. It was now a town of Wal-Mart's, Home Depots, and Sam's Clubs.

Behind the wheel heading south, Kerns dodged eighteen-wheel semis on the mud-slicked highway. It was a bit more unsettling than the first leg of his journey in Adriana's competent hands. At the crest of Antigun Pass and dozing at the wheel, Kerns stopped and stepped out to shake himself awake. At 4,739 feet, Antigun Pass was the highest point on the highway. It offered fantastic views from its many switchbacks. Driving again, he passed the farthest north spruce tree above the Arctic Circle. Vandals had carved limbs and bark off it for souvenirs. The stalk of the lone tree was now dead.

Some miles south, Kerns pulled his 4x4 and old slide-in camper a half mile off the road into a small island of living spruce trees. The sounds of the heavy truck traffic, semis and tankers filled with natural gas, would be somewhat muffled. He needed a good night's rest. Wanting to sleep in the open, which was his choice if he had one—and he had that choice tonight—he parked and grabbed his light down sleeping bag. Kerns pushed his way through the struggling black spruce, clinging precariously to the permafrost. He spotted a small shallow pond, mostly swamp, through the scattered rat-tailed trees. On a slight rise he would be dry and comfortable. He would make it into Fairbanks tomorrow.

Kerns stripped down to the raw. He hated to sleep encumbered by clothes. He rolled out his bag and, exhausted, crawled in. The bag was warm from the long drive in the passenger seat of his 4x4. It felt good. The late September sun had gone into hiding behind Antigun Pass. The arctic village of Wiseman, his proposed destination for the night, was still miles ahead of him. *So what,* he thought. *It's only time*. The days were growing shorter. Kerns wouldn't spend much of it admiring heavenly bodies tonight. He checked his flashlight and .357 Smith & Wesson. He had no plans to shoot any barren land grizzlies if one came sniffing around. He was not a picture-taking tourist. A shot in the air would direct the bear's thinking in another direction. Bears possessed a brilliant sense of smell. Kerns felt they could detect the scent of the strong fluid used to clean firearms and stand back. People without guns smelled like prey. Kerns was asleep in minutes.

No dreams would wake him tonight. It wasn't a dream that woke him.

***

Standing now in the swamp looking down at the naked body, Kerns spoke quietly: "Buddy," he murmured to the mess before him. "I can't be gentle, but I got to move you, man. You are as good as dead, or already there."

The body was oozing blood, ruptured flesh swelling from the burst torso sinking in the moss and wet. Everything was broken—bones shattered and protruding—splinters of white and blood. "Shit," Kerns whispered into the night. "Well, that too."

Holding his small flashlight in his teeth, Kerns stepped knee-deep into the mud and slime. He lifted the body in his arms. The body opened its eyes, or at least one of them. Kerns, amazed at the sign of life, kept walking toward his camper. He laid the mud-slick, bloody load on his clean sleeping bag.

"I got you this far, or what's left of you this far. Can you tell me anything before you leave?" The eye was still open but chalked a dull off-white shade. "I guess it's too late for that, huh?"

The man convulsed. The body managed to take a deep breath, the first breath Kerns saw him take, and the last one. Bloody air and mud bubbled from the shattered lungs. It exhaled: an angry blast, and with it came his final and frustrating words. "Midnight Poison!" was the cry. The body was now truly dead. Kerns turned the flashlight on the face of his watch. It was twelve, midnight, September 17, 2013. *He's right on time*, Kerns thought. *That's something.*

***

In the darkness of the arctic night the journalist was now stuck with a double problem: writing the article "Birds of Darkness." So far all he had accomplished in that direction was to come up with the title and a few hundred digital photographs. Now he had Midnight Poison from the sky. He was committed to "Birds of Darkness." Midnight Poison might be better left in the swamp. That was where it was meant to be. He couldn't believe the depositor of the dead wanted the deed, let alone the dead discovered. Kerns had no desire to involve himself in the bloody situation, and it was bloody. But what to do? Should he simply replace the body, burn his ruined sleeping bag, and drive out? That would be the best exit for him. But what about this poor fucker lying at his feet, his broken arms tied behind his broken back? He would have to turn the body over to somebody, somebody in questionable authority, at which point in the scenario Kerns would be definitely involved. He couldn't just drop it off on a doorstep in Wiseman. He had a useless cell phone with probably a hundred messages on it. There was no service on the Colville and there would be none on his phone until he arrived in Fairbanks, an estimated two hundred and sixty-some frost-heaved, rough miles south on the Dalton Highway.

While battling with his frustration, he cut the rope tying the man's hands together. As he did so, he noticed the skin on the wrists had burned away as if battery acid had been poured over it. And the rope—it was not nylon, but an old hemp rope—was being eaten away. The strands were turning to mush. While contemplating this, he realized his hands, which had touched the rope, were burning as well. He quickly went back to the muddy water of the swamp and rinsed them over and over until the acid, or whatever, was neutralized.

Why in the hell had the rope been meant to disintegrate? There would be no sign of it if the body were discovered in a week's time. Kerns nodded his head in understanding. The perfect crime. Despite the blood and guts angle, Kerns' curiosity was tweaked. The whole bizarre episode was becoming dangerously intriguing. He filled the camper's sink with clean water and soaked the rope in it until there was no reaction. He sealed the clean strands in a plastic baggie. At some point he would have to give the body up to authorities. The rope was evidence of some sort. The ambiguity fit in well with the rest of this Midnight Poison bullshit.

Kerns didn't trust the FBI or the CIA, and the locals could well be as incompetent, or corrupt, as those mentioned. *Probably are*, he thought. But right now, what to do with the body? The scent of blood could and would draw in scavengers. If he was going to turn the mess over to the law, he would have to keep the evidence as uncontaminated as possible. His sleeping bag was ruined already. *Okay, the bag is fucked. I've got to leave this wingless, bloody bird wrapped in my no-longer-any-good down bag somewhere*, he thought bitterly. The blood and offal would dry and stick the body to it. Who would want to sleep in it after that? "So be it." He turned to the dead man. "Listen, buddy, you are not only fucking up my life by flying into it with your Midnight Poison, you're fucking up my new hundred-and-eighty-dollar bag."

Even in September, above the circle, the arctic nights were short. It was now well after midnight. Arctic fall was seeping into the picture with color and cold. The only advantage to this picture: the body would keep—at least it wouldn't disintegrate in summer heat. Best he get it to Fairbanks. He would think of someone to turn it over to on the way.

His friend, Hap, bartender at the International Bar—the Big I, it was called—would know of an honest lawman in this country, if there was one. His mind made up, Kerns left the body to stiffen a bit, making it easier to handle. He scrambled up a batch of eggs and dried onions for breakfast. *It's going to be another long fucking day*. He brewed up a thermos of strong coffee, remembering, as he did so, that there was a public phone in Wiseman. It was the one thing in that arctic village that, if not friendly, was at least neutral and was said to work. It was in a box nailed to a tree a hundred yards from the nearest cabin. He could use a credit card to pay for the call. He would be in Wiseman soon. It was now two in the morning. Dawn would be breaking in the northeast when he got there. No one of a dozen hearty souls left in Wiseman for the winter would be up to question him. He would call Hap in Fairbanks and fill him in as to what was happening. Hap knew everybody. He would think of someone to handle this situation quietly. *Good bartenders are like that*, Kerns thought. *They know more than anyone else about what's going on in any town*. Kerns loaded Midnight Poison and drove back out toward the Dalton Highway. A soft rain was falling. That was unusual here this time of year. Hell, the weather was changing everywhere. Kerns needed some sleep, but right now he was too wound up. He was wide-awake as he pulled onto the rough, half-paved pipeline road. He held his speed between thirty-five and forty in the misting rain. If need be, he would sleep in the cab of his truck an hour or so after pulling into Wiseman.

***

The phone in Wiseman was dry in the makeshift box. It worked. No one answered at the Big I. Kerns left a rather detailed message for Hap and drove on. It was the best he could do.

The rain was steady enough to turn the fine Alaskan dust to mud when he filled his tank with gas at the Coldfoot Roadhouse. He managed to sleep for an hour then filled his thermos with strong coffee at the cafe and moved on. The road was slimy when he carefully negotiated "Oh Shit Corner," a ninety-degree turn at the bottom of a mile-long 12 percent grade. The Alaskan green sign with white lettering stood out officially as Kerns rounded the turn at a safe twenty-five miles per hour. That was fast enough with the top-heavy camper loaded as it was and lashed to the bed of his pickup. It was probably a day like this when "Oh Shit Corner" was named by a truck driver as he went over the steep embankment. "Oh shit, indeed," Kerns murmured. "Oh shit" had been the driver's last words. Kerns pushed on, thinking of the trucker jackknifed in the twisted steel.

It was well after noon when he pulled to a stop at the crossroads in Fox. He went into the Howling Dog, a bar he remembered from twenty years in the past, and ordered a double rye. Alaska had changed a lot in the past twenty years: more roads, more people, a Sam's Club. But in some respects it was still the same. This bar was the same. The Big I was still the same; new clientele and different music, but the bartender was still the same. Kerns thought of the stiff in his camper. He looked at the bars on his cell phone. Service. He punched the number of the Big I. Hap answered. It was after two p.m. and still misting rain.

"The bar's open and has been since seven. Who did you want, or what do you want?"

"It's me, Hap—Kerns," Kerns said. "I'm in Fox, at the Howling Dog. Did you find someone to help me out? I'll be there in half an hour."

"I got your message and your man—Slim Dickerson, Chief of Detectives for the State Troopers. Slim is definitely interested in falling bodies. He's waiting for my call now. He'll be here when you get here. Don't stop too long at the Howling Dog. That bar can screw up a good man's intentions."

"I'm on my way." The bartender set Kerns's drink down in front of him. "Well, I'm almost on my way. It's been a dry month, Hap. No booze in Deadhorse and Coldfoot only has beer." Kerns pushed the "end call" button. He took a few minutes to sip his drink. He paid with a generous tip and was back at the wheel.

***

It was three p.m. The body was now firm but aging as Kerns drove into Fairbanks. He pulled up in back of the International Bar. He cracked the door of the camper and shook Flyboy's leg. Kerns had named the body Flyboy. You don't carry nameless bodies around in your camper. Flyboy's leg was stiff. The whole bundle shook, emitting the early scent of death. Looking about, Kerns relocked the camper and headed into the Big I by the back door. His friend Hap sat with a medium height, heavyset man at the south end of the bar. Patrons were scattered in an orderly fashion sipping red beers and Bloody Marys or sleeping, their heads wrapped in the arms of last night's dream. Hap silently led Kerns and the heavyset man with him to a table at the back of the room.

"This might be the man you want, Kerns, but beware, he's honest and so not to be trusted. He goes by the name of Slim Dickerson. As a state trooper, he carries a badge and a gun. The troopers are fish and game enforcers in this state as well as people cops. You want the usual?"

"Rye and soda."

"Right, splash of soda." Hap nodded to Slim. "Mr. Dickerson drinks coffee."

"Nothing wrong with not drinking. You a trooper? Fish and wildlife?"

Slim set his eyes on Kerns. "That covers murder, mayhem, rape, child abuse, mate beating, traffic tickets, and shooting a moose out of season. The moose comes first. What have you got, Kerns?"

"Mate beating?"

"Husband brutalizes his wife/girlfriend, boyfriend, or vice versa. It carries through to lesbians and homosexuals." His eyes still on Kerns, Slim sipped his coffee.

"I got a dead guy out there in my camper," Kerns said. "He was pushed out of a moving vehicle north of Wiseman at midnight last night."

"At midnight? You saw it, or rather, you witnessed it?"

"I was a few minutes late. The gentleman made mention of the time just before he died." Kerns thought a moment. "Maybe he said it after he was dead."

"He was still alive?"

"Spruce trees and mud broke his fall. If he was alive, he was not well."

Hap set Kerns' drink down on the table. Kerns took a healthy sip. "What's the fish and wildlife got to do with human murders, Hap?"

"You asked for an honest lawman. Out-of-season moose murder is the heaviest crime in this state, Kerns. It's the one law that has not changed here since you left the state twenty years ago. It carries a heavy sentence—up to twenty years. You shoot me, or your mother, I doubt if you get five." Hap returned to the bar.

"With good behavior, you'll be out in two," Slim said. He set his coffee down. "I've heard a lot about you, Kerns. Most of it, be it legal or illegal, is good. Now fill me in on this vehicular homicide, and then we'll take a look at the body in the truck."

"The vehicle was, I believe, a plane." Slim's eyes didn't waver. Kerns went on. "As the male body was naked, his hands tied behind his back, I don't think his descent was unassisted."

"This is a stupid TV cop question, Kerns, but out of curiosity I got to ask it. What were you doing under this plane fifty miles north of Wiseman?"

"Sleeping."

"How close to you did the body hit the ground?"

"Close enough to wake me up." Kerns finished his drink in one swallow. Slim set his cup down and got up.

"Follow me out to my place. It's private. We'll take a look at him there then go to the landing site." Slim headed for the back door, waving to Hap on the way.

Kerns followed him out. Hap was fixing a Bloody Mary.

***

"Holy shit."

"I don't know how holy it is, Slim, but there is a lot of it. My sleeping bag is fucked." They were at Slim's homestead on Chena Ridge north of Fairbanks. Slim's log cabin was quite secluded.

"That is too nice a term for it, Kerns. Let's get this mess out of your camper. I'll photograph it. We'll load it in my truck and I'll take it to the trooper's morgue. I don't think you should be seen with it. You are involved enough as it is. Incidentally, and to keep you in the ring, this is the second body we've found like this."

"The second?"

"The first one I found. Spotted it from a helicopter. It was nothing but bones. There was some shredded fiber with it, but no clothes."

Kerns snapped. "Rope soaked in acid."

"Rope?"

"Yeah, the rope the guy's hands were tied with. It was soaked in what smelled like battery acid—sulfuric acid. I got it in a baggie in the front." Kerns brought it out and handed it to Slim. "These might be the fibers you mentioned. It would be all that was left of them if whoever it was who tied him up used the same acid. It smelled like sulfuric acid. There should be enough of it in the residual left in the baggie to analyze it."

"That's very thoughtful of you, Kerns. Thanks." Slim looked at the baggie. The rope was still together. "I'll have them check it out in the lab."

"Thanks for not taking me with you. I'm going to air this damn camper out before I go. I'll be around if you need me. Just check with Hap."

"Wait here, if you would. Make yourself at home. The door's open. I want to look at the landing site. I'll be back with a chopper. We can fly up there if you don't mind. I need you to identify the location and which direction the plane flew in from."

Kerns shrugged. "Okay with me. I might be asleep when you get back. You think you got a serial killer?"

Slim shrugged. "There may be a tie-in between the two. The rope you salvaged might help prove that. That, and the fact that the first one seems to have come from the sky as well. Perhaps we can identify this one thanks to your being in the right—or wrong—place at the right time. I'll get on the road. Be back soon. Help yourself to my recliner in front of the stove."

Flyboy loaded and covered with a tarp, Slim got into his state pickup. He rolled the window down. "Kerns, there's a can of aerosol in the bathroom. It might help you get rid of the stink in your camper." Slim headed back toward town. Kerns tied the door of his camper open and headed into Slim's log cabin for the stink eradicator. It was an hour later when the *pop, pop, pop* of chopper blades cutting up the air above him snapped Kerns to his feet. He and Slim headed north. It was a smoother trip than on the ground—faster, too.

***

CHAPTER 2

The Major

Major Almas A. Cooper III, a New England Son of the American Revolution, was a flying ace in the US Air Force and father of a soon-to-be first lieutenant graduating this year from the Air Force Academy in Colorado. Major Cooper was married to the same woman for twenty-five years.

The major was not a happy camper. It was the second time he had been passed up for a promotion. Major Cooper felt he should be Colonel Cooper this afternoon, but the official notice in the envelope in his hand proved him wrong. *It's that goddamn woman*, he thought bitterly. *We should have killed her instead of trusting fate to do it for us*. That was years ago. *Better her ghost to haunt me than to have the shade of her bogus accusation blot my record*. "Fuck her!" He crumpled up the paper angrily in his hand but thought better of hurling it randomly into the blowing leaves of an early Alaskan fall. The air force had been shopping him around for the past five years. So be it. But why the hell had he been shipped to this godforsaken post to disappear in the darkness? *That is probably her fault, too*. Cooper's thoughts were not pleasant.

Velma, the major's wife of twenty-five years, standing back in the shadow of the kitchen in their living quarters, watched him through the bleak venetian blinds of the window. She cringed, murmuring to herself, "He didn't get it. May the lord help us." She crossed to the cupboard where they kept the liquor. "God help me, anyway." She pulled down the mixing for martinis: gin for the major, vodka for her. She splashed vodka into a fluted glass. She needed it right now. She drank and rinsed the glass in the kitchen sink. *He'll be in a foul mood.* She heard the front door slam open and shut. *He already is.* She jerked, nervously spilling some of the crushed ice she was chilling the glasses with. Then he was standing before her, his solid six foot two inches framed in the kitchen arch of their allocated base apartment. He took the glass roughly from her and spilled gin over the ice. Furtively she set garlic-stuffed olives on the table and chilled him another glass.

"Bad news?" she said foolishly. He strained the first gin through his slightly crooked teeth and rolled the crumpled envelope out on the table.

"In there." Trembling, Velma noticed the compressed envelope start to relax and unfold. Quickly she rattled ice into the shaker and measured two shots of gin over it. She splashed in a dash of scotch. His "signature" drink. He called it an Edinburgh Martini. Everything he did had a signature, it seemed. She stirred the drink gently with his gin spoon—another signature—a long-handled sterling spoon she had carried for him as long as she could remember. The crushed envelope had almost flattened out. She took the major's crystal martini glass, swirled the ice three times, and dropped the cubes into the sink. She strained the mixture of gin and scotch into the glass. The drink measured out exactly to the rim. He lifted it without spilling a drop. Velma saluted him hesitantly with her empty glass.

"I'll be in my study," he said, turning his back to her. "If the phone rings, don't answer it." The major's study was the basement of their apartment, the apartment they had waited over six months to move into. The first months in the north they had lived off post in a foul-smelling apartment in the little town of North Pole, twenty miles south of Fairbanks. This, even as a duplex, was far more to his liking. He set up his space in the basement. It was dark, quiet, and comfortably overheated. The basement was his domain—his signature domain. The cleaning lady was not allowed in the basement unless he was there to oversee her work. A Sesame combination padlock only he knew the combination to kept the basement door locked. Velma never stepped into the basement. Under orders, she was afraid to. Her washer and dryer were on the first floor, as was the sewing machine she never used. One of three small bedrooms was established as her sewing room. The kitchen and sewing room were her stations. The washer and dryer fit in next to the back door. She had, as yet, no friends on the post. Velma was resigned to the fact that she never would have any real friends on post. As yet she had not spoken to their next-door neighbor. She could sometimes hear her, or the lady's husband, through the thin interior walls. Velma thought he was a captain. They listened to TV late at night. Velma had little curiosity concerning them. If their television or arguments bothered her, she turned up her TV to drown it out.

Reaching for the outside world, she sent email messages to her son and her older sister from a laptop in her sewing room. Velma's life was, in her silent words, "a fucking bore." She watched the major close the door behind him as he descended into the darkness. She wondered what he did down there. The thought of masturbation flashed through her mind. They hadn't had sex in years. Veta, her sister, presented Velma with a nine-inch dildo, complete with instructions. It was a going-away present, she said, when she heard Velma was heading for the Arctic. Velma feigned shock. She did, however, when she was flown north by the US Air Force to join her husband, pack it in her overnight bag with an extra set of batteries.

Velma poured herself a vodka and prune juice in a coffee cup, dropped in a couple of ice cubes, and sat at the kitchen island sipping and trying not to think. She was pretty good at not thinking. It passed the boring time, especially if she had a sip or two of vodka to chase it down. A fucking bore. She never said the "f" word out loud, but it pleased her to think it. She had written it once or twice to her sister. Veta used it all the time. Veta was older and stronger.

She took her drink into the sewing room and opened her laptop. There was a note from her sister. She snapped it to the screen eagerly.

Velma, it read, *get your buns into gear or you are going to die up there. That guy you are married to is an asshole. I've told you that before. You need someone young and fresh. Did you try to get on any of those sex sites I listed for you? The major won't believe you're doing it, although I am sure he is rooted into a number of them right now himself. It would do him good to see your longing face staring back at him from the little screen, crying out to be laid by a young private. Try the "married but horny" site. The major would be afraid of that one.*

Now, hold your breath, little sister. (Velma was already doing that.) *I never told you your major came on to me once some years ago. Your major has a major problem, Velma, besides ED—erectile dysfunction. When faced with an open door, he couldn't get it up. I laughed in his face. That was a mistake. He didn't think it was funny at all. He's strong. He hit me with his fist, a glancing blow, but it knocked me down and he then tried to strangle me. Now, that turned him on. Raping me, Velma, turned him on. He got off on it. I was pretty beat up. I told you I had fallen down the stairs. He is a double-sided dangerous animal that major of yours. I gave in so he wouldn't kill me. After the few seconds it took him to ejaculate, I swore to him I would never tell you—or anyone. The time has run out on that promise, Velma. You deserve better. You need to know these things.*

It was long ago. I hope you're not pissed off at me.

Your loving sister, Veta.

***

Dumbfounded, Velma stared at the screen. Two silent minutes later, still somewhat founded, she got up and stumbled into the kitchen where she poured another cup of vodka. She ignored the prune juice this time as well as the ice. She drank the vodka. It didn't do anything to her. She was already numb.

"I always wondered how she fell down those stairs," Velma said to herself. "Veta is always so well balanced." She poured another vodka and stared into it bleakly.

"That son of a bitch fucked my sister." She said the word out loud this time. She got up and walked to the basement door. She snapped the padlock shut on the major's cave. "Fuck him!" She smiled. It wasn't a happy smile.

***

CHAPTER 3

Adriana

Kerns sat at a table in a dark corner of the Big I making mental notes of the happenings of the past few days. He never wrote down his thoughts, unless on his laptop when doing an article. His mind was his notebook. He couldn't read his handwriting anyway. Being dyslexic, he had, as a cover-up for this mental twist in his distorted brain, discovered a cover-up. It was simple. In high school Kerns adjusted his penmanship so it was illegible. It worked. None of the teachers could read what he wrote. He failed many tests, but at least he felt confident they didn't know he couldn't spell. Kerns still couldn't spell. The spell-checker on his laptop was, in most cases, a godsend. In other cases—like "two," "to," and "too"—he often used "as well." Kerns could spell "as well." He used it redundantly. He passed his manuscripts on to his daughter, Salome, for a final edit. Salome straightened it out.

Salome's mother, who originally edited his manuscripts, died giving birth to their second child, stillborn, on a cold, dark, winter day. They were living in a log cabin deep in the wilderness north of Fairbanks. No phone, no water but melted snow, and no electricity. They bathed in a small sauna he built. One night, six months pregnant, Salome's mother started having cramps shortly after they went to bed. Kerns relived that dreadful night many times. At first she didn't wake Kerns, thinking the cramps would subside. They didn't. Silently they grew worse until they were unbearable.

Kerns awoke in a screaming nightmare. The bed was soaking wet with blood and the water of birth and death. His wife was on the floor crying out in pain. Salome, four years old, was trying to comfort her. Kerns, in a panic, grabbed the battery for the truck. He kept it inside to keep the charge hot.

A fine, sand-like Alaskan snow, in a light wind at sixty below, was packing hard drifts in the narrow drive. He swept the hood of the 4x4 clean and flipped it up. He connected the positive and negative cables. The freezing engine wouldn't turn fast enough to fire. His fingers numb with cold, he grabbed the small propane tank outside the cabin door. A torch was attached to it. From the drifting snow beside the sauna he dug out a six-foot length of stovepipe with a ninety-degree elbow screwed on at one end. He scooped snow out from under the truck. Frantically he thrust the pipe beneath the oil pan with the elbow turned up. With fire from the propane torch at the outside end, the flame was meant to heat the engine oil in the pan without setting it on fire. After ten or twenty minutes of this treatment it would usually kick over.

He opened the valve on the tank and struck sparks at the end of the torch. The tank was full, but there was no gas in evidence at the torch end. There was no fire. The gas would not flow. It never occurred to Kerns that propane could freeze. He took the tank into the house to try to find the problem. The white tank was quickly covered with a blanket of hoarfrost, which slowly melted away in the warmth of the cabin. In half an hour, as the tank warmed, the gas flowed when he opened it. He raced back to the truck. This time the spark struck into flame. Heat rushed through the length of the stovepipe and warmed the oil. It worked. In twenty minutes he had the truck running. But it was too late. Frantically he bundled up his dying wife and four-year-old daughter. Kerns bulled his way through drifts for thirty miles. When they reached Saint Joe's hospital across from the Big I, Salome's mother was gone. The premature baby son was a dead fetus.

Kerns never forgave himself for his actions, for selfishly taking his pregnant wife and daughter into the wilderness with him. Even today, twenty years later, he was not forgiving. Kerns learned a terrible lesson that day. Propane gas freezes at fifty-five below zero. He learned later it had been sixty below in Fairbanks and surrounding areas.

Kerns married again, but it didn't last. To fill the vacancy, he settled for a vasectomy and numerous affairs. The hurt never healed. The guilt always dug at his heart. His sister and friends helped with the raising of Salome. His daughter, when grown into a woman, forgave him. To his great pride, Salome was now working on a master's degree in journalism in Pennsylvania. *She is a much better writer than I am. She always will be*, he thought.

Hap, who had been there the night of that tragedy, came up behind Kerns. He laid his hand on his friend's shoulder gently. "Kerns, you are thinking dark thoughts again. Here's another shot of rye. The bar isn't giving it to you. I'm running you a tab."

"I'm all right."

"I know. Under new skin of the present the past is always a running sore." Hap pulled back a chair and sat to change the lingering subject on his friend's mind. "What did you and Slim find up there north of Wiseman? Anything new?"

"Just as I left it. Slim needed to walk the area so he could tell the story with some assurance. He did comment that it was not the finest place to body surf. Jesus Christ, Hap, that poor fucker ripped a furrow in the moss and mud about forty feet long. In the dark I never saw it. He must have been dead before I found him. The words were just planted in his brain when he hit the ground. They were packed down his throat with mud and his last gasp of air. The reverse pressure built up so high they just burst out." Hap shook his head.

"Midnight Poison, right?"

"I checked my watch. It was right on the stroke of midnight. The bombardier had perfect timing. Jesus, what a way to go. He had to see it coming."

"Hell, it was dark, Kerns."

"Those kinds of things you can see coming, even in the dark, Hap." Kerns thumbed through his mind clogged with history. "You ever read that story written about our Civil War, 'An Occurrence at Owl Creek Bridge'? About a civilian rebel hung from a railroad bridge. They just put a rope around his neck and dropped him through the ties. In the story, the rope snaps and the hanged man escapes in a nightmare of survival. He scrambles thirty miles through a raging flood and a hallucinogenic forest to his home where, as he reaches to embrace his wife, he comes to the end of his reality rope. They made a movie about it I think. It was a bullet, not a rope. *Passion Play*. Megan Fox and Mickey Rourke. Well this guy I found up north had over a thousand feet to think on the way down. That's a lifetime of hope."

"And no rope."

"Christ, Hap, you think of the damnedest angles to any story."

"I'm going to make the movie." Hap grinned. "*A Thousand Feet to Think*. You like the title? Ambrose Bierce wrote that 'Owl Creek' story, didn't he? And he came to his mysterious end in a Mexican Civil War. No one ever found a trace of him." Hap shook his head in wonder. "At least the other guy came to the end of his rope, Kerns, or faced the bullet."

"Thank God you brought me another shot of rye to go along with your bullshit, Hap."

"My pleasure, your tab." Hap got to his feet to tend to bar business. "I must write this shit down, Kerns, so I don't forget it. I'm making notes for a film script that takes place in Alaska. This will spice it up."

"Good luck with your fantasies, Hap." Kerns fell back into his solitary thinking.

The back door of the bar opened. Gray light cut sharply around the shadow that walked in. The light from the open door blinded Kerns for a moment. He strained to see who the shadow was.

"Kerns," a voice said. It was a female voice and familiar.

"Who is it?" Kerns asked. The door closed and shut the blind out of his eyes. "Adriana?"

"What are you doing here?" the voice answered. The body with the voice moved over to Kerns' table. "I left you in Deadhorse."

"With my truck and camper, right. I drove down. It's slower, but it works."

"You're lucky you got here. There's a front coming in over Antigun Pass. I don't think the truckers will even be able to make it through to Coldfoot. I'm supposed to pick up your friend on the Colville today, but I'm not taking off in weather that I can't see through. I'll fly up as soon as it's safe. Mind if I join you?"

"Sit down." Kerns pulled a chair out for her. "It's early for snow, isn't it?"

"It always is." She pulled her flight jacket off and hung it over the back of the chair. Hap came up to the table.

"The same, Adriana?"

"Just coffee, Hap, thanks." She turned back to Kerns. "How's your article coming? 'Birds of Darkness,' isn't it?"

"I've been sidetracked."

Adriana sat and pulled the chair up to the table. "Is it love, drink, or madness that did it to you, Kerns?"

"A little of each. Thinking of an old and deep love and drinking Hap's good rye whisky. The madness has always been there. And you?"

"No old and deep loves to think of. The rye might be good, but I'm waiting for a weather report. I'm concerned about your friend Curtis. I don't think he wants to winter on the north slopes. When the weather breaks, I'll make a dash for the Colville and pick him up."

"I'll go with you if you want," Kerns said hopefully. "Four eyes are better than two."

"I'm taking the Helio. There is room, but I don't need the extra weight. It may well be a short landing and takeoff. I don't know how much baggage he'll have—and his birds. He at least has the three gyrfalcons—your birds of darkness. He had them when I flew you out. We'll leave his boat behind as well as all the stuff he can spare."

"How are you going to get in? You can't land on ice with pontoons and there's not enough snow yet for skis."

"Alaska bush wheels. Alice, my mechanic, is putting them on now."

"Bush wheels?"

"They're those big bush tires." Hap set a cup of coffee and a pot to refill it on the table. Adriana looked up and nodded her thanks.

"This lady can land anywhere, Kerns," Hap said. "You fly with her, you're safe as you can get in the air."

"As long as I can keep you in the air. It's hitting the ground that messes you up."

Kerns had a sudden flash of truth in his mind. A picture of the naked body, eyes and ears open as he flies toward that sudden stop. The falling man's mind fast-forwarding, editing slices of life, cutting razor sharp onto the screen as he makes his dark descent.

"Those tires help, Kerns," she said. "I can land in a foot of snow or on a damn rough gravel bar, soft as into a goose down bed. I can also mount wheel skies to them. But right now the snow is not deep enough."

"Christ," Kerns intoned quietly.

Hap looked at him. "What's the matter, Kerns?"

"I was thinking of that sudden stop."

Adriana glanced up at him. "It would be a killer, Kerns."

Like the "Oh Shit Corner" on the Dalton Highway, Kerns thought quietly. "Can you get your bartender to bring me another Rye, Hap?" Hap raised his arm in the air and snapped his fingers. The Rye was on the way. "Thanks," Kerns said. "With this conversation, I'm going to need that." Adriana glanced from Hap to Kerns. She took another sip of the hot black coffee.

"I must have come in on a dark moment," she said. "Sorry about that. I think I better get out to the hangar and see how my friend is coming with the bush wheels. I'll try to gather up your friend Curtis before he freezes for eternity. I'm not terribly fond of men, but he's a good one—a good person." She pulled a small thermos out of her leather shoulder bag and filled it with the coffee in her cup and in the pot. "What do I owe you, Hap?"

"Nothing. I put it on Kerns' tab."

"Thank you, Kerns. You're not a bad guy either. And, Hap, you are a goddamned jewel." She screwed the cap on her stainless thermos and slipped out the back door of the Big I.

"She is an interesting lady," Kerns murmured.

"Be careful," Hap said. "She is a dynamo. I don't think she is too fond of the male sex. Other than me when she orders a drink, you are the only man she has ever spoken to here."

"Some women like women. I can't blame them. I love them myself."

"She doesn't talk to women either."

"Adriana O'Donovan." Kerns sighed. "It's a beautiful name."

"She's a beautiful woman." Hap picked up the empty cup and coffee pot. "Tread lightly, Kerns."

Kerns nodded, his mind turning slowly. The ice had melted in his drink. He picked it up and trailed Hap to the bar where he left the glass. He followed Adriana's path out the back door. He wasn't following her. He was headed home, such as it was. Adriana was gone when he closed the door behind him. A light granular snow was coming down. It reminded him of that cold night twenty years ago. He studied the gray sky. He didn't think it would amount to anything, but he'd keep his eyes and ears open for the report. He was thinking of Curtis on the icy banks of the Colville. The Colville was named after Andrew Colvile, a governor of the Hudson Bay Company, Kerns thought idly. The British explorers who named the greatest river to flow into the Arctic Ocean spelled Andrew's name wrong. "Probably dyslexic," Kerns said into the gathering snow and laughed. "Hang on, Curtis. That luscious Adriana will pick you up on the banks of that ice-crusted, misspelled river in the morning." Kerns got in his truck and headed for Chena Ridge. He would stop at the Pump House, where the rye was more expensive, and have a bowl of their fish chowder and maybe half a dozen shucked oysters. His mind was spinning. The rye had nothing to do with it. Adriana O'Donovan. He smiled as he headed for his truck. "A bird of darkness," he said softly. "I sure hope she likes men and doesn't migrate south."

***

A few minutes after Kerns left by the back door, Slim came in the front. He ordered a cup of coffee. "I can't make any money off this goddamn caffeine," Hap told him as he brewed up a fresh pot.

"Hell, Hap, I only come in here for the company," Slim said. "I'll pay you for that if it will make you happy."

"I'm not a whore, Slim. Fourth Avenue isn't my line."

"You'd never make a living as a whore, Hap. You are too damn generous."

"A whore with a heart of gold, that's me. It will take it a few minutes to brew, Slim. I haven't read anything in the papers about your recent exploits. What's the story?"

"As far as I am concerned, there won't be a story. It's too delicious to let it leak out. The media would have it all over the lower forty-eight—or fifty—or however many states they got now. I know you and Kerns won't say anything. I have convinced the FBI and the E-I-E-I-O to keep it in the cage for the rest of the month. It will show up in a couple of weeks on *Good Morning America*, dumped in the arms of the media by some agent, speaking on the condition his or her name be withheld because they are not authorized to speak."

"As long as you keep me informed, I won't say a word, Slim." Hap kept his eye on the pot, waiting for the first rich cup to squeeze out. "After all, Slim, I need to know. I am a bartender, for Christ's sake. It's my business to know."

"I'm with you, Hap. Hell, I wouldn't know if you hadn't known first. Anyway, we all know the same thing, and that is that we don't know a damn thing, except one or two bodies dropped out of the sky. As a consequence, they hit the ground. An unpleasant landing, to say the least, but an inevitable one. Ask Sir Isaac."

"Where do you think they will drop the next one, Slim?" The hot coffee had started to seep into the pot. Hap hadn't taken his eyes off of it.

"You're the bartender. Midnight Poison," Slim mused aloud and shook his head. "I have no doubt you will be the first to know."

"Right." Hap held a thick clay mug under the hot water tap to warm it up. "Kerns said he was staying out at your place."

"He is. I like that guy. I want to keep him around. We off-loaded his camper out there. Got it up on stilts with an extension cord running to it to keep it from freezing."

"Midnight Poison," Hap said quietly as he poured Slim's coffee.

"It's a perfume, for Christ's sake, Hap," Slim said. "Kerns and I Googled it. Why in hell was perfume the final thought of this guy who gets pushed out into the sky?" Hap shrugged and handed him the cup of coffee. "Thanks." Slim took a grateful sip. It was too hot. He winced. "We might have a lead on who, or what, this guy is." Hap said nothing. He poured a cup for himself and listened, blowing steam from the black in his cup. "He's military," Slim added.

"Really?" Hap said, sipping his brew cautiously.

"Really," Slim responded.

"There are enough of them up here," Hap said.

"It's moose season. He could have come from anywhere to shoot a moose." Slim reached inside his vest and pulled out a folded piece of paper. He flattened it out on the bar. "This is an artist's rendition. The guy's face was too disfigured to get an honest photo, but this is close to the truth." He sipped his coffee. It was still too hot. "You know, Hap, there was a microchip embedded in that poor bastard's shoulder. No pictures on it that we can find, but a jumbled list of encrypted information. We are trying to break the code now."

"Why not ask the military? They are the ones that plugged the chip into him. Who else would?" Hap was studying the artist's copy of the headshot. "I never saw this one."

"I'll leave you the copy. You might tack it up later with the rest of your rogue's gallery over there on the wall. Someone might recognize him. You never know."

"I might never know." Hap slipped the copy behind the rye bottle sitting by the coffee pot.

"Someone knows," Slim said. "I'd give that chip to the military, but we'd never get it back, or any answers with it. This goddamn government will be planting those chips in everyone pretty soon. Talk about drones tracking us. Google Maps has a picture of everyone entering this bar, Hap, and the government has a copy. The US government thinks information is a great tool—even if it's incorrect." Slim laid a two-dollar bill on the bar. "Give me a call if something comes up."

Hap put the two in the empty tip jar. "Seed money," he grunted. Slim had left. Hap handed the bottle of rye to Molly, his number one bartender. She'd been entertaining at the far end of the Big I. "Put Kerns' bottle on the top shelf, Molly. I'm going to the office to do some book work."

It was almost cocktail hour, but then, it was almost always cocktail hour in Fairbanks. Hap picked up the picture Slim had left and studied it a moment. "I've never seen this guy," he said to himself.

"I've never seen him either," Molly said, looking over his shoulder.

"Put it up on the wall, Molly. If someone does recognize him, let me know."

"Is he a lost soul?"

"Yeah, Molly, he is definitely a lost soul."

***

Major Almas A. Cooper III, in the dark hole of his cave, hovered over the keyboard of his computer, writing his son:

> *They are witch women, son. "Don't be afraid to fly," they cry. Don't be afraid to fly, indeed. They have a broomstick to fly on. They don't need a goddamn plane. And they will use that broomstick on you if you give them a chance. One of those witch women in the air force used her witchcraft on me to deny me my well-deserved promotion. I know it was her. Now they got a witch in charge of the Air Force Academy—a lieutenant general?—shit, son, she's a woman. Those women have to be locked up. They are two-faced, lying witches, all of them. They*

made her—a woman—superintendent of the Air Force Academy? You know, son, our ancestors in Salem had the right idea. Drown the bitches.

Major Cooper's son's face flashed up on his father's thirty-six-inch monitor. "Major, your message is coming in on my laptop. I hope it's not coming up on anyone else's screen here. Lieutenant General Johnson may be a woman, Major, but she outranks both of us. All I want to do is finish this year, get my silver lieutenant's bars, and get the hell out of here."

"Just stay away from those women, A."

"What do you want me to do, Major, turn gay?"

"Watch your mouth!"

"Major, I have had plenty opportunities to do that here. Others are watching my mouth, too—and yours. Don't worry, Major, your son will stay out of trouble."

Since getting out of diapers, Almas A. Cooper IV had never called his father by anything but by his rank, starting with lieutenant. The major had insisted on it. His son had little choice in the matter, other than open rebellion. Although young Almas had considered rebellion, he never had the guts to give it a try. Even his mother never addressed his father by anything but his rank. It was a very military family of three under tight control—no dissension in the home ranks.

The Cooper family had been military since the days of Miles Standish. It had always been army, until the major took to the air. Colonel Cooper II, the major's father, had graduated from West Point. Velma's father, young Almas's grandfather on his mother's side, never got the "bird" colonel's wings, but he did make it a step above major. He was killed in Korea by misdirected friendly fire before he got to wear the silver "cluster," which denoted the new rank on his epaulets. Colonel—a big step above the major. Colonel Clusterfuck was what the major secretly called his father-in-law, using the name stuck on George Bush. Bush, of course—both of them—were the major's heroes. The Bush dynasty loved war (as long as they didn't have to fight).

The major had no idea where the "Clusterfuck" title came from, or who it was aimed at, but he felt it fit Velma's father.

Velma only spoke of her father to young Almas when the major wasn't around.

"So much for family history," the soon-to-be first lieutenant said aloud, dismissing the major and his mother from his mind. He shook his head, shut off his phone, and went back to studying for an exam.

His mother's maiden name was Custer.

***

The major spent an hour punching through some of his favorite sex sites, discarding most messages except for those demanding rough sex. Although he seldom answered, he fantasized. There was one profile that especially titillated his latent desire. It was on a rough site labeled Sex, Fire & Ice. He had been rereading it for two weeks—Midnight Poison. Now, after studying it as if it were a presidential order, he saved it once again. The major especially enjoyed cybersex, although he refused to participate with his uniform on. He seldom gave information concerning his rank to sex witches online. He was pretty sure he never had, but there was a nagging fear that in an ejaculatory fit he may have lost control and blurted it out. E-sex was safe sex—if he could just control his tongue. He had, on one emotional occasion, actually visited one of these quite lovely bodies. He had taken a few days leave and flown, at air force expense, to Salt Lake. He told Velma it had been a secret mission to Spelunker, or some such fictional place she couldn't trace him to. Today, in his depressed state, with the exception of the conversation with his son, he just browsed, read and fantasized. He did, via credit card, acquire a gold slot on the Sex, Fire & Ice site. He felt better for it.

After checking his official air force site—there was nothing of interest there—the major closed down his computer. He turned out all but a nightlight and headed up the stairs. At the top landing he threw back the locking bolt on the inside of the door—the door didn't open. He pushed against it—no give. He pounded on the door. No response. His temper rose and broke. He slammed his heavy shoulder against the hollow core door. After a number of blows, he shattered his way through with a mighty body blow that landed him headlong on the kitchen floor. He grabbed hold of the lip of the island in the center of the room and pulled himself to his feet. On the wet Formica top stood an empty vodka bottle and a few melting ice cubes.

He found his wife on the floor of her sewing room. The deep white shag carpet was soaked in blood where she had thrashed around in the last desperate throes of life. The sewing shears she had never used were finally put to her advantage, severing the arteries of both wrists. The major stood for a moment in silence.

"What a fucking mess," he said with a sigh. Being careful not to soil his uniform, the major dropped slowly to his knees and felt for a pulse. There was nothing left in Velma to pulse. "Today is the making of a goddamned clusterfuck right here," the major said vehemently. He stood and looked down at her. "Why, in the name of Christ, do you do these things to me, Velma?" He turned on his cell phone and dialed 911.

***

CHAPTER 4

In Flight

Adriana checked the wheel and tire installation on the new Alaska bush wheels. It was not that she doubted Alice Baily's work or ability. Alice had been one of her number one jet mechanics in the air force. She was one of the best and most devoted mechanics Adriana had ever had. She didn't doubt her work. It was just that as a pilot Adriana always checked everything. She had a pilot's eye for beauty and a pilot's instinct for locating possible weaknesses in her plane's structure and signs of mechanical malfunctions. Having flown US Air Force fighters and light bombers for five years in the service, she had learned to trust these instincts. In her personal life, her instincts had been severely disrupted, her reasoning derailed to the point of driving her to refuse a major promotion and to welcome an early discharge rather than fulfill her life's ambition.

The beauty of flying still played on its own frequency. When it wasn't a matter of life and death (a situation which held its own excitement in delicate balance), beauty made flying worth the risk. A pilot's knowledge, intuition, and hours in the air balanced the hazards. Adriana had flown in various aircraft thousands of hours. She knew there was nothing better than experience. She had ejected from her jet's cockpit at over ten thousand feet a moment before the fighter she was flying exploded in a gaseous bubble of fire. She had hung on till the last second, thinking there might be a chance to save the fighter. She loved her plane, but not enough to go down with the ship. With that almost-too-late exit, the flash of the explosion singed her protective covering and melted a few holes in her parachute. The chute held up. So did Adriana. She had to admit, that experience brought her the closest she had ever come to praying.

After resigning her rank, under protest, Adriana chose Alaska for her home. Her discharge from the air force had been cloudy. It would be difficult to find a job flying passenger jets even if she wanted to, which she didn't. In the air, she feared she would be working with some of the same class of men she had been surrounded by in the service. She wanted and needed, for her peace of mind, independence. Alaska was the perfect location for that. Adriana had her private pilot's license since before she entered the Air Force Academy, from which she graduated with honors. She had hung on to that private license throughout her time in the service of her country.

In Alaska, she could own her own flying service. With her savings she purchased a 1980 Helio Super Courier H295. The Helio had a newly rebuilt engine. It would carry four passengers with light gear, plus herself, or two passengers and two fifty-gallon drums of diesel fuel if need be.

Some sound bush planes flying in Alaska had been in the air for over fifty years. Adriana's plane was not as popular as the Cessna but was excellent for what she wished to do with it. In the service Adriana had spent a year at Ellison Air Force Base, south of Fairbanks, and had flown over much of Alaska. She was familiar with the various terrains of the largest state in the Unites States, but that was at higher altitudes and at much higher speeds than she would be flying in her new career.

When she acquired the Helio, it was equipped with pontoons, or floats, for water landing and takeoff. That suited her. She began exploring out of Fairbanks, landing on various locations on the Yukon and Tanana Rivers. She spent time in and around Bettles on the Koyukuk River and many other small communities throughout the central part of the state before branching out to the Colville and the north slopes of the Brooks Range. Among other arctic rivers Adriana studied the Colville from its source to the Arctic Ocean.

Her headquarters remained in the Fairbanks area. For some months she explored the airways and alternative landing sites. Many she touched down on were gravel bars in the Tanana, Yukon, and Koyukuk in the absolute wilderness. She would pull her floatplane up on shore and make camp. She pitched her mosquito-proof little tent in many of these locations where she would sometimes catch the few hours of sleep she needed.

Adriana felt comfortable enough to open for business in late August. A-Plus Flying Service was the unobtrusive name she chose for it. Her card was a simple black-and-white presentation. She and her friend and mechanic, Alice Baily, who joined her in Alaska on the date of her discharge, rented a hangar where she would have the bush wheels installed later in the fall. In her modest advertisement, Adriana stressed the fact that she was not a hunting guide. She would, however, fly anglers in and out of locations of their choosing. Her main interest was to fly naturalists, environmentalists, and scientists, such as members of the Arctic Circle Research Lab, with ties to the University of Alaska, Fairbanks and Anchorage campuses, to any location they chose in the state. She was not interested in catering to oil exploration. Kerns' friend, Curtis, was one of her first clients. She didn't want to let him down.

Once her bush wheels—or tundra tires, as they were sometimes called—were installed, she tested them in the present rough weather conditions, landing on a gravel bar in the Tanana River a short distance from Fairbanks. She had, that past May, flown to Valdese to observe the STOL—Short Takeoff and Landing Competition—between seasoned bush pilots. Adriana was impressed. These amazing flyers, male and female, could land their planes and come to a stop in less than fifty feet. One made an astounding landing in just over thirty feet. The tail of his plane stood almost erect when the pilot applied the brakes to those huge, balloon-like tires. Adriana knew she couldn't duplicate this feat without hours of practice, but she certainly saw the advantage of those big tires. On YouTube, she watched videos of planes come in skimming through still water, as if floating, to further slow them down before they rolled up onto a gravel bar. They also could land in up to a foot of snow. In winter weather wide skis could replace the big tires or be attached to them with a special harness.

On her third test landing on a Tanana gravel island, while preparing to rescue Curtis, she brought her H295 Helio to a stop in a little over a hundred feet. She spun around and, full throttle, left the ground just as she hit the water line. Adriana was ready. There had to be a break in the weather. She flew under the low-hanging mist, radioed ahead, and got clearance to land from the Fairbanks tower. She pulled into the hangar where they had installed the oversized wheels. Adriana and Alice checked out the Helio carefully. All was well. Adriana topped off the tanks and stowed her light camping gear, a small tent, a propane cooker/heater, a sixty-below-rated sleeping bag, and a tin of buffalo jerky—provisions for a day (precautions against a forced landing in no man's land). If she went down and couldn't get off in twenty-four hours, she would be there for archeologists a thousand years down the road. She couldn't afford—for Curtis's sake and hers—to go down. She left word with Alice to be awakened if the weather broke up north and curled up on the couch in a corner of the hangar where she and Alice had erected plywood walls for a makeshift office. If visibility on the Colville River was a mile or better, Adriana was ready to fly. Alice, always wakeful for her friend, fit padded earphones to her ears so the continuous weather forecast wouldn't keep Adriana from sleep. Alice's eyes never closed.

***

Kerns was checking the weather, too, in Umiat, on the banks of the Colville, and in Deadhorse. That was the closest he could get a forecast to the headwaters of the Colville where his friend was camped in the cold. Snow, possibly partial clearing in the next twelve hours, was still the word. *This weather, as predicted now, won't kill Curtis, but he needs to get to hell out of there*, Kerns thought.

Zero visibility was no place to fly when you were so close to the North Pole that the needle on your compass didn't know which way to point because of the crazy magnetic field. At least that was the way it used to be. Kerns thought back to his time as a guide on the Colville. *Maybe they have an instrument now that overcomes that inconvenience.* Kerns wondered a moment about that. *Of course they do. They have everything else.* He poured rye into a cup of hot coffee. "Why the hell didn't I ask Adriana to call me when she headed out? If she headed out." Now he was talking to himself. "Balloon tires, tundra tires, Alaskan bush wheels, whatever the hell they are called." He had Googled them. "I hope they work." The coffee wasn't sweet enough. He poured in another shot of rye.

***

Kerns was awakened six hours later by his cell phone buzzing in his ear. It was Adriana. "Kerns, I am taking off," she said, recognizing his voice. "I will fly by instruments to the emergency landing strip in Umiat. Umiat has no navigational device as it used to have in the '50s. That would be completely outdated now. I have all the GPS equipment set up in the Helio. It is top of the line. Don't worry. Curtis doesn't have equipment I can connect to, but I will find him if I have five hundred yards of visibility. I am filing my flight plan with you and the tower here in Fairbanks. Umiat used to be a US Navy installation on the Colville River. They capped a bunch of wells there in the early 1940s. It is now peopled by the oil industry who, with a special dispensation from Washington, hopes to punch more holes in Mother Earth and further frack it up." Kerns had spent time in Umiat. He knew the history. He also recognized a slight bitterness in Adriana's voice. He was glad to hear it. "These oil people are using the strip daily," she said. "I can lock in on it with my GPS equipment and land—no problem. My GPS is good anywhere on the planet." Kerns didn't point out that he had used Umiat as a home base in the late seventies when he was a guide. The lady had it down.

"I will refuel in Umiat. From there, at a low altitude, depending on the weather, I hope to be able to follow the river west. Curtis is supposed to be camped in the open where I can see him on the river and where there is a somewhat level strip for me to land. I'll spot that bright red tent of his and pick him up with his birds of darkness. This Helio is fully controllable at 27 mph at landing. I have a cruise speed of 130 mph for 1,100 nautical miles. Fairbanks to Umiat is only 336 miles. I am flying almost empty, so that will stretch. I don't know why I am telling you all this shit, Kerns, but maybe it will make you feel better."

"Anything you say makes me feel better, Adriana."

"Okay. On returning, if the weather is still inclement, we may stay in Umiat for a day or so to wait it out. Don't worry, Kerns. I'll drink some rye with you when I get back with your friend. I'm looking forward to it. Do we have a date?"

"We got a date."

"I must be crazy talking to you like this."

"I got the rye. Thank you for the call." Kerns had said barely a word since he lifted the phone to his ear and answered. Then he had a thought. "Adriana, does the Aurora have any effect on your instruments?"

"The Geophysical Institute has studied this phenomenon for years in conjunction with the US Air Force. No data has been made available. It is government BS."

"You are in control, Amelia Earhart. Goodbye, love, and good luck."

"Love?" Kerns picked up on a harsh change in her voice. "Love? Where did that come from, Kerns?"

"It just slipped up on us."

"Us? Maybe it slipped up on you, Kerns," she barked. "Just keep it to yourself."

"Right. Sorry about that."

"I am sorry about it too—you don't know how sorry." Adriana cut their connection.

"You take care," Kerns said quietly into the empty cell phone. He kicked out of his sleeping bag and got up. He looked out into the yard. Slim's truck was parked there. Kerns hadn't heard it pull in. *I must have slept—I can't remember. Was I dreaming?* Perhaps he had been dreaming. Perhaps he was crazy. He turned the flame on under the coffee pot. "What the hell is the matter with the word 'love'?" he said into the cramped space of his camper. The rye bottle was empty.

***

The word "love" had snapped Adriana angrily five years into the past. A US Air Force major, holding her facedown on the cold, stainless steel table by her throat, whispered hoarsely in her ear, "You love it, Captain Adriana O'Donovan. Don't you love it? The five of us are filling you with the love you deserve, Captain bullshit O'Donovan and love, love, love is what all of us are giving you—right up the rectum, Captain! Right up that tight little bunghole of yours! And that is where you can stick your promotion, too."

An officer on both sides of the table had her arms pinned down. Her ankles were duct-taped to the table legs. Another officer at the foot of the table gave vent to a coarse sigh of relief and fell back. Another, laughing, took his place. The major, reeking of scotch and gin, leaned over her drunkenly. "It's love." He slurred the word. "Anyone want seconds?"

Adriana screamed in the confined space of the Helio's cockpit. Her vision cleared. Shaking the picture from her head, she pulled the nose of her plane out of a slow dive and stabilized her flight. "Midnight Poison," she sighed quietly. "Three to go."

"I lost it," she continued thoughtfully to no one but herself. "One word and I lost it. Kerns didn't mean anything by the word." Slowly her breathing steadied until she was in control. She studied the bank of instruments before her. That helped. She had broken into a cold sweat. But she was herself again. She was alone with her instruments. The GPS tied in successfully with the Umiat location. She climbed steadily through the clouds until she came out safely above them. There would be little chance of her wings icing up in the drier atmosphere. The first leg of her journey would be safe. She should be over Umiat and the Colville River in less than three hours. She was.

"Midnight Poison," she repeated. "Three to go."

***

CHAPTER 5

The Writer and the Cyber Pimp

"You know, Sam, Sammy boy—whatever your name is—you wanted the job. You wrote a glowing pornographic piece of shit. So I called you in. Young buddy, I am a cyber pimp. I get paid to lock these poor suckers down, to make them gawk at the 'hot & horny' sites and porn stars, deprived housewives, rejected lovers for whatever reason. Nude pictures of what they think are horny housewives, the husbands holding down jobs to keep the ladies sucking on the sugar tit. It's all bullshit. Sure there are a few legitimate quims—not that they are not all horny—but this few admit it and go for it. Young buddy, you wouldn't want to have intercourse with any of them. We got close-up pictures of thousands of asses, shaved and bearded quims—"

"Quims?" The young would-be writer was slightly astonished by the word. "Quim is a coarse term for a lady's vagina used by François Rabelais, the great French doctor and writer in the 16 or 17 hundreds."

"It was the sixteenth century, Sammy boy, the 15 hundreds. Rabelais died the ninth of April 1553. Rabelais, it was, who showed me the humor and absurdity of this business that's making me a living better than teaching. I have a master's degree in English and French literature, Sammy boy. What the hell do you have that you can even spell? Do you want the job or not?"

"I'm broke."

"You got the job—for at least one day. See the humor in this, Sambo. You will go a long way. Follow me." The corpulent Saul Billings led the naïve Samuel Charles Bellefonte down the hall of the large, now somewhat dilapidated brownstone mansion in Cincinnati, Ohio. They entered what had once been the Grand Ballroom, a suitable name for the location. The high-ceilinged, thirty-by-sixty-foot hall of the chopped rock building was divided into what might have been box stalls for horses in days gone by. Here and now it was eight-by-ten-foot box stalls for sexual cyber programmers, writers, bullshit artists, whatever. The high walls were covered with photographs of young nude girls, obvious whores, homosexuals, and gangbangers from the age of fourteen (eighteen was the callout) to eighty-four, or maybe a hundred. It was a rogue's gallery of sick fantasies. Young Samuel looked about in shock and wonder. Saul Billings laughed.

"Rabelais would love it, Sammy boy, to say nothing of the Marquis de Sade. Here is your office." He ushered Samuel into one of the cubicles. There was a wall-to-wall table at one end with a hard wooden chair in front of it. On top of the table was a stack of cheap copy paper, an HP printer, an Apple keyboard, and a flat-screen monitor. There was also a set of headphones. The eight-foot wall behind the table was painted black. The other three walls were painted a greenish off-white. More pictures were pinned to the interior walls of the cubicle. "The artwork is for your inspiration, Sambo."

"Jesus Christ," Samuel murmured under his breath.

"Christ is not one of our clients, although we would not discriminate against him were he to apply and give us the number of his MasterCard. You could write a hell of a profile for that gentleman using some of his actual quotes—or quotes attributed to him. Many of our clients claim to be very close to Christ, and his father, Rambo Sambo."

"Mr. Billings, my name is Samuel. I would appreciate it if you would call me Samuel or even Sam. My name is not Sambo."

"You are not Black Sambo? Right, you are White Sambo, but if you object to that moniker, I will call you Sammy. Will that work, Sammy boy?" Samuel turned away and said nothing. He knew he could walk away. But he desperately needed the work. At least in this job he could tell friends he was making a living as a writer. He would actually be writing for a living. He just would not go into the details of his assignments. As far as Samuel was concerned, even this was a step up from the golden arches of McDonald's. He had walked out of McDonald's, too. Actually, he didn't walk out, he just never showed up one day. He didn't even go back for his final paycheck. When writing, Samuel's words could be very positive. Face to face, especially with eye contact, he was a wimp.

"Sammy will be fine," he replied, submissively. He looked down at the equipment on the table, picked up the headset, and studied it absently. Although made in China, it carried the trade name of an American company. Samuel wished he had a set to match it. He finally looked nervously back to Billings. His new boss smiled.

"Well, Sammy," Billings broke into the silence, "let us see how you do your first day writing profiles for Whores & Housewives, or one of our other sites. We are a worldwide organization with many handles. In addition to Whores & Housewives, from this office we people seven other sites, as well. Bear in mind, every client's profile you write will be channeled through my office for approval and/or editing. I want these sites to shine, Sammy."

Samuel turned away and winced. *My work is going to be graded, even here at the very bottom of the literary ladder.* "I understand," he answered.

"At present," Saul continued, turning Samuel around to face him, "we have about fifty or so stock phrases our clients may pick to dress up their profile. Many clients can't spell shit—well, maybe they can spell 'shit,' but not much else. Sammy, your job is to dress up these profiles. On the other hand, some of our clients, if not discreet, are very intelligent. They can trip you up. Some enjoy doing that. It is a game to them."

"I have all the equipment needed, Mr. Billings. Would it not be possible for me to work at home? I'm really a morning person. I do my best work early in the morning, and—"

"No!" Samuel was cut short. "This is a nine-to-five-thirty job. The extra half hour is for lunch, if you are so disposed.

If you choose not to lunch, you may leave at five." Billings reached out and touched Samuel's arm to bring his eyes back into focus. "You might have noticed, in the center of the black wall is a wide-angle surveillance lens." Samuel turned away and spotted it, dead center in the black wall, a startling view emanating between the kneeling legs of an amply endowed woman. "Any further questions, you may ask of the lens. I or one of my staff will get back to you with an answer." Billings stepped into the arch of the doorway. There was no door to shut or lock for privacy—not that, as Samuel realized now, there would be any privacy. Billings turned back to his mentally disoriented new employee. "We are very open here, Sammy. Every dark wall has its lens." Billings stood a moment in amused silence, then: "Look to your monitor, Sammy, you are on. It is a new site of ours. I have named it Sex, Fire & Ice. It is a nice mix—a bit rough and doing quite well. The client is typing in his or her profile. Take care of it." And Billings was gone.

Samuel was on his own—so to speak. His critic was at the other end of the lens. On the monitor was the image of a large man who Samuel judged to be in his fifties. He was dressed in a military uniform. Samuel guessed it was air force. Sam sat and pulled on the headphones as he read what the man was typing. There was no sound on the phones, only words on the screen. Samuel read aloud:

"Searching for Midnight Poison."

***

CHAPTER 6

The Funeral and Umiat Lost and Found

Adriana left her plane with the three men who manned the unincorporated village of Umiat, Alaska, and walked through a slowly swirling impenetrable ice fog. An icy sleet was falling through it when she reached the bank of the Colville River. The major river flowing into the Arctic Ocean on the Alaska coast was three hundred and fifty miles in length from its source at the merging of Thunder and Storm Creeks in the De Long Mountains at the eastern end of the Brooks Range. From the headwaters to the delta at Harrison Bay, it dropped a bit over two thousand feet. The current could be quite swift in places. The Colville was entirely within the Arctic Circle.

Adriana found ice forming along the banks of the mighty river. Close in, it was thick enough to hold her weight. It would reach a thickness of four to six feet and be used safely as an ice road to bring semi-tractor and trailers with supplies to Umiat during the winter. *In this fog, one could wander off the trail and be lost here forever*, Adriana thought. She stepped off the ice and got back on the dim track to the Quonset hut metropolis of Umiat.

Adriana had dropped Curtis off in the De Long Mountains, somewhere north of the Continental Divide. She had brought Kerns in to join him a week later. When she picked Kerns up to fly him out, he and Curtis had reached a location close to the main flow of the great river. Adriana calculated in her head that Curtis now should be within a hundred miles of Umiat. "Damn the weather," she said, keeping her eyes on the dim trail beneath her. That was just about as far as she could see. The sun, if and when it could be seen, was getting noticeably lower on the horizon every day. This time of year far above the Arctic Circle each day lost at least five minutes. By the time Adriana reached the arched Quonset huts, the trail was completely whited out. The sun, if it was up at all, was out of sight. She hoped for a break in the weather tomorrow. There was little else she could do but hope. The GPS would be little help in locating Curtis. She would have to actually see her client, or his red tent.

***

The funeral for the major's wife would be a small success, if such a thing can be called a success at all. *I mean*, the major thought as he purchased flowers that would freeze before they reached the base chapel, *what else can I do?* It had all taken time. There had to be an autopsy to prove, beyond a doubt, that death was self-inflicted: standard procedure, but time-consuming. Then there was the cremation: more time. It would be over tomorrow. His son was flying in. And Veta. *What am I going to do with that bitch?* The major's twisted thoughts churned in his mind like meat in a sausage grinder.

His son had called his aunt and asked her to be there for him. The major had had no intention of calling his sister-in-law until after Velma was in the ground or in the air. Velma was—her ashes, that is—already at the chapel in an expensive urn. At least it wouldn't be an open casket. The major had had the shag carpet in the sewing room replaced with one close cropped to the floor. He had a new basement door installed, as well—a solid core door with a keyed lock. The major stepped into the undertaker's suite of offices, laboratory, and chapel. He left the flowers on the roof of the car where they instantly froze in the near-zero temperature.

"Major Cooper?" It was Captain Quebberman, the post PR officer, there to greet him. "We are so sorry for the sad occasion of our meeting, but the news is good. The coroner's report found no misconduct on your part. This happens in the service to more wives than you would expect. We grieve for you. It was an unfortunate end to a long and fruitful marriage."

"Thank you, Captain." The major belatedly returned the PR man's salute. "I will miss her terribly," he said without conviction.

"I have no doubt. I am so sorry we had to wait so long for these services—the report and all. And this loss coming on the heels of you not getting your promotion. It's tragic."

Major Cooper swung about, glaring at the captain. "How the hell did you hear about that?"

"I'm so sorry, sir, it just slipped out. I learned of it in the coroner's report. Those reports are very informative."

"So that information will be in the obituary, too?"

"No, no, no. I shall see that it is kept quiet. I will edit the obit, Major. I will glean pleasant information from your son when he arrives. He has been excused by the academy and is in flight as we speak. We have a car assigned to meet him on his arrival. Your wife's sister, you will be happy to know, is here already. She is presently viewing the—well, the urn."

"Veta is here already?"

"Yes, I believe that is the name she gave me."

"Shit." The word was spoken softly, but with meaning. The captain picked up on it.

"Well, oftentimes," Quebberman stammered, "family members are not as welcome as they might be on these occasions." He heaved a sigh of remorse. "I'm sorry, but I understand. In-laws are sometimes a travesty."

"How true, Captain." It was the major's turn to sigh. "Well—I suppose I must go in and face her."

"The undertaker is with her," the captain said. "It won't be as hard as if she were alone."

"Thank you, Captain, in advance, for keeping that bit of information out of the obituary. May I see the copy before it is released?"

"Most assuredly, Major. You may edit it as you wish." The captain saluted his superior. The major returned it smartly and stepped into the viewing room.

The urn was placed prominently on a gold-painted lectern. Veta was on her knees before it, her eyes closed in sacramental prayer. The undertaker was kneeling with her. *How appropriate*, the major thought. He stood in silence for a full minute. His sister-in-law, feeling a heavy presence in the showing parlor, opened her eyes. They locked on the major in angry recognition.

"Are you suffering, Major, or just satisfied?" Veta said in a cold voice, getting to her feet. "It is difficult to interpret the look on your face." She smiled. "Where is your son? He called me with the news. You didn't. I doubt if you would have still."

"Veta." The room filled with silence. The military undertaker rose to his feet. He laid a cool hand on Veta's shoulder.

"I'll leave you two alone with your loss. I understand its depth," he said in a couched tone. "If there is anything I can do, I am at your total disposal. That goes for you, too, Major." The quiet man started for the door then turned back. "Your son should be here soon, Major." The door closed softly behind him. Neither Veta nor the major made a move. Major Cooper spoke first.

"It has been a long time, Veta. Will you bury the hatchet?"

"In my sister's grave?"

"Don't be bitter, Veta. It is all water under the bridge. I have put that episode out of my mind."

"Not only are you a cliché, Almas, you speak in clichés." The major winced at being called by his common name.

"That's enough, Veta. This is a solemn time."

The front door to the viewing parlor opened with a silent swish through the fiber of the heavy gray carpet. Captain Quebberman stood in the opening. "Your son has arrived, Major."

"He's here?"

"Armstrong is here?" Veta echoed the major.

"He was here, Ms. Custer," the captain addressed Veta. Veta had married, but on her divorce, three years later, had the married name eradicated from the records. "But," the captain went on, "your nephew said he wanted to remember his mother as he last saw her, alive and well. They were very close, I take it."

"Was here?" the major questioned abruptly. "Where did he go?"

"He had the driver take him to your residence, Major. He said he would be waiting for you there."

"But the door is locked," the major said, concerned. "A knows I wouldn't leave it open." Major Cooper always called his son by the first letter of his first and middle name, Almas Armstrong, A, or son. He refused to call him Almas Jr., or just Junior, and he hated the middle name.

"He said his mother mailed him a key."

"Wise of her," Veta said. "Velma was a smart woman in many ways. She loved her son."

"I loved him, too, Veta," the major snapped.

"Why don't you say it in the present tense, Almas?"

"I just don't like people wandering into the house uninvited."

"Jesus," Veta said under her breath. "Well, let's go. I am eager to see that young man. And don't you worry, Major. I won't be staying there. I have booked a room at the Best Western in Fairbanks."

"That was unnecessary." There wasn't much conviction in the major's voice.

"No, it was necessary, Almas."

Without a look back at the urn full of the ashes of a sister and wife, the two left the funeral parlor.

***

Adriana flew low over the freezing shoreline of the Colville. The fog had lifted to a cloud about three hundred feet above the open waters. The main channel of the river was separated by shifting gravel bars in many locations. The plan had been for Curtis to camp on the south shore with a smoking fire going during the shrinking daylight hours. Adriana would be on the lookout for the signal and his red tent.

Close to Umiat were low shale bluffs on the south shore, some of them lost in the clouds. As she flew west, the bluffs gave way to rolling tundra, now brushed with four or five inches of light snow cover in the freezing weather. Adriana favored the south bank of the river, but her eyes covered the north shore, too. The outside temperature readout on her instrument panel was minus ten degrees. The cloud of ice fog was showing signs of breaking up. That was good, for what it was worth. No one knew what the weather would do. Weather was in the hands of Mother Nature, and damn the forecast. There was little or no wind. Things looked favorable, but Adriana wasn't holding her breath.

Within the first hour, she spotted Curtis. He was not on the shore. He was floating the center current of the wide Colville. He waved anxiously. He had seen her. She dipped her wings in recognition. Curtis relaxed back to a sitting position in his canvas boat. Not being able to get to the shore because of the converging ice, he had been on the water all night. Adriana realized his problem. She had been concerned for the same reason. Curtis couldn't break through the thick shore ice to reach landfall. Adriana would have to break the ice for him. It was a crazy idea, but it was an idea. The question was, could she and her plane pull it off? If she could find a gravel island in open water long enough for her to make a landing the chances were better. The current from upriver was stronger and the ice in the faster flow was not quite as thick, so she might, she thought, hit the growing ice cover with her new big wheels and break it up for him, making a path of open water to the gravel shoreline. *Am I crazy in my thinking?* she asked herself silently. She circled Curtis, hoping he would read her mind. The broken ice would give him the open water he needed to get his boat to the shore of one of the shifting gravel islands. He had been floating all night in the below-zero damp and must be suffering from hypothermia as it was. Another night of the same, Curtis wouldn't make it. It would take him two nights to get to Umiat and be faced by the same iced-up problem if he did make it that far.

Adriana would have to make her move now if she was going to save him. It was an extremely dangerous operation, but this was a life or death matter. When close to stall speed, which was where she would have to be as she broke the ice, everything would be extremely delicate. The unpredictable drag of the ice would make the risk of stall unreasonably high. Was there a choice? She thought not.

Adriana flew on ahead and found her spot. She circled back, giving Curtis time to close in on her chosen gravel bar. When he neared her proposed landing strip, Adriana cut over to give herself the longest landing pattern on the small gravel island. She judged her envelope to be a little over two hundred feet long. Her plane circled the target three times, touching down in the snow, feeling for solid footing beneath. Curtis figured out what she was doing and guided his boat into her pattern. If he went into the water, he would freeze before he got ashore. They both knew it was a one-time shot. Adriana, hoping for the best, circled one last time and came in a few feet over Curtis's head. The balloon tires touched the thinner outer ice as she settled. She felt it give beneath the Helio's weight. "Keep it steady, shithead," she told herself. Adriana only called herself shithead when there was a good chance of fucking up. She slammed the throttle full forward. Between the lifting effect of the full span flaps, the flotation of the oversized bush wheels, the Lycoming engine powering her plane through the thin ice at five knots above stall speed, she thought it might work. It was a dangerous gamble and was going to be hell on her new tires. Sharp shreds of ice could slice through the thinner rubber and it would be over. "Go for it, shithead," she cried and lowered the nose to increase speed. She used power control to manage the altitude just above ground level—all of which might be normal in STOL landings, which required experience, total attention, and lightning fast reflexes. In addition to which Adriana was dealing with the variable drag of breaking ice, ice of questionable strength and thickness. Delicately she monitored the controlled pitch and power on her approach. *Let us hope the rubber holds out!* She plowed on, breaking a clear water path for Curtis and his fragile canvas boat. Her client was worth it. Curtis got a private, dramatic display of aerial virtuosity, a beautiful woman flying the hell out of a beautiful plane. It was working.

Adriana forced the big tires of her plane deeper into the breaking ice. If the wheels caught beneath the surface, the plane was toast. It would flip and she would be headfirst under the freezing water herself. She held the throttle forward and kept the nose down. She needed to push the weight down to break the steadily thickening ice in the shallower water. At shoreline, the ice was almost strong enough to support the weight of her Helio H295. Water splashed up on her windshield, freezing in the subzero temperature. Blind now, she held the stick solid. Then she felt the rough gravel beneath her balloon tires. If a large rock didn't knock her off course as she pushed through eight inches of new snow on the narrow gravel bar, she would make it. She hoped Curtis was following her in. The prop wash was undoubtedly wetting him down, but it wasn't as bad as going under the ice. She applied the brakes to the big wheels. They were still on land, if close to the edge. She braked the starboard wheel and gunned the engine. The Helio spun about, ready for takeoff. She had made it. Had Curtis?

Adriana grabbed a can of deicer and climbed out of the plane. Ahead of her Curtis dragged his boat out of the shattered ice. He was wet and freezing, but alive. Adriana was exhilarated and very much alive herself right now. She had made it this far and knew she could make it out. She shut the door on the heated cabin of her plane and ran to help Curtis. Adriana hugged him. He was the first man she had hugged in over five years. "Take your birds and get them in the cockpit," she ordered him. "It's warm. After all this I don't want you to expire from a case of hypothermia, or pneumonia. Is there anything else you desperately need, Curtis? I'll get it on board. We are going to leave the rest of your shit right here."

"My notes." Something was struggling about in the burlap bags he held close to him.

The birds, she realized. They were alive, if not well.

"Get them in the cockpit, Curtis," she cried.

"My notes are in that waterproof case. The rest can stay behind," he answered and headed for the plane with his birds. The case Adriana grabbed held his laptop, the solar charger for it, and an extra pair of dry long johns and wool socks. She shoved all this in the warm cabin of the Helio with the birds and ran back to push the boat out of the path the plane would need to take off.

"You will have to give me a hand with the ice on the wings," she yelled to Curtis. He quickly climbed out again into the cold. Adriana pulled a length of rough hemp rope out of the storage compartment. "Sorry to get you out of the warm, Curtis, but I can use a hand here." Curtis knew the procedure. Adriana tossed the end of the rope over one of the wings. Curtis caught it. They sawed the rough hemp back and forth, breaking the ice free that had frozen to the wings on the wet landing. The Helio's special hydraulic airlifts shielded in the wings could now protrude on takeoff. They definitely needed the lifts to make it out of the snow. The fins were a huge help in a short run takeoff. She and Curtis repeated the procedure on the left wing, and they were ready to go. Both in the plane now and buckled down, Adriana lined the H295 up for the longest possible run. The hydraulic airlifts extended fully when she pushed the throttle to the wall. In fifteen seconds they were in the air.

"Thank you, Adriana," Curtis said. "You are amazing." He crawled back to check on the status of his birds. Hooded with leather head-helmets that kept them in the dark, the young birds were quiet in the ice of their burlap sacks. Curtis took them out of the damp to dry. Hooded, and so still in the dark, the birds shook out their feathers and settled. His birds tended to first, Curtis changed into dry socks and long johns.

Three hours later, they were on the ground in Fairbanks.

***

CHAPTER 7

Frozen Flowers

When the major arrived at the mortuary, or military funeral home, he absentmindedly set the flowers he had bought for the occasion on the roof of his car. On coming out with his sister-in-law, he grabbed them and ran back in to place them on the urn. Veta watched him from the passenger seat. "Is that the first time you have ever given your wife flowers, Almas?" The major ignored her comment as he drove off for his quarters. Veta was an unpleasant cog in the wheels.

I will have to make the best of the bitch, he thought. *Only time will clear her out of here.*

It was a short drive to the home he and Velma had shared on base. The door was unlocked. Veta pushed it open before the major could get there. She went on in, calling for young Almas. He answered from his mother's sewing room. Veta raced in and embraced her nephew. Tears welled up in her eyes. "You poor darling," she cried out. "What a shock it must be for you."

"For all of us, Aunt Veta," young Almas said quietly, holding her close. The major stood in the doorway, waiting. He was glad he had changed the carpet. His son broke free of his aunt and saluted his father, who returned the gesture formally before shaking his son's hand.

"She's gone, son," he said. "I don't know why. I don't know why these things happen to me—to her. It was her choice. She hurt me."

"She hurt us all, Major," Almas said softly. "Something must have hurt her pretty bad to make her do it, Major. Perhaps we will never know what, but we must take the blame. We are the guilty ones."

"How—how can that be, A?" the major stammered. "What could you have done to bring this on her? What could I have done? I loved Velma and cared for her all these years. Twenty-one—was it? No, twenty-two. How old are you, A?"

"He's twenty-four," Veta said with ice on her breath. "You and my sister have been married twenty-five years this December. Reason enough, Major." She turned away. Sitting on her sewing machine was Velma's laptop. Guilt caught in her throat along with the words written so hastily to her now deceased sister. "When, exactly, did Velma—did this unfortunate thing happen, Major?"

"Exactly? I don't recall. Too much has happened in the last weeks." He turned away. He couldn't look Veta in the eyes. The major walked to the liquor cabinet in the kitchen and took out a gin bottle. There were three of them there. There was no vodka. "A," he called to his son, "would you like a drink? We will drink to the memory of your mother." Veta was staring fixedly at her sister's laptop.

"When exactly did Velma—did she do it, Major? I need to know!"

"How the fuck should I know? Look on the goddamned death certificate, Veta, if you must be so demanding."

Almas Armstrong Cooper looked in wonder, from his father to his aunt. "What is this all about? The tragedy is that Mother is gone, not when. And she was obviously terribly distraught when she went, lay the blame where you will. We are all responsible—in one way or another. We may never know the reason—the absolute reason." Veta turned, threw her arms around her nephew, and burst into tears.

The major poured a double shot of gin in a water glass. No ice. He bolted it down.

***

Curtis made arrangements to fly his birds to Seattle after he had them inoculated. Wild gyrfalcons were susceptible to many diseases in captivity, as most wild creatures are. Curtis had taken two hours or more each day to train the birds as he came down the river. Even before they could fly, which they could do now, he held them on a leather gauntlet to feed them. They were fast learners. They would now fly to hunt but would be back in his care to feed. Kerns had been amazed to see this take place with the first birds taken before he left for Deadhorse with Adriana. He had some interesting photos of the training process.

Curtis called Kerns on arrival in Fairbanks but begged a time to rest up before a visit. He slept twelve hours straight at the airport motel. Kerns waited him out. They were having coffee now in the motel lobby.

"She is phenomenal," Curtis said. "I was wet and freezing in that damn leaking boat. I couldn't get to shore, Kerns, because of the leaks in the canvas and the closing ice field. There was no way to get ashore. The thin ice at the edge would not support my weight. And the sharp ice slashed at the canvas. If I fell through, I would be a dead man in minutes. I bailed continuously all night to keep myself and my birds afloat."

"What the hell did she do?"

"She broke up the ice with that plane of hers. She took one hell of a chance, Kerns, dipping her plane right down into it. She broke the ice up with the weight of her plane. As she neared the shoreline, she forced it deeper. The big wheels of her Helio cut through it as she skated on the thicker ice nearing the shore. It was incredible. I paddled in right behind her on the broken trail she made for me."

"Christ." Kerns shook his head, listening in amazement.

"If Christ was there, he definitely was on her side—and mine."

"How long will you be here, Curtis?"

"I'll be here forever. Kerns, I will live forever after that one." Curtis grinned. "I am a lucky man. However, I am flying out to Seattle with the birds today. I want to find Adriana before I go and thank her again."

"Her A-Plus Flying Service is in a hangar close to the runway. I'll go with you." They dropped the paper coffee cups in the hotel trash and headed across Airport Way, toward the Fairbanks International runway.

***

Adriana and Alice were reading the local newspaper with rapt attention as Curtis and Kerns approached the hangar. "You know this guy in the paper well, right, Adriana?"

"Alice, I doubt that there are two majors of this name, Almas A. Cooper III. I had lost track of him and he's right here under my nose." She tapped the leading headline in the obituary section of the *News Miner* with her pen. "So Velda, Velcro, Velma, whatever her name, finally summoned the guts to leave him. Sewing scissors." She looked up at her friend. "Sewing scissors? I am reasonably certain she had a bottle of vodka to give her a boost into the hereafter. That poor woman. I only met her once. That was enough time to understand her situation, married to that guy. I believe they have a son at the academy." She glanced back down at the obituary. "And this guy, Captain Albert D. Cummings." Adriana shook her head. "He flew north for the funeral?"

"Tomorrow. The funeral is tomorrow."

"I used to fly with those two, Alice. Real nice guys. You might remember them." She tapped the newspaper again. "Will you please attend? Pay your respects for us? I'd like to go to see the look on their faces, but I'm flying tomorrow. You don't have to say anything, Alice. You're going just for her."

The office entrance of the hangar swung open. Adriana looked up. Kerns and Curtis headed in their direction, their heels echoing across the smooth, clean, concrete floor. Adriana folded the newspaper and slipped it into a drawer of the table that doubled for a desk. "Will you be there, Alice?" She sighed. "That poor damn woman."

"I'll be there for us, Adriana."

Adriana got up to greet the two men.

***

The funeral went without a hitch and with very few words. There was no priest or minister. Velma's son said the words. Alice appreciated the honest grief the young man showed in his presentation. The lieutenant struggled to hold back tears. The major and his friend, Captain Cummings, stood by at silent attention. Alice slipped out the moment the service was over.

Captain Quebberman, the PR man, shook the lieutenant's hand as he stepped from the podium. "Very moving, Lieutenant," he said, with practiced feeling. "Your mother would be proud of you. The US Air Force is proud of men like you."

"Thank you, Captain." His Aunt Veta swished up to him as young Almas saluted his father and the captain standing with him.

"Thank you, Son," the major said, returning his salute. "I don't believe we have to be this formal in situations like this, but I appreciate the gesture." The major turned to the PR man. "Captain, thank you for the moving obituary. Well done. But can you tell me who brought flowers? I would like to thank them."

"Certainly. Your son and sister-in-law each brought an arrangement. Another woman brought a beautiful assortment of wildflowers. She dropped them off before the service and left. She returned to the chapel just as your son began to speak. She also left a small bottle with a black ribbon bowed around it. I believe it is still there on the urn. And by the way, Major—"

But the major had walked off to the urn. He picked up the delicate vile with the black ribbon, glanced at it, and slid it in his pocket as the undertaker stepped up to him.

"It was a beautiful service, Major," he said. "Your son gave an admiral presentation. I must admit when the lieutenant asked for his mother to not be represented by a member of the clergy, I was a bit shocked. Is he planning to study for the clergy himself?"

"He hasn't mentioned it to me."

"I see. Well—oh, by the way, Major, are you taking the urn with you, or would you rather I deliver it to your quarters?"

"Would it be too much to ask you to hold it for a few days? I have so much going on right now—company, family, and all."

"Certainly not, Major. I will see to it. Just call when you wish for delivery."

"Thank you." The major headed back to his party.

"Major," his son spoke upon his arrival. "Aunt Veta and I are going in her rental car. We will be at the house a bit later."

"Permission granted, Son. We shall see you there." Young Almas and his aunt left the chapel. The major turned to his friend, Captain Cummings. "What do you think of this, Captain?" Reaching in his coat pocket he drew forth the black beribboned vile of perfume and handed it to the captain.

Captain Cummings put on a pair of dark prescription glasses. He would have to give up flying soon if his superiors discovered the deteriorating condition of his eyesight. He glanced down at the bottle in his hand. Obviously impressed, he looked about the near-empty chapel. The undertaker was picking up the urn and flowers. All others had left. "Major," he said in a muted whisper, "where did you find this?"

"On top of the urn, Al. Someone left it with the flowers."

"Who?"

"I don't know. But I plan to find out." He took the bottle back and pocketed it.

"Midnight Poison?" The captain mouthed the words silently.

"Right, Captain. Midnight Poison." The two officers left the chapel.

***

At his quarters, the major and his friend poured a quick drink and descended to his basement studio, or cave, as Velma had called it. They opened his computer and browsed for Midnight Poison, getting the same results as Kerns and Slim had before them. However, the two men inaugurated a deeper search and came up with a name they sought in the site that held it. In his inbox, there was also a note from an old comrade in arms.

> *Look for me in Fairbanks, Major. Will be there in a few days. JB.*

Above them, they heard the major's son and his aunt Veta. The Young man was gathering his things for his flight back to Colorado Springs. It would leave in a few hours. Veta was going through her sister's email. She guiltily eradicated the letter she had sent to Velma concerning her affair with the major. She felt much better for it being wiped from the record. After hasty goodbyes to the major, Almas and his Aunt Veta left for the airport. The major and his friend dove back down into the cave.

***

CHAPTER 8

The Galloping Banana

Samuel Charles Bellefonte, in his private cell in Cincinnati, completed his second fantasy profile of the day. This was his sixth week on the job. He was alternating weekends with another writer, an older man with a jaded outlook on sex and a bureau full of worn out clichés. Samuel worked on his "novel in progress" on his days off. Saul Billings was pleased with Samuel's profile creations. Samuel had a good rapport with the real participants—that is, honest housewives, those who cried out for attention. Samuel was a good listener, without taking too much of the company's time. Samuel was a good salesman, as well. He wouldn't do cybersex, only voice contact. Eye contact was not for the ex-McDonald's handler.

Samuel believed his literary work in the sex line, or market, was quite good: certainly better than average. After all, he sat back in his chair and thought, Anaïs Nin and Henry Miller, when writing for survival in Paris in the 1930s, wrote pornography for a living and, in Samuel's mind, Anaïs and Miller were literary giants. *What will be will be*, he thought. *We artists will do as we must to survive*. His eyes flashed up to the screen.

Samuel had one problem client, and here it was again—Midnight Poison, Sex, Fire & Ice, a rough trade client. Saul Billings had turned the client and her correspondence over to Samuel. Midnight's attitude frustrated the naïve young writer. It was not that the client was dumb or stupid that bothered him. Quite the opposite. She was just difficult. Midnight Poison would not allow him to "doctor" her profile, a profile he considered ugly, or "gargoylish," as in gargoyle. His last description of it was a word of his own invention. He was quite proud of it. From the picture she submitted to accompany her profile—a beautifully toned body (unfortunately, the head was cropped)—he judged the woman to be in her well-preserved thirties. He had advised her to show her facial features. She refused to pay him any mind, even so far as to give him an answer. She ignored him completely, except to demand he make changes in her profile as she called for them. Among other things, she would change the date of her birth. This was not unusual. Most clients lied about their age. At times they lied about their sex. Midnight Poison changed her birthdate and profile much too often, Samuel thought. Why? What was she hiding? What was she after? Saul, too, had problems with this client.

Saul Billings's previous life had been solely academic and a bit lackluster. Teaching French and English literature in a small college in Quebec, Canada left him an abundance of time to browse the Internet. While doing so he absently stumbled across a number of sex sites—not online dating sites, but raw sex sites. Membership in these and dating sites was touted to be free. Under an assumed name, Saul joined an online dating site and two obvious sex sites. After working the sites for less than a week, he discovered that many of the participants on the sites were, in fact, fictitious. The sex sites were more inclined to seed their numbers, and profiles, with tantalizing allusion. After a month of online intrigue, Saul, a citizen of the United States, applied for a business license in the States and started his own site, Raw Wives in Need. After a few weeks of editing the rough profiles submitted by his clientele of supposedly married women in need of extramarital attention, he was in business. The homosexual lesbian factor came on in passable numbers as well. The site's financial stability grew.

Saul, following the path of preexisting sites in order to text the "ladies of the site," as Saul Billings billed them, male members, as well as the ladies, had to submit a legitimate credit card number to pay a monthly fee if they wished to communicate with other members of the same or opposite sex. As the dollar factor grew, so did Saul's intrigue in his new business. He was soon taking in as much as or more online than he did teaching. He turned in his resignation in Québec and moved back to the States where he was born. Under the same business license he started a new site, Cum With Me. Another success. And now, Sex, Fire & Ice. A somewhat pseudo-poetic heading for such a business endeavor, he had to admit, but it was catching on. He had to remind himself of the type of mind he was dealing with.

Saul kept his sense of Rabelaisian humor, but he had to hire help to keep up with the work demand. He loved it.

***

Sex, Fire & Ice professed to be a free site. As far as Samuel could see, all sex sites offered this false enticement. To attain the "five-star service," that is, to contact other members on site, one had to make a monthly payment. Once Saul Billings, or some like-minded site owner had "your number," it was made very difficult to break free—to "unsubscribe" from the cyber morass you had plunged yourself into. The automated payments were withdrawn monthly until the disenchanted client instructed his card company to cut off the connection. More than once a distraught husband or wife who did the family's bookkeeping discovered the glitch and divorce, or worse, was the outcome. In other cases, the only way out of this morass was for the client to cancel the credit card.

Although fascinated by the twisted directions Midnight Poison took in her profile's presentation, Saul had problems with her blunt delivery. In the profile she placed on his Sex, Fire & Ice site, she demanded no poetic justice. She wanted it straight, hard, and rough with a capital R for rape. According to her profile, Midnight Poison claimed to have been abused as a child by her father and two uncles, all members of the military. The newly submitted profile stated up front that she wanted to be raped as she had been as a child. It was the only way she could "get off," she claimed. Also, she demanded military personnel, preferably US Air Force officers, to answer her profile requests.

There had been numerous replies, but Midnight Poison was extremely selective in her choices.

Saul turned the troubling case over to his new writer, Samuel, but monitored it closely. Samuel had "ethics" even in the cubicle of this questionably literary and definitely limited outlet. Surprisingly enough so did Saul Billings. If there was no intrigue or humor in the client's profile, he objected to it. It was no longer a game. There definitely was no humor in Midnight Poison's Cum With Me or Sex, Fire & Ice profiles. Samuel was directed to talk the client into accepting the fact that she needed to lighten up. Neither Saul nor Samuel had a problem with the military bent of Midnight's profile, but both were appalled at the violence of rape. Saul had never had to face Midnight Poison's situation before. In Saul's mind and heart (Samuel was surprised he had one), rape of any kind was an odious act. To Samuel, sex, as he fantasized it, was supposed to be, if a bit kinky, still a thing of beauty. Rape was brutal. He wanted no part of it. He sent a sharp reply to Midnight Poison, expressing his thoughts concerning her new profile. He told her that, in no uncertain terms, Sex, Fire & Ice would not condone rape.

Samuel fully expected his boss to crack down on him for his open display of sensitivity. It had burst from him in an uncontrolled display of emotion. Once in cyberspace, there was no calling it back. Samuel knew his boss personally monitored the interplay between him and Midnight Poison. Yet Saul made no reply. There was a reply, however, from Midnight Poison.

My dear SB (does this stand for Son of a Bitch?),

If these are indeed your capitalized initials, as you represent them to be, what right have you to edit, cross-examine, or otherwise interfere with my rights on your fucking disgusting porno site?

I have paid for the right to use it as I will and so I shall, or I shall sue your tight little faggot ass, which I am very capable of doing.

Samuel sat back in his chair and waited for more. There was no more.

"Well," came Saul's hushed voice over the private intercom, "I guess that settles it, Samuel. Midnight Poison is an educated woman. She is definitely a woman and knows her rights. Do nothing! Do not answer her last transmission. Let her profile stand as is. That is all, Samuel."

Samuel sat, his mind swirling, and obeyed his orders. He did nothing.

***

Having access to Midnight Poison's credit card information, or what he considered to be her credit card information, gave Saul access to her real name and station in life. It also gave him access to her credit report. The report gave her top honors. Financially Midnight Poison was a no-risk client. Saul had this same credit information, excellent, good, bad, and indifferent, filed on the thousands of members of his sites. Credit information and the card numbers themselves were strictly guarded and touted to be absolutely secure. Messages between members of his sites were absolutely confidential. In fact, they were closed to his staff. Only Saul himself could hack into them as he wished. Saul Billings feasted on information and enjoyed doing this. He now wished to know, in truth, what Midnight Poison was up to. Also, why was she referring to the Sex, Fire & Ice site as a fucking disgusting porno site? She was a part of it. He tracked down all who answered her profile. There were many that reached out for this luscious toxic morsel, but almost no queries were accepted by Midnight. The latest acceptance was an Air Force captain stationed in Germany. The captain's message, terse and to the point, had been in response to the rape request in her profile. In an unauthorized manner Midnight Poison gave the captain a private email address. That was a "no-no" on all sex sites. Money could be lost. The message from Midnight to her client read:

Email any and all messages to MP—only at this address: ATownsend @gallopingbanana.net.

It took but a moment for Saul to pluck and search the name. He was an expert at it. But it was confusing, definitely puzzling. ATownsend? Who the hell was that? Neither did he recognize gallopingbanana.net. Saul was bothered. He would lose a client's income. He did not appreciate his client's correspondence going to addresses other than those provided through his sites. They seldom did. He didn't push it, but he didn't like it. Midnight Poison obviously didn't trust the security of Saul's site. Smart lady. Saul set to work. It took him almost an hour to break the code and hack into gallopingbanna.net. He had foolishly started his search in the tropics and then Gallop, New Mexico. That was too easy. The galloping banana threw him off. He took a blind stab and discovered that Southwestern Alaska was referred to by hard-line natives of that state as "the Banana Belt." Saul had locked on to something here. *Galloping fucking bananas*. The thought rankled him. He pushed the thought from his mind—but then reconsidered. "That's it," he cried aloud. He was on to something. More absurd connections had sprung up in this business. Why not? He thought a moment, drumming the rubber eraser head of his #2 pencil on the oak surface of his desk. Then he wrote it down. He had found it. Saul never took notes on his keyboard. Too permanent. Even eradicated, the worldly ghosts could be dragged from the grave to incriminate him. Notes taken with #2 lead went into the shredder—and from there to the Cincinnati alley behind the "Fornicarium," as Samuel had so aptly christened the sexual office space. From the dumpster in the alley all penciled notes went to the garbage crematorium, a fitting destination.

"No," Saul said aloud. "All sites of mine are secure!" Although substantial offers had been made to share his clients' information, he had never been tempted to sell credit card numbers or other personal identities he possessed. Saul, the Rabelaisian clone and admirer of Marquis de Sade, had never sunk that low. Saul Billings considered himself a man of honor—in business transactions. And sex was his business right now. He would transact it with honor. Saul might hack into a few accounts. It was his right, he felt. But the information he fed on would go no further than his #2 lead. Gallopingbanana.net. So be it. Saul Billings laughed aloud.

Saul glanced up at the bank of video screens over his head. Samuel was still staring blankly at the screen in front of him. "Forget about the Poison, Samuel, and get to work!"

Samuel shook his head sharply. It cleared to some extent. "But it's rape, Saul."

"Mr. Saul Billings to you, Sammy."

"Right." Samuel looked about at the naked men with shaved balls and cunt-shaved women on the walls of his cubicle. They were in his face all day. Some photographs, like the pictures of Midnight Poison, possessed no heads. Just tits and ass—"And cunts," he murmured. Samuel was calling them cunts now, instead of quims. They were his clients. They deserved honesty. "Fucking cunts!" he yelled.

"To work, Sammy boy."

"Right, Mr. Billings."

"Yours is not to question why."

"Right, Mr. Billings." Samuel pulled up the next profile. It was an Irish girl, standing slim and naked in a field of green grass. She claimed to be safely over eighteen years of age. Her small abrupt breasts stood out, nipples erect, her blue eyes wide and pleading. Samuel read her proposed profile:

I am 22 years old. I am five feet 4 inches tall. For you, I will play the role of a total slut.

I have blue eyes and brown hair.

Force me to have sex.

Make me a victim.

Strip me naked.

Tie me up.

Talk nasty to me.

Blindfold me.

I am a student.

Teach me.
Use me hard.
Make me cum.
Please make me cum.
Force me to cum.
Force me to be a total slut!

"Oh shit. She wants to be raped, too. And she's Irish." Samuel dropped his head into his arms and sunk lower in his chair. "Another one. I might as well move to Washington where the lying and deceit is worse, but more profitable."

***

CHAPTER 9

Truth Will Come Out

Kerns turned his 4x4 into Slim's freshly snow-covered drive. No one shoveled snow in Alaska. It was just packed down until spring thaw when it melted to expose the truth of last year's garbage melting through it like the legendary middle finger. Right now everything was white and beautiful as a virgin's breast. It was cold enough for the snow to be dry as chalk. His Ford crunched to a stop as if it were on a bed of gravel. Chalk would make more sense right now. His throat was dry as chalk. He remembered he had left a half-full bottle of rye on Slim's kitchen table last night. He slammed the pickup's driver door shut and headed through the cold for the log cabin.

Slim's fifteen-year-old son, Roy, by his only marriage, was spending the weekend with his father. The kid was a sophomore in high school and pretty bright. *Maybe too damned bright*, Kerns thought. *Like most high school kids, he probably thinks it smart to drink*. He hoped the boy hadn't finished off his bottle of rye. Slim and his wife had named their son Roy so he wouldn't be stuck with a nickname like Sammy or Frisky or Leroy.

As Kerns swung through the heavy plank door, Roy jumped guiltily to his feet and blocked the view of the screen on Slim's computer.

"What you watching, Roy, pornography or football?"

"Well," the boy stammered, "I was doing some research."

"Pornography, right?"

Roy put on a crooked grin and shrugged. "You and Dad were trying to find out about Midnight Poison. Maybe I found it—or her. From what I can see of her, she is something else. But I can't see her face. They cropped her head off." Kerns brushed past the boy to look down at the screen.

"Holy shit, Roy, do you study this stuff in school?"

"Sex education? It doesn't cover porn. I wish it did. We might learn something."

"I don't mean naked women, but computer shit. I had to make do with *Playboy* at your age."

"It's all fantasy, Kerns."

"Smart ass. Your mother know you are doing this—research?" Kerns sat down at the table and studied the screen. "They did cut her head off, didn't they?"

"It was a cyber cut. Nothing serious. She says she wants to be raped. Now that is serious."

"It's her choice. She's over eighteen—she wants to be raped?" That was a new one for Kerns. Kerns had perused a few porno sites, but he wasn't particularly turned on by them. Why hadn't he thought of them in connection with Midnight Poison? *This kid is smart*. "You haven't reached the age of consent yet, have you, Roy?"

"No. I'm still in the pimple age. But Dad says I'll grow out of it. I'll be sixteen in December." Roy stood silent for a moment. Kerns wasn't listening to him. "You like that picture, Kerns?"

"Just doing research, Roy."

"Right."

"Kids are too damn smart these days. Why don't you make yourself useful and fix me a drink—if there is any left in that bottle."

"Same as you left it. I think maybe I'll be a bartender when I graduate from high school." The boy stepped down into the kitchen. "I'm already an expert at pouring Rye."

"Your dad doesn't drink."

"Neither do I."

"There's nothing wrong with not drinking, Roy." Kerns was only half listening to Slim's son. His mind was on Midnight Poison and her blatant sexual profile. It was more outrageous than he had expected. More negative than positive and not exactly celestial—certainly not morally sexual. Other than the words uttered by a dead man on the shores of an Alaskan swamp, there could be no connection. *Does it have anything to do with falling bodies? That is a bit off the wall. What does she want? Rape? The question: Is she too intelligent for that? Or is she intelligent enough to make it work in her favor? Or am I dreaming bullshit?* The picture definitely had fallen into a crack in Kerns's mind. Kerns shook his head out of the reverie of a mental forest.

"I smoke dope instead."

Snapped back to the present. "You what?"

"I don't touch that meth shit." Roy set Kerns' drink down beside the keyboard. "It's poison."

"So I understand. Worse than Midnight Poison?"

"Midnight Poison looks pretty good to me, Kerns," the boy said smugly. "What do you think my dad will think of her?"

"I don't think you should be writing her any love notes, Roy."

"I don't have a credit card. You need a credit card on those sites. You think I could use Mom's? You got to give Sex, Fire & Ice a card number."

"Sex, Fire & Ice? Where did you come up with that name?"

"Research, Kerns. Do your research."

"What time will your dad be back, Roy? Did he say?"

"You going to tell him?"

"Tell him what?"

"That I did your research for you."

Kerns took a thoughtful sip of his drink. *This kid is too much*, he thought, reflecting on the Rye in his glass.

"I put two ice cubes in it. That's the way you like it, isn't it?"

"It's perfect, Roy. Thank you."

"My dad used to drink, Kerns. He used to drink a lot more than you do. He quit after they got the divorce. I still wonder why he didn't quit before he and Mom split up. They are friends again now. That is where he is now, with Mom. My old man gets me to come up here and visit him, and then he sneaks down to see Mom. They think I don't know. What do they think I am, stupid?" Roy picked up Kerns's Rye and smelled it, then set it back down on the paper napkin he had brought with it. "Do you think I am stupid, Kerns?"

"You are definitely not stupid, Roy. You do a lot of thinking for a boy your age and thinking is definitely not a stupid thing to do."

"Yeah. I do research, too."

"Right." Kerns took a long slow sip of his drink. *This kid is too much*, he thought again. *Thank Christ we had a girl.* Kerns dipped into melancholy for the moment, wishing his daughter Salome could be here with them, wishing, after all these years, his wife were still alive. He finished his drink. "Right," he said again. "You are definitely not stupid, Roy—and you do great research."

"Did you know that Midnight Poison is a perfume, Kerns? It's made by Christian Dior. I think I will get some for my Mom—if I can afford it. Or I could use her credit card. What do you think?"

"I think using her credit card would be a little stupid, Roy, for whatever poison you plan to purchase."

"Yeah. You're right. I'll get her flowers. She likes flowers, especially in the winter. It's almost winter here. I'll let Dad get her the Midnight Poison. I'm glad they are friends again even if they are keeping it a secret."

***

Captain Albert D. Cummings had used up about all the leave time he had coming. He and the major had perused the bars of Fairbanks on two or three occasions, the Airport Motel Lounge, the Pump Station, the Switzerland. They tried the Red Fox but found it much too noisy for their taste and the patrons a bit slovenly for the spit and polish of the air force. Tonight was Cummings's last night out in the north before returning to his base in Texas. He was dressed in civilian clothes, dressed down, as it were, pressed blue jeans, etc. The major had pulled night duty on the post. The captain was on his own, slumming it, lowbrow.

The taxi dropped him off in front of the Big I. He was looking for prey. The cab driver suggested this location. "Lots of GIs," he said. "Male and female. You should do all right, Captain." The cabbie had taken him out before and knew what he was looking for when out of uniform.

One of the many things in the northland that was distasteful for Cummings was the tobacco smoke in most Fairbanks bars and restaurants. Although smoking was banned in public places throughout the US, Alaskans paid no attention to the law. The Big I was no exception. The captain braved it and chose an empty stool at the bar. He ordered Irish whisky on the rocks—with a splash of Coke. Molly, who was on duty, choked at the thought of Irish whisky mixed with coke but managed to fill the order.

It was still early Friday evening. A local gathering of writers, actors, and artists and would-be writers, actors, and artists, happily bright on a potluck of various wines and anti-political conversations, entered by the back door. Cummings observed them with distaste as they made a rather boisterous entrance. They moved forward onto a raised platform behind the seated officer where tables had been unofficially reserved for them. There was one rather inebriated, but lovely, lady in her twenties who did fetch his attention. *She must be legal*, he thought. *No one carded her*.

A rather distinguished gentleman was handed a guitar and a drink. "Doc's special," the waiter proclaimed. "A Bloody Mary made with Boodles Gin." Dr. Robert Singer nodded his appreciation. Dr. Singer had been Fairbanks's most sought after doctor for many reasons, including the fact that he gave credit to anyone who truly needed credit. Unfortunately, he had been caught performing free abortions and lost his license to practice. The doctor struck a chord. He was also an accomplished musician. Rob Singer didn't need a license to sing and play. The crowd burst into a song about the Lowland Sea, followed by an original about Chena Ridge.

The guitar player then slid into an instrumental blues number. His eye, however, was on Diana Alderman, the pretty, quite drunk young lady. Cummings had attracted Diana's attention as well. The captain picked up on the fact that she was loaded but lovely and attracted to him. She would be an easy mark. Doc, who missed very little, was aware of this interplay. Having helped to bring Diana into this world twenty years earlier, Doc Singer had become, more or less, a surrogate father figure. He was not overly possessive in that he didn't try to run her life. But both her parents had died in the young girl's early teens. She needed some restraint. Doc watched over her. Diana depended on him, yet seldom took his advice.

While Cummings watched her, Diana lost it and slid under the table. Her friends propped her back up in her chair. Hap brought her a cup of coffee. Captain Albert Cummings was at this point distracted. On the wall behind Diana Cummings was the artist's rendition of the man Kerns had found in the swamp above Wiseman and the Arctic Circle. In the dim, smoke-filled room, Captain Cummings crossed to it. He set his drink down, unpinned the drawing from the wall, and stepped back to the bar where the light was better.

Hap picked up on Cummings studying the headshot. He circled behind the bar, set down the coffee pot, and watched the man with the drawing. Strangers were watched closely in the Big I. Cummings ordered another drink. Hap moved in to take the order. "What kind of Irish, stranger?"

"It's all the same. Just put some Coke in it." Molly had moved in to overhear the conversation.

"Poured him Tullamore Dew the first time. There is only one kind of Coke." The customer was studying the drawing again.

"It's on the house, Molly." Hap turned back to the stranger. "You're only a stranger here once, mister, until we buy you a drink. Good to have your company."

Cummings looked up. "You know this guy?" He tapped the drawing.

"Know him?" Hap said. "No," he said truthfully. "You?"

"No," the man said. Hap knew he was lying.

"The lady over there, the one that was under the table, she made the drawing," Hap lied. "She's a fine artist. She knows him—maybe." Hap was good at lying.

"What's her name?"

"The under-the-table lady?"

"The under-the-table lady."

"Diana."

"Here's your drink, mister. My name is Molly. What's yours?" Molly had moved back into the scene.

"Take care of him, Molly. I got to go check my plumbing." Hap slipped his iPhone from his pocket as he headed for the restroom. The customer in front of Molly leaned in on his elbow, studying the drawing. Thoughtfully, he bit down on the skin on his forefinger. He smelled the wet, tonguing it. It pleased him.

Bizarre, Molly thought, *but I have done it myself. Sort of a masturbation hang-up. This guy isn't bad looking, just got bad taste in liquor. Irish whisky with Coke?* "What's your name, mister?"

"Albert, Al," the captain said without thinking. "What's yours?"

"Molly. I told you."

"And that's Diana, over there, asleep in her chair?"

"Diana, the artist?"

"And she sketched this portrait?" Cummings held up the artist's conception left by Slim.

Why the hell has Hap passed along that bogus information? Molly wondered. "She's the one."

Hap stepped back into the conversation. "Do you know this guy in the sketch, mister?" Hap asked, trying to draw him out.

"Albert," Molly said. "His name is Albert."

Captain Albert Cummings picked up with the next question. "And do you know him?" Albert asked pointedly. Hap shook his head. "Thanks for the drink," Albert said. He got up and, taking the drawing with him, walked over to where Diana was passed out in the chair. Hap figured Diana wouldn't wake up. Doc had a protective eye on her, too. The rest of her group was singing another song led haphazardly by the disbarred doctor with the Boodles Bloody Mary. The song was something about a Kegler lost in the woods. Albert stood a while over Diana. He shook her shoulder gently. As Hap figured, Diana did not respond. Hap walked around in front of the bar so he could be closer to them. He did not feel comfortable with the situation. *Why the hell did I tell that guy Diana made the sketch?* He could see that Doc was concerned, too. Hap knew he had set it up and could kick himself now for doing so.

The stranger shook her again—this time roughly. Diana blinked back to wakefulness. Doc stood quickly, setting his guitar down. The singing stopped.

"Who the hell are you?" Diana mumbled, trying to focus on Cummings.

"A friend, lady," the man said, sizing up the situation. "You need to go home, Diana. I'm going to take you there."

"That's the best proposition I have had all night." Diana started to get up. Doc reached to steady her. Diana pushed him off and turned to the captain. "Your car or mine?"

"Shit," Doc said quietly. Things were not going right. He knew the story.

"You got the keys?" the man said.

Hap took the captain firmly by the shoulder. "Where you taking her, soldier?"

"I'm not a fucking soldier, buddy. I'm an officer. I'll take care of her."

"You heard the man." Diana pushed Hap aside. "He'll take care of me, Hap. An officer and a gentleman. Don't mess up my date. Who do you think you are, my father?"

Doc took Diana by the arm and spoke softly. "We'll take you home, Diana. You don't know this man!"

"Take your hands off me." Diana was drunk, and when drunk, she really got drunk. Her friends, of whom she had many, put up with it. "I make my own path," Diana yelled at the guitar player. Doc backed off. Diana grabbed her purse and found the keys to her car. "You drive!" She shoved the keys into Captain Cummings's hand. "I don't know who the fuck you are, but I trust you. Don't let me down!" she screamed at him.

Captain Cummings held the sketch up in front of Diana. "Did you sketch this drawing? Do you know this man?" Diana snatched the sketch from him and tore it to pieces.

"Are you taking me home or not?" she yelled at the man she didn't know.

Cummings took her by the elbow and headed toward the front door of the bar. Hap stood aside. This was out of his realm now. He looked to Molly. She was on the phone. Hap had been unable to reach Slim. He hoped Slim was the one Molly was talking to. It was not.

Doc Singer left his instrument on the table and grabbed his parka. He followed Diana and the man who led her out into the night. In the darkness of the street lamps he watched them closely. Doc was bothered. He knew, however, there was no reasoning with Diana when she was bombed. He would try to follow and be there if she needed him. He did not like the assertive way the stranger treated her. *Be he an officer, that man is no gentleman.*

As Diana's Chevy pulled out of the parking lot, Doc slid behind the wheel of his old Volkswagen bug. The engine finally caught, sputtered, and came to life. He turned right and, ready to turn again, was cut off by oncoming traffic. When he got on the Cushman Street Bridge Diana's Chevy was three cars in front of him. It made the first yellow light. Doc lost sight of it by the time he got off the bridge.

***

Lufthansa Airline, having flown in over the pole from Hamburg, touched down at Fairbanks International Airport. Captain Jason Blitzweimer, on personal business leave and dressed in civilian clothes, deplaned smartly from the first-class section. He was the first to be checked quickly through customs and was picked up by a driver brandishing a sign bearing his name in the lobby. His destination: Chena Hot Springs. The captain's business was his business. He was antsy to get to it. His driver told him of the picturesque log cabin near the resort and of the pleasures awaiting him within. The captain told her to just shut up and drive. Alice was happy to comply. The drive took a little over an hour. Alice led him to the cabin door and opened it for him. In the near distance a generator purred.

Captain Jason Blitzweimer stood in silence as the heavy door to the old log cabin closed behind him with a silent but solid finality. Slightly confused, he turned to it and reached for the latch. He found the door locked. He swung back into the dimly lit room. More of an entryway, it was low ceilinged and measured, perhaps eight feet by ten. There was a door on the far side, which must open into the main cabin, he thought. Heavy acorn hooks were screwed to the logs beside the door. A fur-lined coat with wolf fringe hood and a couple of heavy sweaters hung there. He crossed quickly to the door and swung it open. Warm air flooded in from the main room of the cabin. A bright light was directed in his face. Someone was sitting at a finished plank table in the center of the large room. He threw his hands up to shade his eyes from the sudden brilliance. The "someone" was familiar and staring straight at him. She was holding what appeared to be a pistol in each hand. As his eyes became accustomed to the light, he recognized her. "You," he said blankly.

"Me," she answered. Her right hand jumped in recoil with an almost soundless *blip*. The large animal tranquillizer struck Captain Jason Blitzweimer in the chest. He looked down at it in disbelief. "This time we won't go through the dehumanizing embarrassment of a trial either, Captain."

"Adriana—the bitch from hell." His eyes glazed over. As he reached for the dart, he knew it was too late. "The air force can track me to your door, bitch."

"The chip off the old block, Captain? Your implanted tracking chip? The 'sign of the beast'? A Satanic symbol? The USDA approved the technology. However, your little satanic microchip was scrambled at the Fairbanks airport. You are here alone."

"How?" He was fading fast. "You can't get away with murder, Captain O'Donovan."

"And you won't get away with rape, Captain Blitzweimer. Not this time!"

Jason Blitzweimer crumpled to the floor.

***

After leaving the Big I, Diana Alderman was nowhere to be found. At least she was nowhere to be found where people looked for her. Doc was still looking for her car in the dim light of late morning dawn. He found it frozen in the early ice of the Chena River. Doc called 911. The first person to show up was a reporter with earmuffs and a cowboy hat. Doc had nothing to say to him.

***

The victim was fully dressed, the sketchy article in the *News Miner* said, but badly bruised. It continued: *Diana Alderman, a promising young local artist, had, evidently, made no attempt to get out of her seat belt. A coroner's report is pending. Foul play may be involved*. The reporter was guessing at this. There was a quarter-page photograph of a wrecker pulling Diana's car from the ice-crusted Chena River.

Hap put down the morning paper and poured himself a drink. It wasn't his first. Hap never drank on the job. He wouldn't today either. Hap was drowning his guilt. Why had he told that asshole Diana had drawn the picture Slim left in the bar? Hap poured another drink and announced to his customers that the Big I was closed for the day. He escorted early drinkers out the front door and locked it. He didn't get to the back door in time. Slim and Kerns were there ahead of him. Dr. Rob Singer was there as well.

"I'm closed, goddamnit," Hap said. "Throw the bolt on that door and I'll put the coffee on. The Rye is on the bar. Help yourself, Kerns. I got your guitar behind the bar, Doc. I thought maybe you followed them last night."

"They lost me," Doc replied. "I knew that son-of-a-bitch was a phony."

"There was nothing you could do to stop her last night, Doc," Hap said quietly. "Diana was drunk and that lady drunk is impossible. But I set her up—telling him Diana drew the picture you left here, Slim."

"No," Doc said. "That guy had his eye on her long before he saw the picture. I saw it all happening. She was pounding those drinks like her mother used to long before we came into the Big I. I should have taken her to my place. It was my fault, too, Hap. I keep a room for her at my place," Doc said. "She stayed there the night before. She got a key to the door. Not that I lock it. You never know who might have to get in out of the cold. I waited for her there until four this morning. She never showed."

"What will be, will be," Slim said. "The city police are on it, too. What we need to do now is fill in the blanks—try to track down the guy who was supposed to be taking her home."

Hap was building the coffee by rote. He rinsed out what was left in the pot from last night and ladled fresh grounds into the gold filter.

"His name was Al," Hap said, "or Albert. No last name we know of." Hap thought for a second. He had dumped in three extra scoops of grounds. Hap wasn't counting. He added an extra spoonful and hit the on button. Hap wasn't thinking about coffee. The pot started to growl. "The man was in civvies but claimed to be an officer. Army? Air force? I don't know. He didn't say. Molly might know."

"I talked to her," Slim said. "Molly knows no more than you do, Hap. She'd never seen the guy before. He just came in out of the cold," she said. "He ordered Irish whisky and Coke and complained about the smoke. He wanted to know where the non-smoking section was. Molly told him it was outside."

"Sounds like a self-important son-of-a-bitch," Kerns interjected. Kerns had been up and dressed when Slim was leaving the house on the ridge. Slim was glad to have him for company on the early morning call. Headquarters told him when they called that Doc had found her at the site of the old ice bridge on the Chena.

"I would have gone in after her if I thought there was a chance," Doc said. "Shit. I left the house a little after four. My cabin is by the university," he explained to Kerns. "I drove back to the Cushman Street Bridge and crossed there. Christ, Hap, they got ten bridges over the Chena now and she takes the old ice bridge—with no ice on it."

"It's not your fault, Doc." Hap had fixed him a Doc Special Bloody Mary. He slid it across the bar. Doc took a long, red drink.

"I searched every place I thought she might have ended up, Hap. The ice bridge was my last thought. Hell, she used to be the first one to cross it in the fall and the last one to take a chance on it in the spring. That kid was crazy. Somebody gave her a car and she was driving it when she was thirteen." He turned to Slim. "How many times did you stop her?"

Slim shook his head. "I don't know, Doc. I was drunk half the times I stopped Diana. How could I, a drunken cop, in good faith give her a ticket? I couldn't take her driving license away." Slim smiled in spite of the situation. "She didn't have one."

Hap joined in the smile. Doc took another long drink of the red and laughed bitterly. "I don't believe much in the Almighty, gentlemen," he said, "but if there is a life after death, Diana Alderman would be right here laughing with us—or at us—right now."

Slim turned suddenly serious. "Well, she sure could answer some questions." He turned to Doc. "You were there when we pulled her old Chevy out of the Chena, Doc. I got an early report from the coroner. There was no water found in her lungs when he did his preliminary check. Diana Alderman was dead before she hit the water." There was a long silence. "That is not for publication until we know more."

Slowly Doc put his empty glass back on the bar. "I am not a believer in capital punishment either. I have even lobbied against it a number of times, but that rotten, mother fucking, son-of-a-bitch deserves to die! Preferably burned at the stake." Doc made a quick run for the men's room. He was sick. Five minutes later, he came out and motioned to Hap to open the back door. "I am not well," he said quietly to his friend. "I've seen death a hundred times in my business, but the thought of Diana just got to me. I hate violence. I have been a pacifist all my life, but then so was Einstein—until Hitler came along." Raising his hand in salute to those at the bar, Doc headed for the back door. Hap opened it for him and slid the bolt back in place when he left.

"That hit him hard," Hap said.

"It hit us all hard," Slim said.

Slim continued, trying to put the picture together: "Did this guy Al come in with Diana?"

"He was alone," Hap said, "but looking. He spotted Diana as an easy mark and went up to her table. That was when he spotted the picture."

"What picture?"

"The one you left, Slim. I had stuck it on the wall behind where Diana was sitting. This Al guy took it down and brought it back to the bar where the light is a bit brighter."

The Big I coffee pot was still growling. Black water was dripping into the pot. "He, this Al guy, started asking questions about the artist's sketch. Wanted to know where it came from. Who drew it? Stuff like that."

"Did he say he knew the guy?"

"No. But he did. Why would he be asking these questions? He was acting real shitty about it, too. I tried to call you. No answer."

"I know. I got your message too late."

"And then I really screwed up, Slim. Why? I don't know, but I told him Diana drew the picture. This guy wheeled around and went right up to her. He shook her awake. She had passed out. That's when the ruckus started. She started yelling. She grabbed the drawing and tore it up. And then she demanded that the guy take her home. She gave him the keys to her car and ordered him to drive her home. Doc got real upset. Diana told him to shut up. And then she and this Al went out together. Doc left his guitar behind and followed them. Christ, Diana doesn't even have a license."

"Yeah, but she had the keys," Slim said. "Not having a license didn't stop me from driving either. I was damn lucky they kept me on the force." Slim took a sip of Hap's overly strong coffee and gagged.

"You are the best man they have, drunk or sober," Hap said.

"I'm a better man sober, Hap. I haven't taken a drink in three years, but this coffee of yours might drive me to it."

"How do we find this Al guy before he's out of the country?" Kerns asked to get everyone back on track. "If he's guilty, he'll be on a plane and gone already. It's only a ten-minute walk from the old ice bridge to the Fairbanks International Airport."

"We're checking that out. If he did, he would have had to pick up his baggage. He had no car here and his stuff wasn't in Diana's Chevy," Slim said. "Diana was passed out, or already dead. He could have picked his bags up anywhere. The city and state cops are checking everywhere." Slim sighed. "Al—Albert. Molly said she washed the glass he was drinking from. We can't even get fingerprints. The car was wiped clean before it hit the water and then smudged by the gloves of everyone who pulled her out."

"I never saw him before," Hap said. "Could he be stationed here?"

"He had to be. Who in the hell would come up here unless he is ordered to? This is not exactly paradise." Kerns reached for the Rye. "Think about it, Hap."

"I'm thinking," Hap said. "Maybe we should put his picture on the wall, too." Hap was making a new pot of coffee. "Get your artist, Slim, to draw one up. I can give him a description. Molly can, Doc can, as well as others who saw him.

"How'd he get here, Hap?" Kerns asked. "Did he walk or come in a cab? Somebody must have seen him."

"Cabbies don't talk in this town," Slim said.

"We'll check around," Hap said.

"But right now there is no real evidence that there was any foul play on his part. There were no witnesses—no prints." Slim added hot water to his coffee. "That crazy lady could have kicked him out of her car anywhere. Anyone could have put her behind the wheel, opened the windows, started the car, and jumped out. The key was still in the on position, the windows were open so it would sink quickly, and the car was in gear."

Hap broke in: "There was no water in her lungs. The paper said there were bruises." He held up the daily with the picture. "A possibility of foul play."

"There's always a possibility of foul play. Who else was in the game? And no witnesses to prove it, Hap. That was said to sell papers. Nobody knew anything at that time. That damn cowboy reporter dreamed it up. We didn't know there was no water in her lungs until later."

Slim's cell phone went off. He stepped away to answer it, taking his doctored coffee with him. Kerns picked up the paper. He scanned the article and turned to Hap. "That ice bridge was close to the airport, right, Hap?"

"A short walk."

"A quick getaway." Kerns glanced back at the paper. Over the picture of them dragging Diana's car up through the ice there was an insert of Diana on a happier day. "She was a beautiful lady, Hap."

"Diana was a talented artist, too, but she couldn't stay off the sauce. In her blood, I guess. Her old man was an alcoholic and a junky. He swallowed the evidence and OD'd in the local jail. He tied up the few ounces of heroin he had on him in a condom and swallowed it. Figured he'd crap it out later—but he didn't tie the knot tight enough. Her mother—they found her frozen in a snow bank out by the university. Diana was living with friends and going to high school. She was a freshman or sophomore. She was always staying with friends, but sometimes they weren't the best of friends."

"I guess not." Kerns put the paper down and turned to Slim. His friend was pocketing his iPhone. The look on his face was one of suppressed shock. Kerns waited.

"We got another one through the ice, Kerns."

Hap set a fresh cup of coffee on the bar. "The coffee's hot and right, Slim. You look like you could use it." Slim set down the cup he was holding and picked up the fresh one. Kerns and Hap waited while Slim tested the coffee. It was too hot. It was always too hot. He set it back on the bar.

"Another surprise from the sky," he said quietly. "He came in about midnight. Dropped like a bomb and went through the ice. Into Red Slough—some people call it Red Slough, or Blood Slough. At Manly Hot Springs, below Minto where the Elliot Highway bridges the old boat landing cut in from the Tanana.

Riverboats brought supplies in there before the highway was pushed through." Slim tried the coffee again.

"Who found him?"

"There was a couple on the bridge when he came down. That's how we got the time. They didn't see the plane, but they heard a scream coming out of the sky and then silence. No one spotted the body until an hour ago. Naked—hands tied—frozen in the ice. The new ice won't support a man's weight. We'll take the chopper with a lift to break him free. You ready for this one, Kerns?"

"Didn't they try to find him last night?"

"Said they didn't know what the hell it was, Hap—maybe a Halloween prank, they said. It's a new married couple up there to soak in the springs. They didn't get out of bed until noon, so we didn't know sooner. You ready, Kerns?"

"To go swimming? I'm not a polar bear."

"I'll do that. They are packing a dry suit for me and a set of tanks if I have to go under."

"I'm game, if I can do you any good."

"You were there for the last one. You might recognize something." Slim pulled on his jacket. "The chopper will be waiting for us." The two men headed for the back door. Hap went with them that far.

"I'll keep the coffee hot," he called after them as he relocked the door.

The Big I would stay closed today.

***

CHAPTER 10

Blood Slough

Even through the crust of new ice on the slough, the water had a bloody tinge of color. There was no movement. The ice was clear and still. The six-foot slice of white flesh, with arms and legs akimbo, was easily spotted from above. Slim instructed the pilot to circle the body above tree level and safely above the height of the old steel one-lane bridge. A number of people had gathered on the bridge to watch them come in.

"You're not going to keep this one out of the news, Slim."

"No. But we'll keep the other two out as long as we can." Slim instructed the pilot to bring the chopper down in the camping area east of the bridge. "Don't want this to be another 'shoot-out in the Alaskan wilderness' like that business in '84. That was a nut case—the Spree Killer, they dubbed him—shot John Myers, one of our troopers. Shot him in a damn helicopter. It was a long shot. Killed him. Myers was in a chopper much like this one. Michael Silka, on his spree, killed at least nine people, including a two-year-old, the kid's pregnant mother, and her husband. He dumped them all in the river. The wife of one victim found her husband seventy miles down the Tanana in the spring runoff. Nobody knows for sure how many this Silka nut killed. One, for sure, in Fairbanks. The rest were here in Manly. There may have been a few in the States before he moved up here. Silka wanted to be a mountain man. He was a good shot, or at least a lucky one."

"I wasn't in Alaska that summer," Kerns said. "I heard about it. It made the History Channel, didn't it?"

"It was good copy. People love to hear about tragedy."

The chopper was on the ground and unwinding. The two men ducked out. Thomas, the trooper on the ground, met them. He had been keeping everyone off the ice. Slim hastily introduced him to Kerns.

"There is no current in that slough," Thomas said. "It's freezing fast, but not fast enough to trust it. Ice got a good grip on the body," he added. "He's not going anywhere." Slim was pulling his dry suit on over his winter gear. The pilot had taken a door off the chopper. While they talked, Thomas helped him hook up the drop cable to lower Slim and bring up the body. Kerns stood by, but out of the way. There was no rush, but it needed to be done and they knew how. Slim talked quietly to Kerns as he snugged himself into his diving gear.

"Where's your oxygen tank, Slim?"

"I don't think I'll need it."

"I'm not your keeper, Slim, but wear the goddamn thing."

"I got it right here," said Thomas, "and Kerns is right, Slim. Wear the goddamn thing."

"Is the tank full?"

"It's ready to go, but you check it, too." Thomas grinned. "You, Slim, are the safety instructor who taught me to always check my own gear. Now take your own advice."

"All right, guys, that's enough." Slim turned to Kerns. "While we are up there or I am in the water with my tank on, nose around, Kerns. Talk to the couple that heard the plane and the man screaming down. Ask them if by any chance they recognized the sound of the plane, twin-engine or single. Or if they would recognize it if they heard it again. A lot of people in Alaska fly. They might be able to do that. And see that guy over there in the cowboy hat with earmuffs? He's talking to the guy with the video camera. Channel 7, or whatever number. They must have flown in. Stay away from him. That's the cowboy who was out there when they pulled in Diana this morning. This is a bigger story. He's hungry." Slim checked the small ax strapped to his waist. He would have to cut the ice.

"The cowboy is shooting us now, Slim. You're going to be on the national news." Kerns grinned.

"Listen, Kerns, that cowboy will be busy covering the drop and the body being chopped out. This is a big one for him. While he's doing that, see if you can round up that couple that was there last night and talk to them."

"Don't fall in the wet."

"Thanks, Kerns."

The pilot was back at the controls. Slim and Trooper Thomas strapped themselves in. The big prop wound up slowly and caught. The craft rose like an unlikely dinosaur in a cloud of snow and dust. People scattered, Kerns with them. As the chopper lifted through the trees, Kerns saw the reporter's hat sail off in the down draft. The hatless cowboy was on camera at the time. *Nice shot*, Kerns thought as the cowboy anchorman ran after it.

***

Kerns walked out on the bridge as the chopper hovered over the white blotch of flesh that used to be a man. *Screaming all the way down*, Kerns mused. *Maybe he didn't have time to think with all that noise straining through his head.* A young couple stood looking up at the chopper as Slim, on a thin cable, dropped out of it. Thomas, attached to a safety belt, was leaning out and slowly letting Slim settle to the ice. It held. Slim didn't break through, although the clear new ice spider-webbed under his feet. On Slim's command, Thomas gave him more slack. The command was a hand signal; his arm lifted, Slim wound his hand slowly down. Kerns saw the cable belly out. Slim dropped to his knees and started chopping around the body. The ice opened. Red water spurted up in a small geyser. Slim went through it and out of sight. Those on the bridge and shoreline screamed. The chopper hung solid. Thomas reeled in the cable. After a moment Slim bobbed back to the surface. Hanging waist deep from the safety cable, he continued with his task, working his way around the body.

There were twenty or so curious observers on the bridge, among them a young couple at the center edge. They were lined up with the body and holding their mittened hands together.

"Newlyweds," Kerns said softly. *There is no one else in this town holding hands*. He stepped up behind them and tapped the man on the shoulder.

"I told you," the man turned and yelled in Kerns' face. "The sky is full of planes here day and night. So one flew over at I should judge to be about a thousand feet. Is that unusual? Night and day they fly here. Hell, I fly my own plane. I flew it up here for our honeymoon. And now you got me locked down for questioning because I heard a plane flying over and some animal screaming in the woods. It was dark. We didn't see a goddamned thing!"

Kerns stepped back, raising his hands up in denial. "I'm not a cop, or an undercover narc. I'm sorry."

"I'm sorry, too. Sorry I ever came to this place. If you're not a cop, what the hell is your beef?"

"I don't have one."

"Then fuck off."

"Honey," the woman with him spoke up, "the man isn't accusing you of anything. And the officer who asked you to stay around even said please. We are not under arrest."

"It's our honeymoon, Judy. I paid for a luxury suite. Better than that, I paid for a private cabin after we got here so we would not be disturbed on the first night of our marriage. It was our night, Judy, and then this happens. Some naked asshole jumps out of a plane without a parachute. Am I to blame for that?"

"Sweetheart."

"And then some cowboy asshole from the newspaper wants to know the intimate details of our first night together. Christ, he will probably post it on Facebook. People post the date, weight, and time of their bowel movements on Facebook, Judy."

"They do not."

"Your brother does, for Christ's sake."

"He does not!"

"Well, some people do. They post everything else." The new groom turned at last to Kerns. "I guess I'm sorry, Officer," he said. "I saved and saved for this night—actually, we were going to stay for a week. I can't afford a week."

"You can't, honey? You promised me a week."

"I'll pay for the rest of the week," Kerns interjected without thinking.

"But I'm not married to you," Judy cried. "It wouldn't be fair. Oh shit." She turned to her new husband. "Is this all going to be posted on Facebook? I feel like throwing myself off the bridge."

"Go ahead, Judy. Make a fool of yourself. I'll post that on Facebook."

People had stopped watching the dead body being sucked up into the helicopter. They were all gathered around the marital dispute. *One goes where the excitement is in Manly Hot Springs.*

Kerns was ready to flee the scene, but he had learned that the man was a pilot. Perhaps he could give them some positive information on the plane that dropped the body. "You are evidently an expert," Kerns said to the groom, soothing his ego. "Could you please tell me if it was a twin-engine plane or a single-engine plane you heard?"

"It was a single-engine plane," the man turned and yelled in his face. "It was a Helio Courier 295, or a Super Courier. They both drive a three-bladed prop that has a distinctive sound to a trained ear. From the stress of the engine, I would judge the pilot was doing fifty to sixty miles an hour air speed. I fly a Cessna 185 myself, but I can tell the difference in a heartbeat. It was a Helio, a Lycoming engine powering a three-blade prop. Take my word for it, copper. Here's my card if you have any questions." Kerns took the card.

"Thank you, Mr. . . ." He looked down at the card. "Mr. Right?"

"That's spelled with an *R*, right? R-I-G-H-T. Right Flying Service, that's my company." Grabbing his wife's hand, the groom dragged her off through the crowd. On the periphery, he turned back. "She's my wife, mister, and I pay for our own room!"

Kerns had nothing more to say.

***

The chopper was dropping Thomas and Slim, with the frozen body, in the parking lot at the east end of the bridge. The body, after a quick exanimation, would go on to Fairbanks. The cowboy, his hat recovered, was directing the filming of the event. Newspaper reporters were on hand as well. The one thing Slim wanted to know for sure was if the body had a small puncture, not much more than a needle prick, in the chest area. There would be discoloration around the puncture. The body that was dropped in Kerns' camping area had that hypodermic puncture and bruise around it. The coroner suspected it was from a large animal tranquillizer shot into him to knock the guy out. Slim checked and found the small wound roughly in the same location. These two guys went through the same introduction. *What the hell is going on here?* He wondered. *Was there a computer chip in this guy's shoulder too?* Slim kept his mouth shut. They would find that out in the lab. Slim kept these thoughts to himself. With all the media attention enough, rumors would be flying as it was. As the copter came down Slim had cut the rope binding the body's arms behind its back. He slipped the strands in a plastic baggie and sealed it.

***

A computer rendering of the head and shoulders of the character, Albert—whoever took Diana for a ride—was sketched by the police artist. He drew from Hap's and Molly's descriptions and then enhanced it to their satisfaction on the computer. Molly hung copies of it in various bars and restaurants in and around Fairbanks. The Fairbanks newspaper carried the rendition on the second page. The first page totally focused on the Blood Slough episode. Slim was featured in each article.

The police lab proved the rope to have been soaked in battery acid as Slim suspected. The pathologist who examined Diana found she had indulged in rather rough anal and oral sexual activity shortly before death. He definitely proved there was no water in her lungs. Reason enough to believe there had been foul play. He ruled she had died of asphyxiation prior to immersion in the freezing water of the Chena. Slim's investigation showed that her car was parked at the crest of the steep bank of the Chena with the motor running and the heater on for some time. It had then, with windows open and in first gear, rolled out onto the thin ice where it broke through and sank.

The search for the missing officer, Albert, was intensified.

***

Major Almas A. Cooper III was shocked when he opened the Sunday paper and saw his friend's likeness on the second page. As he read on, he became more agitated. *How could Al have gotten mixed up in this shit?* was the major's first and prevailing thought as he read on. *The presumed officer (air force or army unknown) is wanted for questioning in the death of local artist Diana Alderman.* The major rolled the paper up and slammed it on the Formica-covered island in his kitchen. Three nights ago, between midnight and four in the morning, Al had pulled up in front of the major's quarters in a car the major, looking from his bedroom window, didn't recognize. There was someone slumped down in the passenger seat in the car with him. Albert had gathered his belongings, dropped off the key to the house, and left. His flight was to leave at six a.m. The major assumed he was headed for the airport. Cooper looked back down at the picture in the Fairbanks paper. *This is a good likeness. People will remember seeing him with me at the funeral.* The major poured a second cup of coffee. He considered gin but left it out of his breakfast menu.

It was now three days since the girl's car was dragged from the icy waters of the Chena. The major calculated the date of Albert's departure. *If anyone asks, I'll say it was four days ago he left—as I remember it.* "It must have been three days ago." The major was speaking to the walls of his quarters as he wandered from room to room. There weren't many rooms in his quarters. He was going in circles. "Al, you put me in deep shit. I am not involved in this clusterfuck of yours! I have got enough shit to deal with." The major knew Captain Albert D. Cummings well enough to know he was capable of being involved in this rape and murder, if that is what it was—and that is what it looked to be. The major added a hefty splash of Scotch whisky to his coffee.

Other things in the Sunday news were a bit distracting as well, but not distracting enough for the major to dwell on them. Somebody was dropped or jumped from a plane. *A rather terrifying trip down without a parachute*, he mused. *That was a stupid move*, he thought, and thought about it no more.

The major missed flying. This military life behind a desk was not for him. He needed to sit at the controls of a jet where the excitement was the joystick of life. Major Almas A. Cooper III was nearing fifty. He was long eligible for retirement. He had been encouraged to do so by his superiors but had no desire to take the plunge. What would he do? He had no family, no place to go. Flying was his life.

Cummings was younger and still flying. The major envied Cummings the years and his aerial freedom. The major had nothing to do behind his desk but count the days—the hours, et cetera—until the end. The end of what? A game of Tiddlywinks? He unlocked the door to the basement and stepped down into his cave. He would play with his keyboard for an hour or so before retiring for the night. In that time, he would drop a line to Captain Cummings. *What has that asshole done and, worse yet, done in my territory? It can amount to nothing but trouble. Someone on the post is bound to see the drawing in the paper, recognize it, and question me.* "Shit!" That scatological thought plugged his brain waves.

Major Cooper was worried and confused. Maybe he should retire. It didn't look like he was ever going to make colonel, a substantial monetary dollop in his military retirement pension, but what else? He had invested in a pair of silver oak leaf clusters in preparation of his expected promotion. He carried them with him daily. Fingering them in his pocket turned him on. Midnight Poison didn't even give him a semi erection right now. What was the point? That goddamn Cummings had sealed his fate. Retire? He would move it into the works tomorrow. The works would work. Cooper knew they wanted him to retire. He was nothing but an incumbent, a useless cog in the military wheel. He had done the numbers. They weren't bad. But what would he do as a civilian? He had no ties to civilian life. The service was his family. He didn't even have a wife to lay the blame on now. And now, this goddamned Cummings thing in the paper . . .

***

Adriana O'Donovan was reading the Sunday paper with interest, too. She had caught the local news last night as well. She also caught a glimpse of Kerns taking to the trooper who chopped the body from the ice in Blood Slough. She sat up, suddenly fully alert. What the hell was Kerns doing, mixed up in this thing? Kerns didn't work for any branch of the law. He wasn't the type, for one thing. And he was a journalist, not a muckraker. She raked up the term from memories of her high school history class on the Civil War. Kerns wasn't mentioned in the Sunday article dedicated to the incident in Manly. She wondered about that as she turned the page. Nothing was making sense to her.

On page two, the artist's conception of the man involved in the possible murder of a young artist set her back in her chair. The caption under the drawing asked in large letters, *DO YOU KNOW THIS MAN?* The man in the drawing Adriana knew all too well. He was an associate of Major Cooper III. Captain Albert D. Cummings was in the air force, a pilot, and stationed somewhere in the state of Texas. Where he was now? Adriana had only a vague idea. Texas was a big state. According to the drawing, and the likeness was a good one, he had been in Fairbanks. She called Alice. Alice said she had seen the man at the funeral of the major's wife.

Adriana put the paper down and walked out into the ten-below temperature and lightly falling snow. The frost crystals had reached the depth of perhaps three inches. The flakes were as light as down. She gathered some in the palm of her bare hand and studied them. Each flake had its independent character. She put her hand to her lips and blew softly. The crystals settled silently as the flakes drifting from the gray sky above. The new white, which had taken hours to build up, had no substance but color, and that was uncertain. The slightest breeze, as her breath had, would reduce it to nothing. She picked up another handful of flakes and pressed it to her face. There was no wet she could feel. The snow just disappeared in a slight chill. If she felt any moisture at all it was on her skin, her fingers and cheeks.

We are like this white ghost we can't hold without it disappearing—feathers in the wind. Feathers with no quills, no substance, empty thoughts in the air. Does anything I do make honest sense anymore? She thought in the bitter cold. *Does justice equal revenge? Is justice what revenge is all about? Or vice versa. Do the courts meet out revenge in the name of justice? Humans love revenge.* She considered that thought for a moment in the cold. *Nature, or God, whatever you want to call it, has given us the power to reason. Instead of using that power as it was meant, we kill, maim, rape, and torture, and all for the pleasure of revenge. Gods we invent cry out for revenge. We hide the horror under the name of justice. Little Alice, cowering in the rabbit hole of her existence, cries out. The red queen calls for justice: "Off with his head!" The Mad Hatter joys in it. These thoughts are blind*, she reasoned, *blind reasoning*.

"I'm flying backward. I'll get nowhere thinking this way," she said aloud.

Adriana went back in her cabin. She threw another log on the fire and heated up the coffee. Depressed, Adriana wouldn't drink alcohol. Alcohol brought on the darkness she didn't want to deal with, couldn't understand. She was depressed right now. She poured a cup of hot black coffee and sat to read the entire front-page story. She thought maybe Kerns, as a journalist, had written it, but no. Three other names were listed as the authors. Adriana was glad of that. She would get to page number two later. A line in the front-page article caught her attention. *The man on the bridge at midnight in the dark claimed he could tell the difference between the sound of a two- and or a three-bladed propeller slicing through the air—creating thunder, as lightning did, or as a jet broke the sound barrier with the same result—the big bang*. "Although," she whispered quietly but aloud, "the jet was well ahead of the sound when the split air reassembled with that thundering crash."

Yes, Adriana reasoned, *he could have deciphered the difference. Yet there are many Helio Couriers H295s in the air here. In the air, the fingerprints are flight plans*. Had she filed a flight plan? Adriana flew at times with her radio transponder turned off. She flew low, which would void any trace of her flight path had she filed it. Had she been in the air that night? She knew she had. It had been her dark choice, her revenge. Her plans were laid carefully. There were only two left to go now—only two and she could find her way through the dark. Her mind would be free and healthy once again. Adriana tried to shake these thoughts from her thinking.

She turned to page two and Captain Albert Cummings. Should she turn this man over to the law a *second* time? When she first did, the military court, as such, had let her down with a devastating crash. The law was in her hands now. Should she take a chance and trust the law of a civilian court? If so, who should she give her Cummings information to? The name and number of the good Captain Cummings? Adriana definitely did not want to become involved. Nor did she want to mix her friend Alice into this soup any deeper than she already had. Adriana realized she had taken advantage of Alice's love for her, a love that went deeper than friendship: a physical love Adriana was not interested in. However, Alice was the kindest and most thoughtful friend she had. She was the one friend she could depend on. Adriana knew that in a minute a civilian court of law would convict Alice as an accomplice to what they would consider multiple murders—what Adriana considered, in her darker moments, to be justifiable homicide in return for a heinous act of ugly, obscene, inhuman proportions, an act the US military condoned—the rape of a fellow human being.

Adriana knew, as did Major Cooper, that Cummings was capable of pulling off this act, and if he did, he would consider it a successful stunt and nothing more. The girl—the artist,

Diana—meant nothing more to him than a momentary sexual jolt, soon forgotten, or recalled only as a fantasy to feed his midnight dreams.

Kerns, she thought. Kerns somehow had a tie-in with the law and Kerns could be trusted not to bring her name up in the process. Or could he? She considered this thought for some time. The thought of Kerns was somehow easing her depression. Should she call him? It was now after midnight. Adriana poured another cup of coffee. She knew she wouldn't sleep tonight. She would wait to make the call. The night was long. Adriana read both articles through a second time. They did not put her to sleep. She was somehow responsible. She felt guilt creep into her being. Why? What was she guilty of?

***

Kern's phone sounded off at five a.m. It didn't wake him. He had been up since four organizing his photographs and trying to get a grip on the article "Birds of Darkness." He jotted down the title thirty times. The opening line following it read: "These warriors of the night cut the darkness with their wings, sharp as razors, cold as ice." *That carries a good ring—but I need a second line to continue the story*. He had inserted twenty of the hundreds he had on his computer and deleted them all as many times. His mind kept slapping back to the blood-red waters of the dead lagoon—the blood of Dead Man's Slough. *No, Kerns, that is not the name of this article. Jesus Christ, what am I writing?* The phone rang again. His ears rang with it. His brain hung up. The Rye bottle was empty, the inspiration gone. He thought of something his daughter, Salome, the journalist student, told him: "If you can't start at the beginning of an article or story, start in the middle. Don't try to create the first page until you have written the final page and are satisfied with it."

"That makes sense, Salome." Kerns was talking to himself, or ghosts, all night. He heaved a sigh of relief and wrote down *Page number 34*. "Okay, I am in the middle of it, Salome, what now?" He plunged on, hitting the keys furiously.

“The falcon sat on the icy ledge and contemplated her nest site. Was she satisfied, she wondered?” Kerns now had decided to write the story from the bird’s point of view. It would be an entirely new approach—startlingly original—at least he hoped it was original. He couldn’t see how a publisher could refuse it.

The phone rang again. Kerns picked it up. “Who the hell is this?” he yelled into the little black box. “I hope you realize you have completely derailed my train of thought.”

“Kerns? Is that you?”

“Who?”

“You, Jack Kerns?”

“Who is this?”

“Adriana.”

“Oh.” Kerns did a double take.

“Did I catch you at a bad time?”

“I have been up all night, and all of that time has been bad. Is this really you, Adriana?”

“I’ve been up all night, too.”

“I am out of Rye. I need something to ease my pain, Adriana.”

Adriana ignored Kerns’s need. “Listen,” she said urgently. “I have a question for you. I need to know if you can keep this question and the answer to it in confidence. And I want to know if you are speaking the truth. Okay?”

“Sure, that’s okay,” Kerns said. “But what the hell is the truth?”

“The artist who was murdered in the Chena River a couple of nights ago. The one they wrote about in the Sunday paper with a picture of the guy who murdered her.”

“He may have murdered her, Adriana. There is no proof of anything.”

“There was no water in her lungs, right?”

“Go on.”

“He raped and murdered her.”

At Kerns’ end of the airways there was no answer for a number of seconds. Adriana kept breathing. She was breathing anger. “You know he murdered her?” Kerns asked. “You know this creep?”

"Kerns," Adriana answered intensely, quietly. "I don't want to go into my relationship with this gentleman. He is not a nice person. He is a piece of shit."

"I see." Kerns waited.

"I will give you his name and enough information about him to locate him. But only if you will promise me I will not become involved, that I will remain completely clean and clear of any investigation. Is that a 'yeah, right'? Or do I cut you off right now and swear we never had this conversation?"

"Adriana, you can depend on me. You will never be mentioned."

"You may think of me, Kerns, and mention me in your dreams, if you wish, but not in connection with this episode. Got it?"

"Got it."

"You got a pencil handy?"

"I got a piece of lead in my brain. It records everything."

"Do you have an eraser in your brain, Kerns? That eradicates certain episodes?"

"Adriana, you can depend on me."

"The man's name is Captain Albert Cummings. He is a pilot in the US Air Force. Cummings is stationed in Texas. I don't know where, but he is a close friend or acquaintance of a Major Almas A. Cooper III. The major, also in the air force, is stationed at Fort Wainwright, south of Fairbanks. The major has something to do with the aviation squadron there, the drones, I think. The major's wife recently died. She committed suicide. Cummings flew up to attend her funeral. He has no interest in the wife. His connection is with the major. They go back a long way. You take it from there."

"I don't know how you got this information, but it is amazing and on point. This is definitely the best lead we have gotten so far."

"If that picture in the paper is right on, this is the guy, Kerns."

"I'll pass it on as an anonymous tip."

"Thanks." Adriana cut off her phone. Kerns tried, but there was no getting back to her—at least not right now. He kicked off his sweats and pulled on a pair of long johns, Carhartts and mukluks. Five minutes later he was in Slim's kitchen. He had forgotten about "Birds of Darkness."

***

"How do you get through to the military? Especially if you are trying to investigate one of them?" Kerns asked. He and Slim had adjourned to the Big I to confer with Hap before the bar opened for the day. Hap heard their problem and was standing quietly by, wondering why they had dragged him out of bed at eight in the morning. The three of them were drinking coffee.

"The military has its own security and its own set of laws," Slim answered Kerns' question. "It is as if they are not a part of the United States."

"They got their own set of ethics, too," Hap interjected. *Hell*, he thought, *I'm standing here. I might as well say something.* "Granted," he went on, "they are very stringent within their confines, within their own walls. They have their own judges, sort of like the Vatican. Things might be immoral in civilian circles, but that doesn't necessarily apply to the military. In the military, image comes first. The image is as the commanders imagine it. The image must be clean—on the outside. Sexual abuse in the service is a perfect example. The civilian world can't get a grip on it, as much as some scattered members of the House and Senate would like to. The military has strong masculine support in the US legislature, as well as in the governments of other countries. Women are allowed in the ranks, but they are heavily outnumbered, or at least outweighed. The consensus within the ranks, and in the legislature, is that the female sex must be kept in her place. As more women are elected to political office, this wall is starting, at last, to crack."

"It's been starting to crack for centuries," Kerns said. "Look at *Lysistrata*, a play written four hundred years before Christ, for Christ's sake. It's about women in a time of war. Aristophanes wrote it for the Greek theatre. It is a serious comedy about a very serious subject."

"*Lysistrata*?" Slim shook his head. "Hap, you are the theatre buff. What the hell is he talking about?"

Hap laughed. "It's a damn funny play, Slim, but as Kerns says, the subject is very serious. We did it at the Riverside Theatre here a few years ago. *Lysistrata*? She would be classed as an activist today. As a matter of fact, she was an activist then. The military wanted her head on a platter. This brilliant lady talked the women of Athens into going on strike."

"A strike against what?" Slim said, pouring himself another cup of Hap's coffee.

"A sex strike. That is," Hap continued, "don't give our men even a taste of it until they do what we say. Just cross your legs and keep them locked until the damn fool men stop making war."

"Did it work?"

"Use your head. Of course it did. Men were just as stupid then as they are now, and just as horny. I played a general in our production. The generals foolishly swore they would not give in to these angry women." Hap struck a Napoleonic pose and burst into lines from Aristophanes' ancient satire—lines that stand unchanged today, the lines of war.

For through man's heart there runs in flood
A natural and noble taste for blood—
To form a ring and fight—
To cut off heads at sight—
It is our military right!

Kerns applauded. Slim bowed deeply to his friend's accomplishment. "You are a ham, Hap, as well as a fine bartender, and a bit of an agitator yourself."

"I do the best I can."

"So tell me, Hap, do we organize the women of Fairbanks?" Hap shrugged. Slim pressed on. "How do we deal with the military, Hap?"

"I just serve them drinks until they get too rowdy, and then I throw them out."

"Thanks, Hap. That's why we dragged you out of bed before eight in the morning."

"No problem."

Kerns burst out laughing. Hap continued:

"I have found, that when in doubt, go to the top. Were I you, Slim, I would go directly to the commanding general of Fort Wainwright, home of America's Arctic Warriors. Just drop in on him unannounced."

"Are you crazy, Hap?"

"I have been accused of it."

"Just drop in unannounced?"

"Why not? You'll never get an audience if you ask permission. He may be furious, but he'll let his curiosity overcome that. He'll want to know who this asshole is who thinks he can just barge into a commanding general's office to pass the time of day. I mean, you are a trooper, Slim. You are the leading detective of our Alaskan Troopers. Put on your Sunday dress uniform and play the role."

Kerns burst out laughing again. "You guys should do a stand-up comedy routine."

"I think that is what we are doing, Kerns." Slim sighed.

"I'm serious, Kerns," Hap said. "I wasn't at first, but I am now. Slim, you start off the conversation. Once you get him eye-to-eye, start talking about the body in Blood Slough. You think the body is that of a military man, you tell him. The body might be air force, you tell him. You need this army general's help. You tell the army general you have found the air force unaccommodating in the past—a little slow, perhaps, you tell him. On hearing this, the general will turn to his secretary and order her, or him, to, in the general's name, demand the presence of Air Force Colonel So-and-So to report to his office immediately—on the double—ASAP! The air force on Wainwright is a small squadron in charge of drones. The general in charge of the base is not too pleased to have them there. He will be pleased to use you as an excuse to embarrass the air force colonel, a drone himself, in charge of drones. At this point, be prepared to listen to a few air force jokes and to laugh appreciatively. Within minutes, another secretary will enter and announce the presence of Colonel So-and-So. The general will be in the middle of another air force joke. He will tell the secretary to have the colonel stand by until he has finished his present presentation. At the end of said presentation, the two of you will laugh uproariously. At which time the general will push the intercom button and the secretary will usher the air force in. The general will return the colonel's salute as the laughter subsides and you are free to question the colonel about the major. The general will stand behind you. The major will be brought in. Mission accomplished."

"How do you know all this, Hap? I mean it is a great scenario, but what the hell did you base the music on?" Slim stood waiting for an answer.

"What I hear over the bar. There are a lot of military who pass through these doors. Most of them are not happy to be in Alaska. I have learned from them that the present commanding general at Wainwright has a problem with the air force brigade or squadron commander serving under him with his ineffective fleet of drones and reconnaissance planes."

"What have I got to lose, Kerns? Hap is a hell of a salesman."

"Dress in your best, Slim," Hap added. "They love uniforms. And you will, as you say, have nothing to lose." Hap stepped to the front door of the Big I and threw the bolt.

Kerns and Slim stepped out the back. The Big I was open for business.

***

Major Almas Cooper III had been a troublesome stitch in Air Force Colonel Cornwall's Christmas stocking since a charge had been submitted concerning the officer's conduct and involvement in a so-called "gang rape" of one of the female officers under his command. The easiest out for the air force was to ship the major and his presumably innocent accomplices to distant corners of the earth. The broadside had come at a bad time for all concerned. Sexual assault in the military was in the news, and it wasn't good news for the military. Women were filtering into the House and Senate where the male armed forces had held total sway for years. Politicians were skeptical about standing up for the accused. A rape case raised hackles in the Naval Academy where members of the football team were involved with alcohol and the rape of female cadets. Most women wouldn't come forward for fear of reprisal, but some had the determination to right this wrong, or to try to do so. Many suffered for it.

Where to send these high-ranking officers to keep them out of the media's sight and hearing? Afghanistan held an open hand. Yet Afghanistan was too obvious. Alaska? Yes. Another could be lost in Western Europe. No one could say that the military did not look after her (his?) own. Texas would work. Split them up. They were all good men, but nearing retirement. Get them out of sight and keep them there until they could be offloaded. In the meantime, a committee could be established to prove their innocence. The charges against them were ludicrous—according to the post inspector general where they were accused of this embarrassing minor transgression, or troublesome misdemeanor.

There was the occasional molested female who was not afraid to speak out. This was one of those cases. They were the dangerous "femmes," the women who needed to be weeded out of the service without incriminating fellow officers.

Colonel William Cornwall, air force commander at Fort Wainwright in North Pole, Alaska, was stuck with one of these possible rapists, a major with an impeccable record before this reported incident smudged it: a man his commanding officer felt needed to be retired for the good of all concerned. Clean the smudge, so to speak. And now the colonel had been called on the floor by his commanding general, a non–air force general no less, who embarrassed him in front of a civilian law officer. The law officer, decked out in gold braids, an Alaskan trooper, a glorified traffic cop slash game warden named Slim Dickerson, or dickhead, appeared to be a friend of the general's. Maybe they went hunting together.

The general excused himself, leaving orders that the colonel see to it that the trooper's wishes were complied with. Colonel

Cornwall stood at attention as the general and trooper shook hands warmly. He then saluted his superior and left the general's quarters accompanied by the trooper. He and Slim, or Detective Slim Dickerson, arranged to meet in an hour at Cornwall's headquarters. The colonel promised to have the major in question on hand to answer the detective's questions. Slim thanked him and got in the official cruiser he was driving. Slim headed for the post chapel/funeral parlor. He had a copy of Velma's obituary with him. A Captain Quebberman's byline was under the heading. He also carried copies of the likeness of Captain Albert D. Cummings.

***

Colonel Cornwall had a dossier on Major Cooper. He had studied it on the major's arrival. He knew the charges that had been filed against Cooper. He was fairly certain the major was guilty as charged but would not voice an opinion. He would swallow his convictions and let the major sink or swim on his own. *Get this goddamned cunt-struck officer out of my hair, off my back.* Cornwell had his orderly draw up papers for a thirty-day leave for Cooper, starting immediately following his interview with the trooper. From what Cornwell understood, Major Cooper was not personally involved with the possible rape and murder case here in Fairbanks. But when the media got a grip on the story Cornwell didn't need his squadron drawn into it under any condition. He would use all of his influence to convince Cooper to resign, hinting he might be stripped of his rank if need be. At that point, Cooper might listen to reason. As an afterthought Cornwell phoned his adjutant to see if it was possible to hack into the major's personal email accounts to learn more.

"No problem, sir. We have a man quite good at that. He is an expert at 'cyber manipulation,' as we call it. As a matter of fact, he is in your squadron, a Corporal John Winslow."

***

That morning, Major Almas A. Cooper III had called in sick. He had no desire to face anyone today. He had nothing to do at the office anyway but sit and stare at his computer screen. In the office he didn't dare connect to his personal sites. He did that here at home. Perhaps a little cybersex would distract him from his problems this morning.

His phone rang. He didn't answer it. The call was forwarded to his cell phone, which began to vibrate on his hip. He shut the cell off. The landline rang again. He switched it to mute. He stepped into what had been Velma's sewing room and stole a glance out between the drapes. An official air force car was parked in front, the motor running. The man sitting behind the wheel was listening to his cell phone. "Shit."

As the major started down the stairs into his cave, he heard a knock on the front door.

"Shit again." Should he answer it? The knocking was quite persistent. Feigning illness, the major opened the front door a crack, coughing as he did so.

"Sir." The sergeant standing on the stoop saluted sharply. The major returned it with a limp movement.

"Yes, Sergeant?"

"The colonel wishes to see you in brigade offices, Major. It's quite important."

"I called in ill, Sergeant. I believe I have the flu."

"May I suggest, Major, Colonel Cornwall is quite insistent."

"I see. Tell the colonel I shall be over shortly."

"I was instructed to bring you personally, sir."

"I see. Thank you, Sergeant. I shall be out directly." Cooper closed the door. "What the hell is this about?" He glanced at the paper, open on the kitchen island, and knew what it was about.

***

The major pulled on his boots and black tie, checked himself once in the full-length mirror in the master bedroom and closed the Sesame lock on the basement door. He stepped out into the cold, and locked that door behind him. Now he was genuinely ill. His blood pressure was peaked. The sergeant saluted and held the car door for him. They were off to the execution. On the seat beside Major Cooper was an open copy of the *Sunday News*. Captain Albert D. Cummings was smiling up at him. The major turned the paper facedown. It didn't help.

In squadron headquarters, waving aside a salute, Colonel William Cornwell stepped forward and took Cooper's hand in a solid grip. The colonel's hand was not warm. "How do you do, Major?"

"I may be coming down with the flu, sir. I hope not."

"You have had a difficult time lately, Major. I arranged a thirty-day leave for you. I suggest you return to the States, Southern California or perhaps Florida. If you like it there, you might think of taking your retirement while you are at it. You have given more time to the United States in your capacity as a warrior than many I know of. You deserve the leave and retirement."

"I have recently considered retirement."

"Good. Now, to get down to immediate considerations: There is an investigation being conducted, unfortunately a civilian investigation. The authorities here would like to question you concerning a Captain Cummings. Do you know this captain, Major?"

"I am aware of him, Colonel. I wouldn't say I know him well enough to recommend him for a promotion."

"A member of the local law enforcement organization wishes to ask you a few questions concerning this officer. Are you amenable to that?"

"I should prefer for the captain to answer his own questions. Especially if it is in connection with some violation of civilian law."

"Understood, Major. We are in accord here. I am sincerely sorry for any inconvenience."

An orderly stepped into the room and stood silently at attention. "Yes, Corporal?"

"Colonel, there is an Alaskan trooper out here who says he has an appointment with you and Major Cooper. Shall I bring him in?"

"Please do."

Colonel Cornwall introduced the two men and quickly excused himself, leaving the men in apparent privacy. Cornwall had pre-arranged to have their conversation videotaped. He would view it, live, in the privacy of his office.

Once the colonel stepped out, Slim came straight to the point, laying the artist's likeness of Cummings on the table between himself and the major. "Do you know this man, Major? And what do you know about him?" A long pause. "I understand he flew up here for your wife's funeral."

"His name, I believe, is Cummings. He was stationed in my company years ago. Exactly why he flew up here for Velma's funeral is not apparent to me. Does that answer your three questions?" Slim was quietly jotting down some notes.

"What is his rank?"

"I believe it is captain."

"What was it when he served with you?"

"I would have to look that up."

Slim nodded and scratched that information down. In his office, Colonel Cornwell sat back in his leather swivel chair. There were four cameras hidden in the interrogation room. Corporal Winslow, in a separate room, edited as the cameras rolled, giving the colonel full face as each man spoke. The tape from all cameras would be preserved.

Slim reached into his old soft leather briefcase on the floor at his feet and drew out an eight-by-ten copy of another picture. He slid the color print in front of the major. Major Cooper's face blanched noticeably. Slim let the silence stand for a long moment. "And do you know this man, Major?" The photo was of the man found in Blood Slough taken shortly after being cut from the ice. The back of the man's head was quite mangled, but the frontal view was fairly much together if crusted with blood and slightly twisted.

"My God. What happened to him?" In Cooper's mind the photo registered as that of Captain Jason Blitzweimer. *Jason emailed me that he would be stopping here. What the fuck is going on?* Major Cooper said nothing. He was visibly shaken.

"Look at it closely, Major. We know, from the microchip found in his right shoulder, that he is, or was a member of the armed services, probably an officer. At present, we know little else about him."

The major was pulling himself back together slowly. He stared at a framed photograph on the wall behind the Alaskan trooper staring at him. It was an enlarged and beautifully framed photo of a US Air Force F-15E Strike Eagle jet fighter. The major was very familiar with it. He had flown that model jet thousands of miles over the deserts and jungles of the Far East and on maneuvers in Europe and the US. So had Cummings, First Lieutenant John Noble Ode, First Lieutenant William Bancroft, and Jason Blitzweimer. The picture of a talented pilot by the name of Adriana O'Donovan flashed through his mind. The six of them had flown over the same territories in formation and in active battle side by side. The major was not so proud of some of the things they had done side by side. The past was crashing in on him. *What is going on here?* he thought again. *And who is this fucking civilian cop hurling these questions at me?*

In his office, Colonel Cornwell was on his feet behind his desk staring down at a close-up of the bloody image as pictured from a lens disguised as a sprinkler over the table Slim and the major were seated at. Cornwell did not recognize the bloody facade. *Thank God it is nobody from this squadron.* He sat back down and heaved a sigh of relief. *But I'm still on thin ice. I got to get that major off the premises—off my back.* Cooper held up pretty well under the first round of questioning, but he folded when he saw that bloody picture. Cornwell pondered for a moment. *That has got to be the guy who fell through the ice. And how in hell did that dumb cop know to look for a microchip?* The trooper was talking again. Cornwell sat back down to eavesdrop, wishing he had never agreed to this interview. Trooper Dickerson was back on full-frontal view. Cornwall turned up the volume.

"Think, Major," Slim said, determined to get an answer. "Who is that man?" Slim stared hard at Major Cooper. "You have seen him before, haven't you? You know him." There was a long pause. "That is not a question, Major. That is a statement!"

"I have never seen that man in my life until right now," Cooper said, trying to stare Slim down in the silence that followed. The major's eyes dropped. "It's just that his bloody appearance was a shock."

"You've seen dead men before. It has been your business to kill them, Major. Who is this guy?"

"I only killed people from a distance," the major cried. "The pilot who dropped the bomb on Nagasaki and Hiroshima never touched a body, or even saw one. There is a difference, Trooper—whoever you are. In the air force we don't kill people face-to-face. There is a difference. We are the artists who paint the big picture. We are not down there with little pig stickers. I told you, I don't know. You don't see people from ten thousand feet up, or even three hundred. I have never seen this man before in my life, dead or alive, in my life—or his."

"I see." Slim took the eight-by-ten back and slid it in his briefcase. "Let us get back to the other gentleman. Do you have a name? A number? Even in your records? Who is he?" Slim shifted papers on the table. Cumming's face surfaced. "You said you were acquainted with him. Please give me the information you have. It is not as if you are turning him over to a hangman. From what I understand from you, you are not close to him, Major. You were not bosom buddies. I am not asking you to finger him as a murderer."

This was easier to do and it let the major sidestep the previous question. "His name and rank, I believe, is Captain Albert Cummings. He is stationed in Texas. I don't know the exact address. He is not married, at least I don't think so. I am not his keeper, Constable. You will have to take it from there."

"Do you know when he left Alaska?"

"He didn't make me privy to that information. I believe he mentioned an early morning flight on or about . . ." The major thought for a moment. *When did Cummings leave?*

"The day of the murder?" Slim pressed him.

"What? No, the day before, I believe." The major cleared his throat. "I can't swear to that."

"I think I have taken enough of your time, Major," Slim said. "You must have a full schedule this afternoon." The trooper rose. He looked directly into one of the hidden lenses and saluted. "Thank you, Colonel. Please save this interview as you have taped it. It may well prove very important in the near future. Also, please see to it that Major Cooper does not leave the Fairbanks borough in the near future. We may need to continue this interview at a later date. I'll leave my card and the artist's conception of Captain Cummings's likeness for your records." He turned back to the major. "I thank you both for your cooperation." Slim stepped forward and took the major's hand, which came up automatically. "It's been a pleasure talking with you, Major." Slim checked to see that he had left nothing and made his departure. Major Cooper was looking about, trying to figure out who Slim had saluted and who he had been speaking to.

Seconds after Slim left, Colonel Cornwall stepped smartly into room. "Major," he said. "We need to have an in-depth conversation. Who was that guy in the photograph? It was apparent from the look on your face that you know him." The colonel had given instructions that the cameras continue to roll on Major Cooper.

"The trooper was right. This room is bugged, Colonel."

"I asked you a question, Major. Who is that man who was dropped through the ice?" The major hesitated a moment uncomfortably. He was in a corner. He had to come up with an answer.

"Jason," he said, hedging his bet. "Captain Jason Blitzweimer. He served under me some years ago and is now stationed in Germany. Colonel, I didn't want to let that information out to a civilian without consulting you first."

"I see."

The exit door opened. Slim stepped back into the interrogation room. "Thank you, Colonel," he said. "That is exactly the information we needed." Slim turned and was gone.

"You fouled up, Major." His commanding officer was good at laying blame elsewhere. "You should have stuck to your story. You will apply for your retirement today! I will see that the order is expedited immediately. As a civilian, you can deal with this fuck-up on your own! That is all, Major!"

Major Almas A. Cooper III was left standing alone in front of the cameras. He had only one way to go.

***

CHAPTER 11

A Path Not Taken or Forgotten

Slim pulled into his homestead on Chena Ridge. He had to get out of this monkey suit, into real clothes, and back in his 4x4, all of which would make him comfortable. At home, he pumped the new information he had accumulated into the computer that would relay it to his office. It all started to make sense. But what kind of sense? Slim shook his head.

Cummings and Jason Blitzweimer had previously been members of the same flying group as Cooper. He checked out the other members of the club. Two of them had disappeared, gone AWOL, whatever. Slim punched in the blood type of the man Kerns had discovered and the DNA of the skeleton of the first one that turned up west of Antigun Pass. He had to contact the military to do so. The response from the military was that the information requested would be available within twenty-four hours. Slim was a patient man. He could wait that length of time. Things were looking up—if there was any way things could look up in a murder case.

Slim waited the twenty-four hours and checked again with the military. Nothing. He was advised to stand by. He did. He called again to discover that the US Military was now conducting its own investigation and that no information would be forth coming at the present time. The detective in Alaska was requested to drop the case. The worst scenario for Slim. He kicked himself for passing on the little information he had. The military was now demanding the remains of the bodies the troopers had iced down in the morgue. On Slim's cell there were three additional messages directly from the Pentagon demanding the troopers drop the case. Slim had his office return word that he was in the wilderness and out of cell phone and radio range. That bullshit still worked in Alaska.

***

Slim and Kerns sat in the cabin on the ridge. Slim's phone was turned off. He had given the dispatcher Kerns' number for updates. Nothing new had come in, in over an hour. Then word came that the military had a refrigerated vehicle at trooper headquarters to reclaim their dead. "Kerns, if I was a drinking man, I'd have one right now." Slim sighed. "As it is, I'm stuck with coffee." Slim got up and tossed another log on the fire. "Who's your contact, Kerns? Do you suppose there is any more information there?"

"I can try. But I can't let you know who it is. I promised her I would keep that information under lock and key."

The "her" registered in Slim's mind. He gave no sign of it. He opened the damper in the six-inch stovepipe, letting it suck a bit more oxygen into the fire pit. The coals responded, kindling a light flame, which grew quickly around the fresh log.

Her? How many "hers" did Kerns know who might be able to help them out and yet would not want to be an active part of the investigation? One sprang to mind as the fire grew in intensity. Slim opened the front draft a crack and closed the damper slightly. He wouldn't push his friend. He had the information he needed. That information would go no further than this room, but Slim would follow up on it for his own satisfaction. Kerns had not knowingly broken his word to the lady at A-Plus Flying Service. Slim would respect that. He was, however, eager to follow up on this fresh information. Slim wanted to know for sure if the "her" who slipped out knew this Captain Cummings personally. Where did the "her" know him from? And for how long? There were a number of etceteras that followed that thought. Slim would do a Google search later at the office.

"Why don't you do that, Kerns?" he said. "That is, follow up with your informer, whoever, and see if there is any more information that person can put on our plate. That first taste led us almost through the sticky fingers of military red tape. It certainly set us on the right track. Perhaps there is something more we can use." Slim pulled on his coat. "I got to get down to headquarters. I don't think we can keep the military from reclaiming the bodies, but I want to keep those microchips. They are all gibberish still, but something may come of them."

Slim drove out, heading west on the ridge road. Kerns headed east. It didn't make much difference; the road went in a circle. Kerns would stop at the Pump Station for a bowl of fish chowder and a shot of Rye and then cut over to the airport. He hoped to catch Adriana in her hangar and thank her for the information she had fed them that morning and perhaps take her back to the Pump Station for dinner. He would pop the question about more information at that time.

Kerns had never asked Adriana out. He thought she might join him. He wouldn't mention the word "love." The thought struck him that perhaps love had something to do with her relationship with Captain Cummings. If so, it must have been a strained relationship. He would have to think more on that. *Oh well, what the hell. Take a chance. I'll ask her to dinner first. Right*? "Take a chance," as W. C. Fields used to say in his dissertation on chance: "I had an uncle once who took a chance," Fields drawled. "He jumped out of an airplane into a haymow. Did he make it?" There would be a significant pause in Fields' impeccable timing before he went on: "No, but he might have." Kerns smiled at the great comedian's humor as he had done all his life. Kerns had a collection of all of Fields' movies. When depressed, Fields always cheered him up. It worked again today as early dark closed in on the Arctic.

At the Fairbanks airport Kerns drove directly to the hangar where Adriana kept her Helio. Inside, he found Alice doing routine maintenance on the plane. There was also a Cessna 182T Turbo with "for sale" painted on the side of it. After learning Adriana would not be coming back for half an hour or so, Kerns wandered over to the Cessna, inspecting it. "You selling this?" he asked Alice, making conversation.

"I just bought her. She needs work, but she's in fair shape."

"I didn't know you were a pilot, Alice."

"I fly planes and I'm safe to fly with, but I'm not the pilot Adriana is. That woman is an ace." Alice kept her attention on her work as she spoke. She was replacing a section of the floor carpet in the Helio. There were two or three spots that looked like they had been burned into the fabric. The fabric wasn't new, but except for the holes, it was in pretty good shape. Kerns wasn't paying much attention. He had his eye on the door, waiting for Adriana. Alice cut a perfect square around the holes and pulled the small section of carpet up. She used acetone to loosen the glue, which secured it to the floor. She cleaned the loose strands up with a sharp putty knife. Kerns watched absently, admiring Alice's neat work. Once she had finished the patchwork and cleaned up, he couldn't tell where the original ended and the new began.

Adriana came in with a bag full of groceries. "You're just in time for dinner, Kerns," she said. "Alice and I need a cook here. Are you any good at it?"

"I'll do you one better. I'll take you both to the Pump Station for dinner. Then nobody can blame anyone but the cook there for a poor meal."

"You're on, Kerns. Pack up the tools, Alice. The gentleman is taking us to dinner."

"Not me. I want to get some more work done on the Cessna. The Helio is ready to go whenever it is needed. Oh, and they want you to rephrase something on the site. They think it is a bit strong."

"For the Air Service?"

"The other one."

"Don't touch it, Alice. I'll take care of it." Adriana glanced down at the patchwork Alice had done on the deck fabric. "And good work here, Alice. I'll put the groceries away and Kerns and I will be off."

"You sure you can't join us, Alice?" Kerns asked, not exactly eager to have her, but willing. Kerns wanted Adriana to himself.

"Got my heart set on the Cessna. Thanks, Kerns."

***

Slim arrived at the trooper headquarters complex just as the military was pulling out—with two bodies and the bones of the first air drop victim. *At least now we have the names of two of the victims and the possible name of the bones. If they were all from the same outfit that Major Almas A. Cooper III belonged to in Baghdad we have filled in a blank*, Slim thought. He checked his desk. The two microchips were there in the plastic baggie as he had left them. But what the hell was on them? Slim was no cyber guru. He could send and read mail and he could do a Google search. He still didn't know, nor did he trust anyone to try and decipher, what was on or in the chips—if they could be deciphered. What kind of a signal were they giving out, if they were giving out a signal at all? *Only kids know how to play these games*, he thought. *How much information can be contained in a pill the size of a bean? Did they send out a signal like that thing that was crawling about on the surface of Mars?* "I am a total cyber jerk," Slim said aloud to no one. "What the hell do I know about this cyber stuff? I should get my son to do it. He's an expert." That thought suddenly clicked. Slim got to his feet, circled his desk, and sat down again. "My son might be able to do it, Roy might," he said with sudden realization. "This chip might be just like a game—or only a tracking chip. A tracking chip?" Slim continued, muttering to himself. "Was this chip putting out a signal? If this is a tracking chip, why hadn't the military tracked these men down? I mean, my boy has a raw mind. He spends hours a day on an iPhone. What the hell can you do on an iPhone that takes more than a minute?"—Slim stopped to think—"Other than talk to someone? Or get the weather? Or look at a map? They probably have a GPS system, a compass, and/or sixty other things that I know nothing about."

Slim got up again. He walked to the window and looked out into the afternoon darkness. *Roy is still in school. I can leave a message for him to drop by. The bus goes right by the office*. He turned back to his desk and picked up the office phone before he stopped to think a moment. *If I get my son to check this thing out and he breaks the code, or whatever, do I want Roy to become that involved in this?* He set the phone back in the cradle. *I don't think so*.

Slim tucked the chips in his vest pocket and walked out of the office. He stopped by the front desk and told the dispatcher he was going to cruise some of the back roads branching off the Anchorage Highway.

"We got a call from a Colonel Cornwall," the dispatcher said, looking at his notes. "He said they had the bodies, which we knew, but they were looking for some computer chips that were supposed to have come with them. I told him I would look into it."

"Tell the colonel you did look into it and the chips have been misplaced. If he asks for me, tell him I am beyond cell service. Leave me a message if he calls. Please let me know what he says. And thanks." Slim stepped into the clear cold of the lighted parking area. He unplugged his 4x4 from the winter heating post and drove out. Slim thought better behind the wheel. It burned up a bit of fuel but was well worth it. The Alaskan troopers had a lot of country to cover. It was good for them to show up in unexpected places on occasions and a good excuse for Slim to get into the field. Twenty minutes later he pulled in at Skinny Dick's Halfway Inn. Inside Skinny's, a car full of GIs and their girls or wives were celebrating around the glowing wood stove. They quieted down when the trooper stepped in. Skinny was no longer living, but his likeness and words of wisdom were posted all over the walls. The present owner, Margret, stepped to the bar with steaming coffee for Slim. Slim pulled up a stool and sat. Margret lit a cigarette. She exhaled the cloud of smoke over her shoulder, her one concession to the no smoking laws on the "outside," or lower forty-eight. The sign behind her read significantly:

Complaining
To the management
About smoking in this establishment
Will definitely
Be hazardous to your health!

Slim was not a smoker but knew better than to complain. He took a sip of coffee. A young lady from the now quiet party around the wood stove stepped over to the bar.

"Officer," she spoke up. "I am the designated driver."

"I didn't come in here to break up your party," Slim answered. "If I was still drinking I would be over there with you. Keep having fun—but don't shoot a moose out of season."

One of the celebrants made eye contact with Slim. Slim had seen the man before somewhere. He searched his mind. The young man came over to him. "You knocked them dead at the colonel's office yesterday," he said. "I never saw Cornwall so pissed off in my life."

"That's where I saw you. You were the orderly at the colonel's reception desk."

"Right. When you left I had to stand at attention for five minutes while he ranted at me about not ever letting you back into his office again." The orderly laughed. "And the major, whoever he was, snuck out behind him. That guy is now a civilian. He was retired before the day was finished."

"He's a civilian now?"

"Right, and on his way to the good old lower USA. The colonel had him shipped out this morning. His belongings will follow."

"He's gone already?"

"I typed out his papers. I wish that the colonel would do the same thing for me."

"What was his destination?" Slim asked.

"The ticket the air force paid for got him as far as Seattle."

"What are you drinking? I'll buy you one." Slim nodded to Margret, who was already pouring a double shot of tequila.

"Thank you, Officer."

"The name's Slim." Slim reached out to shake the young man's hand. Slim Dickenson wrote out his name on a piece of scratch paper Margret kept on the bar. "Do you mind keeping me posted with the major's address?"

"No. Be happy to."

"The man who answers this number will be Kerns," Slim said, writing the number down. "I don't want to get you into trouble calling my phone. Your Colonel Cornwall has my number in his files. He's a control freak. He'll be looking for it and might not appreciate you making a call to me."

"He wouldn't. Thanks for the drink."

"The other number is for my son Roy. They can both be trusted."

The young man paused, checking the numbers, and then raised his glass in salute. "Slim?"

"Right."

"And yours?"

"John, Johnny Winslow. I'll get that information on the major to you tomorrow, Slim. No problem."

"Thanks, Johnny." Slim put a bill on the bar. "Keep the change, Margret. I'll see you again in a day or so. And you, Johnny, keep having fun." Slim finished his coffee and left Skinny Dick's. At the south end of Skinny's drive, he crossed the highway and headed down a narrow muddy lane through the woods into moose country and the Tanana River. Six miles down the narrow track a windblown tree was across the road. The 4x4 slowed to a stop. Slim pulled a chain saw from the back seat. He was smiling. "Nothing like good hard birch to keep the home fires burning." On the second pull the saw roared into action. In the lights of the truck Slim sliced the trunk into stove-length pieces and tossed them in the bed of the pickup. The wood road was now cleared. The job done, Slim backed around and headed for home. *So*, he thought, *the good major is a civilian now. I, or my counterparts in the States, can deal with civilians. No problem.*

***

Kerns and Adriana were sitting at the bar. After two Ryes to whet the appetite, they were ready for the main course and a bottle of fine red recommended by the bartender. Outside a full moon was rising over the Chena. The night would drop to below zero, but all was warm here. Kerns hoped it would remain so. Spain's Fundador Brandy finished off the meal. They walked out into the crisp evening moonlight. Kerns had gone out minutes earlier to start his truck and take the chill off the cab. Now what? He had meant to ask a number of important questions about Adriana's knowledge of Cummings and/or Jason Blitzweimer, but could not bring the thought of murder to destroy the pleasant atmosphere. He had learned nothing new, except that he was afraid he was falling in love. He truly longed to hold this lady in his arms, but was afraid the touch might break the spell. Very little was said on the drive back to the hangar.

Adriana seemed nervous. So was Kerns. It was a first date. *Jesus*, Kerns thought. *She's in her thirties. I'm forty-four. What's the problem with me? And what is this woman's hang-up?* Adriana definitely had one. *Hell, I got one, too*, Kerns thought. *I'm not back in high school. What is it?* Kerns parked and they walked into the hangar. Alice was no longer there. The Cessna was missing, too. Kerns followed Adriana to her office. There was a note on the table both women used as a desk. Adriana picked it up. "Alice is test flying her plane," she said. "She tells us to have a good time." Adriana wrote something on the blank side of the note and set it back on the table. "Are we having a good time, Kerns?" She wasn't smiling. "We had a good dinner. Thank you."

"We are acting like a couple of high school kids, Adriana. What the hell is the matter with us?"

"I know what's the matter with me, Kerns. I don't know what the hell is the matter with you."

"I'm afraid to think about it."

Adriana burst out laughing. "Why don't we fly up to my place at Chena Hot Springs, Kerns? Together, maybe we can figure it out."

"I'm game, if you're flying."

"I'm flying."

They opened the big hangar doors and pushed the Helio out into the open. While Adriana started the plane, Kerns drove his truck into the building and shut the doors. "Do you want to leave a note for Alice?" Kerns called to her.

"I already did, Kerns. Let's go."

Except for the smooth turning of the motor and the prop of the H295 cutting the air, it was a quiet trip.

***

LATER THAT NIGHT

"I don't know what you are doing in my bed, Kerns, except that I have got to find out if I can do it without vomiting or striking back at you."

"That is not necessarily the voice of foreplay, Adriana. What the hell are you talking about?"

"What I am talking about is making love—me making love to a man. It has been a few years. I have chosen you for the experiment."

"Experiment?" Kerns rose up on one elbow and looked down at Adriana, lying beside him in her cabin at Chena Hot Springs. Adriana rose quickly to match him eye for eye.

"You are not exactly a guinea pig, Kerns, but I must not get too serious about this or it won't work for either of us. Most definitely, it won't work for me." Adriana stared at a troubled Kerns silently, neither of them speaking. She started shaking visibly, as if ice cold. With stubborn determination she brought herself under control. Color came back into her cheeks. "We had a wonderful evening, floating around in the hot outdoor pool in the nude. I mean, you looked really good to me. I mean sexy, Kerns. It was the first time in years I thought of a man as sexy."

"You looked pretty damn good yourself—and I mean sexy, too, Adriana. You are a beautiful lady, in truth, and in truth, I had a hard time restraining myself from making lo—a pass at you right there on the steaming rocks. I thought you felt the same urge, or am I completely out of touch with reality?"

"You were right, Kerns, I did. It is not easy for me to admit it."

"Then that other couple jumped into the springs and that broke the spell, right?"

"Right. And reality went right down the drain."

"Right. We got out of the wet, toweled down, dressed. We had a drink at the bar and you invited me over here to your cabin, Adriana. I was in heaven." Kerns dropped back onto the pillow. "But then, you invited me here from Fairbanks, too. We flew up here together." Kerns turned to face her. Adriana was staring at the ceiling. "So here we are. And now what? I would like to hold you in my arms, to comfort you, to make love to you—whatever. There, I said it, the forbidden four-letter word. But I'm afraid to. When I touch you that beautiful warm body of yours turns cold."

"I thought it would work. Maybe it was the Rye, Kerns."

"I hope not." Kerns sat up on the edge of the bed. He took a deep breath and stood up. "I'll sleep on the couch in the kitchen." He turned, looking down at Adriana. Adriana was still staring at the ceiling. "I am very fond of you," Kerns said softly. "I know that is a weak word for what I feel for you. Actually, I am afraid to feel. I have only been really in love one time in my life. That love has never died. The lady who nurtured it did. She died because of my selfishness. I have never forgiven myself for that. There is no need for me to go into detail. I am not a Catholic kneeling beside the darkened confessional. I will live with it. Earlier, this evening, I thought I had shed the guilt."

"We all have things we must live with, Kerns. We are all victims of fate. Somehow, we must survive it. I try to convince myself I am not a victim. I am a survivor. I am working at it."

Kerns stood quietly, still looking down at this helpless, beautiful woman on her back, her knees pulled up to her breasts in a tight fetal position. She was trembling as she spoke. "I am working at it, Kerns. I thought maybe this would help, but I am not strong enough yet to make it work." Adriana rolled over, her back to him. She shuddered and lay still, relaxing slightly. Kerns let his silence reach out to her. If she spoke her thoughts, as dark as they might be, he was there—a friend, not an adversary. He hoped she understood. He needed her too. For a full minute, barely breathing, she said nothing.

"I was raped, Kerns. I was gang-raped by five men. When they finished with me, they drove me into the wasteland, a lifeless place, somewhere outside of Baghdad, where I was stationed. I was left to die. Somehow, in the cold of the night, I revived enough to know I was still alive. I was naked and knew I had fallen from grace. Grace was taken from me like my pride. It was I who was responsible for my loss, not the five animals who crawled over and into me. I felt guilty. I was bitterly angry with myself because of that weakness in me: because of my guilt." Adriana looked up at him. "I was shocked and weakened. I was bleeding but I was determined to live. In the distance there was a light, a fire. On hands and knees I crept toward it. It was anger that fired what little strength was left to me. I couldn't get to my feet. I crawled. I slept, or passed out, I guess. I came to. The fire in the distance was reduced to glowing coals. I crawled again.

"If the men who took advantage of me, who viciously raped me, had been strangers, I might never have made it to that fire, but the rapists who laughed and snarled above me were my fellow officers, graduates of the US Air Force Academy, as I was. I had flown with them. I had partied with them before. But this time was different. We were celebrating my decoration—and my promotion. I hadn't officially received the major's gold medallions, but the word had come down. I was now a full step above the rank of captain. We toasted my promotion for the fifth time." Adriana's fists balled tight, the knuckles white and straining.

"That was when they turned on me." Adriana's eyes closed as tight as her fists. She pounded on the sheets in pain and frustration. "At first it was just in rough fun, claiming that, as a woman, I had no right to be a pilot let alone receive the rank of major. I should have laughed it off, as one of the boys, and left. But I grew angry. What they were saying, what they laughed about, pissed me off. I told them what I thought of their macho stupidity." She looked back at the man standing beside her.

"'You are fucking animals,' I cried out. It was the same anger that gave me strength to crawl toward the fire in the sands of the desert. I saw women cooking over the coals. That fire burned in my heart. What had I done to deserve this? What had I done, but fly and fight for my country? I was decorated for that. I was a war hero, they told me when the decoration was pinned on my uniform—the same decoration my fellow officers tore off with my clothes and my pride. They threw me down and held me down on that cold, stainless steel table in the officer's recreation room. They took turns. Four of them holding me as each took his insecurity and frustration out on me—into me. I was helpless. 'We will show you animals,' the major hissed in my ear as he bore down upon me.

"As the anger once again grew in my heart there in the desert, I rose to my knees and gathered the strength to cry out. The women at the fire heard me." Adriana let her fists relax; her tensed muscles loosened. She took a deep breath and let it out slowly. Kerns stood in stunned silence, unmoving. "I remember nothing from that point," Adriana said in an exhausted whisper, "until I woke in a medical facility in Baghdad. I was alive!"

Minutes passed before she turned to the man beside the bed. "It was weeks, Kerns, before I was mentally capable of bringing charges against the men who had attempted to destroy a fellow officer. A fellow officer who, in their minds, was not worthy because of her sex to wear the wings, to own the rank of major. It was weeks before I stood before my commanding officer seated at his desk, the commanding officer of our wing. He listened as, in the tears of that still growing anger, I recounted my story. The men I was accusing, he said, had been shipped out. They'd been transferred to other parts of the globe. It would be very difficult to get statements from them. The general stood slowly.

"'That is quite a tale of woe,' he said. He reached out and took the written report I was about to file. He glanced at the paper. 'Thank you for submitting this to me first,' he said, slipping the typewritten pages into a drawer of his desk. 'I would appreciate it if you kept this quiet until I have had time to study your accusations. You realize, I am sure, that this report, true or false, will reflect badly upon the honor and integrity of the air force, Captain—and upon your honor and integrity. As you must be aware, right now it is holding up your promotion. These men you are accusing of heinous crimes are all men of honor: men of your present rank, or better, Captain O'Donovan. They are well-respected officers of the force, as you are—at present.

"At that I was excused. That was the end of it. Two months later I was made a resignation offer, with full retirement benefits. One has to be in the service twenty years to receive retirement benefits. I wasn't a fool. I agreed to what I was offered—that is, I agreed until I read the small print. When I read the small print, I read it carefully. I tore up the papers. In the small print I was sworn to secrecy. I was to sign an affidavit agreeing that the rape had never occurred. In my lifetime, I was never to mention the episode to another soul. I tore up the papers and left the United States Air Force in disgrace."

Adriana straightened out full length on the laid back sheets of the bed. Her eyes flashed a sharp Irish anger, which still sustained her. "Kerns," she cried out, "at that moment the US Armed Forces raped me for the sixth time. That last fuck by the US Air Force, which I lived for—which I was willing to give my life for—hurt the worst."

Kerns looked down upon this beautiful and distressed woman reliving the horrors of her betrayal by the armed services of the country she believed in. She turned slowly and looked up at him. "I will be a survivor!" she cried. "I will be a survivor, Kerns. I am not a fool. I will not be a victim. Get back into this bed!"

If there was small print here, Kerns didn't see it. Kerns was not a fool either. He felt the fierce, determined anger in her first lovemaking in over five years. Kerns understood. He hung on until she reached her crest, crying out in tears and falling back. He held her gently as she wept in his arms. The second time she gave to him her love. "Forgive me, Kerns," she said again, "for pouring my anger out upon you. I'll fly you back to Fairbanks if you wish."

"That is not my wish. And you have nothing to forgive, Adriana. I'm not a bad cook. Let me fix you breakfast."

"I'm not a good cook, Kerns. Please let me take you up on your offer."

Kerns kissed her gently. "I'll call you when it's ready."

***

The aroma of fresh, strong coffee filled the cabin. On the kitchen wood stove, bacon sizzled. *This is the best morning I have had in years*, Kerns thought. He carried her coffee into the bedroom. Adriana was asleep. On the flight up here, she had said she seldom slept. Kerns didn't wake her.

***

CHAPTER 12

Questions and Answers

Slim might not be genius, but he was smart enough to know his limitations. He had a great respect for them as well. Limitations, he felt, were to be dealt with as silently as possible. The woman Kerns had introduced him to at the Big I had the first name of Adriana. He thought she owned the A-Plus Flying Service in Fairbanks, Alaska. He didn't know how long she had owned it. By browsing the Web he knew he should be able to find a history of A-Plus Flying Service. There was none. There was no website. He was sure he had made a mistake and checked it out again. Nothing. Slim drove to the airport and cruised about until he spied a small sign on a rather large hangar, which gave him the name he was searching for. The name under the sign, however, was Alice Baily. There was no Adriana listed.

"Okay," he muttered. "Maybe I made a mistake. He went back to the office and his computer and searched for *Alice Baily, pilot @ A-Plus Flying Service*. It flashed up on the screen. *Okay*, he thought, *I am not completely stupid*. Alice Baily's co-pilot was listed as Adriana O'Donovan, retired air force officer. Adriana had been decorated in the second Gulf War—declared by President George W. Bush and his vice president, a forgettable man by the name of Dick Cheney. Although Slim classed the name as forgettable, he couldn't shake it from his mind. Slim thought very little of both men. However, he reasoned, his personal beliefs had nothing to do with the search he was conducting on the web. He zeroed in on Adriana O'Donovan. He discovered the lady had been stripped of her rank and dismissed from the air force five years ago. It wasn't a dishonorable discharge, but it left a lot to be desired as far as honor was concerned. Adriana had pleaded no contest, or had pleaded nothing to an unmentioned, ambiguous charge. The pleading was unclear as far as Google was concerned. A blank page was the end of the report. There were no comments posted. There was no space relegated for comments.

Adriana had disappeared, and that was that. Many people came to Alaska to disappear. Slim shook his head and contemplated the results of his search. If Adriana was the informer Kerns had talked to, what was her position in the case? Slim knew, from what Kerns had told him about her, and it wasn't much, that she had flown Kerns into the headwaters of the Colville River and dropped him off. Sometime later, she flew in, picked him up, and flew him to Deadhorse, where she had picked him up previously. In the Arctic wilderness finding a lone man on the North Slopes of the Brooks Range would be classified as fairly precise flying with the eyesight of a peregrine or a gyrfalcon, two of the fastest and most amazing birds of the falcon family. The peregrine, in a stoop, or power-dive for prey, had been clocked in at speeds of two hundred miles per hour. Slim looked Adriana up again under *Adriana O'Donovan/US Air Force*. She had been listed, but that site was now a blank. *Something is missing indeed*, Slim thought. He placed a call to Kerns' cell phone. There was no answer. He left a message to call him when convenient. Slim left the office. When he arrived at the homestead, Kerns was not there. He called Hap at the Big I and left a message for Kerns to call in. Slim was a bit concerned.

He parked next to Kerns' camper and found tracks where Kerns had driven out the day before. There were no return tracks. Slim plugged his 4x4 into the extension cord leading up from his home. The engine would stay warm and ready to go. Lights were on in the log cabin, but no vehicle was parked there. Through the double-paned, frost-proof glass he saw his son bent over the laptop. *Roy is always bent over a laptop, or a screen of some sort*, Slim thought. His mind snapped to the chip implants he still carried. Roy was good on the computer. No one at the office could figure out the chips. What harm could there be to turn them over to Roy? Slim stomped loudly up onto the porch, alerting his son of his arrival.

"Mom dropped me off," Roy said. "She has a meeting in Anchorage and flew down. I'll catch the school bus here in the morning." Slim saw that Roy had filled the wood box and thanked him. "I live here half the time, Pop. As you say, a person should do something for his keep." Slim threw his coat over a chair and gave his son a hug. It was returned warmly.

"So what have you fixed for dinner?"

"That's your department, Pop. My priority is the wood box."

"After the laptop?" Slim fished into his son's priority list. "And your iPhone."

"That's my A list, Pop. The wood box tops my B list. Oh, and as far as dinner goes, I did get a couple of moose steaks out of the freezer."

"Good thinking." Roy was back at the computer again. "By the way, Roy." Slim paused, thinking a moment. "I got a problem." He pulled the plastic baggie with the two chips out of his shirt pocket and dropped it on the desk by his son. "Do you know what these are?"

Taking them out of the baggie, Roy studied the chips, the size of a pinto bean. "Big Brother," he said. "George Orwell dreamed them up in the forties. I've seen pictures of them, but I've never seen them in the flesh, so to speak." Roy looked up at his father. "Where'd you get these?"

"I'd rather not say. Who is George Orwell, Roy? Who is he? How do you know about these, Roy?"

"These are tracking devices, Pop—RFID, radio frequency identification. Possibly a VeriChip. The mark of the beast, Pop. According to Revelation it is a biblical prophecy. Do you know what the mark of the beast is? Look it up on the Web. They shoot one of these into you and the government, or whoever, can follow your every move. A little scary, but amazing technology."

"You can find them on the Internet?"

"Yeah." Roy typed something quickly on the keyboard. A list flashed up beneath his search line. He clicked on one. A photo filled the screen. It was the magnified tip of a human finger. Resting on it was an almost duplicate of the microchip Slim had brought home.

"That," his son said, "is a very small hard drive, a microchip, Pop, like a VeriChip. The USDA has okayed VeriChips for certain medical procedures. Of course, they don't tell us for certain what the procedures are."

"How do you know all this stuff, Roy?"

"I knew some of it. A friend of yours, a guy by the name of Johnny Winslow, called me trying to get in touch with you. We must have talked for an hour. That Winslow knows a lot of computer stuff. But he said I might know more than him. He said something that made me think. Your friend Winslow said young people are the smartest on computers because we don't know there are things computer geniuses have proved you can't do."

"And you do them? Right, Roy?"

"Right, Pop. If you don't know it can't be done, Pop, your friend told me, you can probably do it. I believe those were his exact words."

"That's dangerous, Roy."

"Maybe, but what you have here, Pop, is a piece of the beast. It is, among other things, a tracking device like they implant in credit cards now and passports. It is capable of tracking the implanted plastic or person or animal anywhere in the world. They can break down or be broken down, Winslow said, but that is unlikely." Roy looked up at his father inquisitively. "Where did you get these little toys, Pop? They are pretty high-tech."

"That is encrypted information, son." Slim considered for a moment. "Can anyone read these things, Roy?"

"Anyone with the right receiver and/or the password can." Roy picked up one of the chips. "I wish I had a microscope to go with it. I could maybe see how they made it and what they made if of."

"We got a magnifying glass. It's right in the drawer there."

"Better than nothing, Pop." Roy studied the tiny hard drive through the glass. He glanced back up at Slim. "I can't see what it is made of, Pop, but there are some strange fibers stuck to it. Was this, by any chance, cut out of some animal, or person even, like the guy you pulled out of the ice in Manly? If it was implanted, it could be designed to bond with human or animal tissue."

"What—why?"

"It would keep it in place, like hold it steady, like an artificial hip made out of titanium adheres to the upper leg bone. Whatever that bone is called."

"I see." Slim paused a moment, thinking. "You are right, son. It's from the guy at Manly. We are trying to figure out who the person is—or was. It is a part of my damn business. Right now I need an expert." Roy was back studying the little translucent pill. "Do I have an expert in the house?"

"The guy you pulled out of the Red Slough in Manley, right?"

"Right. Look, you don't have to go on with this, Roy. I was wrong to ask you."

"No you weren't. I am honored that you did. I am very proud of you, Pop. So is Mom. I want to help."

"Your mom told you she was proud of me, Roy?"

"I don't think she ever stopped loving you, Pop." The boy turned back to the cyber pill in front of him. "Now, let's drop that subject and get back to work on this." He brought the magnifying glass back into focus on the pill. "Your computer is picking up a slight signal from it. Tell me everything you know about this guy they dropped into the slough."

"Who the hell are you, Roy, the chief of detectives?" Slim grinned.

"I might be someday, and you, Pop, will be the first man I hire as my deputy."

"Well Jes-us!"

"He's not for hire. Now give me all the information you have on this Red Slough guy, Pop. I'll do an advanced search to see if I can find where he got this pill implanted."

Slim opened up his worn pocket notebook and started giving his son all he had come up with about the body dropped in Red Slough—and Captain Albert Cummings, who may have raped Diana, if the name Kerns got from his informer was correct. It wasn't much. Roy absorbed it and clacked away on the keyboard, starting with the Red Slough drop. Roy had continually loaded all upgrades on his father's Apple computer. It had been, and was still, a top-of-the-line brain. Roy tracked the Red Slough pill to a captain in the air force stationed in Germany. "Ramstein Air Base, Pop. United States Air Force base in Rhineland-Palatinate—Pal-a-tin-ate—well," Roy hedged, "I can't pronounce it, but it doesn't appear Captain Jason Blitzweimer was Charley the military work dog, but he is, or was, a pilot and a star on the base bowling team." He clicked another key. "It says here: 'The mission of the United States Air Force is to fly, fight, and win . . . in air, space, and cyberspace." Roy looked up at his father. "This Captain Blitzweimer knew computers, Pop, and it looks like he had one for a heart." He nudged the tiny hard drive with the lead tip of his pencil. "You have the heart right here." Roy looked down meaningfully at the minute hard drive in front of him. "Let us see if this heart pumps anything out." Roy loved the challenge and worked on it for over half an hour in silence, trying out many combinations as he searched for a password that fit. His father looked on with amazement at first and then with occasional boredom.

"This will never work, Roy. There are a thousand combinations."

"I got it," Roy broke in with muffled excitement. "It's jasonBCap@serv.org." He studied the screen for a moment, puzzled. "But the works in the chip are scrambled, Pop. There is nothing here but gibberish. The tracking mechanism is toast. Pop, somewhere, someone dumped the information contained in the drive and trashed the tracking program. The thing is dead. This guy, Jason, was on his own."

"You mean his mechanical heart expired some time before he did, son?"

"You hit it, Pop."

Slim nodded. "Thanks, Roy. That explains why the military didn't show up to claim the body immediately. But where did the heart expire?" Roy was studying the other tiny, bean-size rubberized chip.

"What about this one, Pop?"

"One at a time, Roy. We don't have a chip for Cummings. He may be still alive."

Slim caught a flash of headlights in the window. Kerns was back. Did he have any information? It was time to put another log on the fire.

***

Kerns was definitely charged up on his return to Chena Ridge and it wasn't on Rye. He did consent to a drink when Slim poured it out for him. "Where the hell you been?" Slim asked as he did so. "But then, I guess that's none of my business."

"You are right there." Kerns sipped his drink. "So what have you two been up to? But then, I guess that is none of *my* business."

"Okay, so we are even," Slim, replied. "Let's make it all our business. Where the hell have you been, Kerns? You were going out to get some information for me. Where did you go, or what did you find out?"

"I have been to Chena Hot Springs soaking in the wonders of life." Kerns inhaled a deep breath and let it out slowly and with satisfaction. "But I didn't soak up any information for you, Slim. So." He looked from Slim to Slim's son. "I guess it's my turn now. So, what have you two been up to?"

"We have—" Slim stopped in mid-sentence. "I should say *Roy* has broken the code on one of the chips. The one found in the body that landed in Red Slough."

"Great. What does it say?"

"Nothing. Someone, somewhere along the line, scrambled that information. But get this!" There was no mistaking the pride in Slim's voice. "My son found the air force base in Germany where this Captain Blitzweimer is—or was—stationed."

"A computer genius." Kerns placed a large, strong hand on Roy's shoulder. "Great, Roy. All you got to do now is find the base in Texas where Cummings is stationed and bring him back here for your father to question him."

"Midnight Poison might lure him back, Kerns."

Slim spun around. "Where'd you pick up that name, Roy?"

Kerns jumped in. He was afraid Slim would be a bit too fatherly if the truth came out a bit raw. "Roy was doing his bit for you, Slim. He did an in-depth search and came up with a porno site listing Midnight Poison. I was here with him, Slim. We were doing it, more or less, together. It's just that your son is more competent on the keyboard. He nailed it. There she was in all her glory—except for her head. The head had been cropped from the poison. The profile with it was a bit rough, though. Your son brought it up on the screen, that was all."

"Kerns loved it, Pop. You want to take a look?"

"Holy Mother," Slim sighed. "No I don't, Roy."

"Okay, Pop. Do it after I leave. I know you will. You have to." He smirked. "It's your job."

"He's right, Slim. It may well have something to do with this case, which is why we looked it up. Midnight Poison. It was a pretty strong accusation when I first heard it."

"Yeah, but Roy—"

"Roy's a man, Slim."

"Okay."

"Okay!" Roy echoed his father's admission. "You said it, Pop. Thanks." Roy went to his father and embraced him. His father let out a sigh of surrender. He wanted and needed the answers.

"I'm proud of you, Roy. I couldn't ask for a finer son."

"I'm proud of you, too, Pop. I couldn't ask for a better trooper. And speaking of better, we had better get back to work."

Kerns looked silently into his glass. He then raised it to them. "I'm not so proud I won't have another splash of Rye. Here's to you both."

***

In Cincinnati, Samuel Charles Bellefonte dropped his head into his arms on the table before him. His problem was Midnight Poison—whoever Midnight Poison might be—she was changing her profile again. A client from Germany was the last to answer. Samuel had heard nothing more from the officer in Germany. He hoped the man was satisfied, or had been satisfied. Cybersex would be the least expensive way out, but Midnight and the officer had cut to a private email address and that was the last Samuel heard from Germany. Midnight Poison did have other clients asking for her. To Samuel's knowledge Midnight never answered any of them—well, perhaps before his arrival on the scene, she had. Samuel, following Saul Billings' orders, had written back to a few promising male clients in Midnight Poison's name. Studying the wonders of her fantastic female body, all be it headless, the young writer made up preposterous lies. Samuel took his work seriously. Letters like that drained him. He hated pretending to be a women, especially in the cybersex market. *I am a writer and it is a living. I make a living writing fiction, not fact*, he kept telling himself. *I am an honest writer!* Billings just laughed.

"Of course it's a living Samuel, and a good living. Who else can make a living fulfilling fantasies of both sexes? Why, you have men and women dildoing themselves to heaven and blessing you for it. All ages, all colors, all sizes, in beds, on bathroom floors, sitting on bidets adjusting the pressure at your bidding, enemas on call, heated seats, massage functioning toys, pulsation function. You are giving them a Disneyland of fornication fantasies, Sammy boy."

"Jesus, Saul." They had reached a first name familiarity.

"Oh, stop calling on him. You are being redundant."

"I can't take any more of this. Sex, sex, sex, all day long. Where will it all lead, Saul?"

"To the bank, Sammy boy. You'll have them masturbating in the master vault. Samuel, you are doing a great job. Keep it up." Without taking a breath, Saul went on, changing the subject drastically. "I'm dying of cancer, Sam. They say I got six months left. The old prostate. It's not even a sexually transmitted disease. The closest I get to a sexual experience now is when that lovely doctor shoves her finger up my ass. Get a sweet young female MD, Samuel. I don't care what news she gives me. It's worth it every time." Billings suddenly turned serious, as he always did when business called. "Your light's flashing, Sammy. It's Midnight Poison. She's been busy lately. Take care of her." Billings left, and then, as he always did, he shoved his head back into the open doorway with an afterthought. "By the way, Samuel, when I die I'm leaving it all to you. Have a ball, kid. Keep 'em fucking, sucking, and rubbing the old worm into an erection. No erectile dysfunction on this site, Sammy." And Saul Billings was gone. God bless him.

***

Saul left Samuel to deal with his last words. The big man did have cancer of the prostate. He knew he had cancer months before he entered Samuel's cubical on this day, but he had no idea he was going to leave everything he owned to the boy until he walked out the door. He knew he had something to say when he stuck his head back in. But he just blurted it out. He didn't regret doing it. There was no one in his scattered family he thought enough of to leave anything to. Saul was a kind and very impulsive person. He didn't say it just to get Samuel to stay on. He liked Samuel. *I must like him*, he thought. He hadn't known he liked the boy enough to leave everything he owned to him in his will. Now that he'd said it, he had better write it down. He made a penciled note to call his lawyer in the morning.

***

As it always was, the forty-eight-inch flat TV screen in Saul's private office was on. It was muted as it always was. Earphones lay on his desk. He could pick them up anytime he wished. Actually there were five sets of earphones on and around his desk. They were all color-coded. Each color connected him to a certain cubical. He enjoyed Samuel's line the most. The kid had talent. Saul had considered kicking him out on the street where he would have to write real stuff, like *Down and Out in Cincinnati*. Samuel would be down and out in Cincinnati, too. He would be working in the bowels of a restaurant, but he wouldn't be writing. Saul knew Samuel had talent. Saul assured himself this life was better for Samuel. Here he could learn his trade. *Now that I am dying*, Saul thought, *not that everyone isn't dying from the day of his or her conception, but I am blessed to have a set date for the event of my exodus. I have time to prepare.* He shrugged and glanced up at the TV screen. They were playing the same media news shit they had been playing for weeks. Some asshole had jumped naked from a plane and crashed through the ice of a bloody slough. That was about as crazy as any news could get. *And news can get pretty crazy in the world today*, Saul thought. Suddenly, blood-red words were splashed over the rehashed picture of a cop chopping a naked body from the ice. The words snapped Saul to attention:

MIDNIGHT POISON

The words flashed across the screen in great jagged red capital letters. Saul grabbed a mike and pulled a green set of earphones over his bald head. He pushed a green button on his bank of buttons.

"Are you fucking with me, Samuel? Or jerking off?"

"I'm sorry you got cancer, Saul. Are you sure? You don't have to give anything to me," was the comeback. "You have given me enough. You have faith in my writing."

"I'm sorry I got cancer, too. But that's got nothing to do with what Midnight Poison is doing on national television."

"You mean we are exposed? Are they going to raid us?"

"Get your ass in here, Samuel!" Saul looked back up at the screen. Midnight Poison had cross-faded into a fantastically made up anchorwoman Saul would love to have for a client. Perhaps he did have her for a client. He would have to check. In any case, she was now dealing with the latest media absurdity, which she was treating as a ladies' aid society news item. Saul slid the volume all the way up. The anchor's velvet voice blasted out of the surround-sound speakers.

"We have the latest breaking news on the naked slough murder and/or suicide in Alaska." She smiled seductively as she waited for the next line to flash up on her teleprompter, and then continued: "As it turns out, an unidentified agent of the CIA speaking on the condition he would remain unidentified, as he has no right to release this information, has come bravely forth with strikingly and bitterly truthful words concerning the Blood Slough scandal." She smiled again. "But first a commercial."

Saul hit the mute button.

***

At the Big I in Fairbanks, Alaska, Hap turned up the volume. *MIDNIGHT POISON* once again in lightning flame, jagged-shaped letters flashed across the screen over a rerun of Slim chopping the naked body out of the red ice of Blood Slough. The local Alaska anchorperson picked up the story:

"This is not a case of WikiLeaks, folks. The CIA has come to the fore with news we can trust." Doc was at the bar with Hap, Kerns, and Slim. They watched the screen closely as did all in the Big I.

"You look pretty good on TV, Slim, even soaking wet." Kerns grinned at his friend's discomfort. Slim turned his back on the video and burned his tongue on Hap's hot coffee. The rest of the patrons in the bar crowded in for a closer look. They had all seen this cut a hundred times but not the large red words superimposed over it.

"It seems," the anchorperson went on, "the local law enforcement officials have been keeping this news under the covers, so to speak. This is the third naked body dropped from the Arctic skies. It is believed all three of them uttered the same cry on the way down."

"Turn it off." Slim made the request of Hap. Cries of disapproval went up from the disgruntled drinkers. Hap turned the volume down.

"All the victims are US Air Force officers and all were jet pilots," went on the anchorperson. "Captain Jason Blitzweimer was the one to take the fall into the ice of Blood Slough. Second Lieutenant William Bancroft was discovered earlier by a local law enforcement officer, as was the first drop, found only as a skeleton. The skeleton will be referred to as John Doe, until notification of next of kin. With the exception of John Doe, all had a small puncture wound in the chest. This wound is attributed to a large animal tranquilizer dart, which rendered the fighter pilots unconscious almost immediately, and thus, virtually incapable of defending themselves. There is no explaining the kind of mind that would dream up such a horrible descent into the bowels of death."

"She's getting pretty poetic, Hap." Kerns indicated the TV anchor.

"It's her or the teleprompter," Hap laughed. He hit the mute button on the TV. "I don't think Slim appreciates it."

***

Doc Singer silently left the Big I for his cabin close to the university. Doc was spending a lot of time on the computer lately. Today he would spend even more. Singer was good at his homework. He had tracked down Captain Albert Cummings's name and rank. He had now only to find the bastard's location. Doc was determined.

"I think he's on a mission," Hap said, watching Singer leave.

Slim stepped into their conversation. "Whatever it is, he's pretty quiet about it. He hasn't asked questions, but he has listened to every word we say. And speaking of silence, thanks for cutting the sound off, Hap. It's only bullshit and we have all heard it twenty times."

"You don't want to catch the particulars, Slim?" Hap asked with a straight face.

Slim just looked at him as one would at a bad dog. "Those government agents keep their minds closed, but they can't keep their mouths shut," he said.

"The media loves them for it," Kerns replied quietly. "Pays them for it, too." Something was nagging at Kerns' mind. "The media hasn't mentioned the kind of rope tying the victims' hands behind their back," he said, "and the fact that in each case the sisal rope had been, or was being, dissolved by acid."

"Why don't you call them up and tell them about it, Kerns? You can get your name and face all over the screen, too."

"Did I miss something?" Hap asked, looking from Kerns to Slim. "You know I hate being in the dark."

"It's nothing," Slim said. "If they thought it important that woman on the tube would be screaming about it."

In Kerns' mind, he recalled Alice patching the acid-burned carpet on the floor of Adriana's Helio. He shook his head, throwing the entire thought out of his mind, and changed the subject. "That woman on the tube loves talking about it and she loves talking about you, Slim."

"Love is always for sale," Hap said philosophically.

"It isn't love that's for sale," Slim snorted. He wasn't quite as philosophical as Hap. "I'd better go into hiding and write a report—a competent lie, that is—that explains why we didn't get the whole story out the day we found the first fallen body. I will keep you out of this, Kerns. Right now there is too much misinformation in too many hands and heads. They will all be scrambling for recognition and glory. God only knows what crap will be spewed up next."

"They will find you at the homestead, Slim," Kerns said.

"I'm not going to the homestead, Kerns. I will tell them at the office what I am up to and have them tell the world that I am in the wilderness. Thank God for poor phone service in Alaska."

"Where will you be?" Kerns asked. "Just in case." Hap stepped out of hearing. He didn't want to know. Hap was good at lying, but he didn't like to do it.

"I'll be at my ex-wife's place. No one will look for me there. Roy will be quiet about it." Slim slipped out the back door reserved for special customers. "Special customers" referred to anyone who knew about the back door. Every local in Fairbanks knew about the back door. They were all special customers.

The TV was replaying the news on the mute setting. Kerns ordered a shot of Rye and thought about sulfuric acid. "No." He shook the troubling thought from his head again. "No way."

***

Back in Cincinnati, Ohio, Saul Billings turned to Samuel. "What do you think?"

Samuel was quiet for a long moment. "Is that our Midnight Poison?" he finally said. "The names match. Can this be getting us in trouble, Saul?"

"It certainly got the three of them in trouble, Sam. I don't think it can get us in trouble, but something here is morally wrong, Sammy. Bring up Midnight's latest profile." Samuel started out of Saul's office. "No, Sammy, sit here. We shall do this together." He pulled out the overstuffed, leather-covered chair behind his desk. "Sit here, Samuel. Bring Midnight up. We need to be prepared."

Samuel sat down apprehensively. The chair engulfed him. He touched the keyboard. The cropped photo of Midnight Poison leapt to the screen along with the new profile the client had submitted. It read:

> *Hey I'm looking to be fucked by two to three guys at a time. You have never experienced a blowjob like mine. It cuts like a knife. You'll cum like a cannon. At the same time, I want to be fucked so hard I can't move. I'm looking for abusive sons-of-bitches to tie me up and slap me around. It's the only way I can get off. I was abused—no, fucked—by my father and uncle from the time I was five until I was fourteen and left home. They were both officers in the US Army—respected men, both of them decorated. Both of them died with honor in Vietnam. They left me with this curse. I can't get off sexually unless I am raped by someone in uniform and in the service. Officers and gentlemen, step right up and take your turn.*

***

In the town of College, Alaska, Doc Singer awakened his Apple and was looking at the same copy. "Christ almighty," he breathed aloud to the empty room. "Midnight Poison. That is the connection. Captain Albert, whatever his name, could be the next to go." Doc got out his notebook. He flipped it open with cool excitement, checking his notations. Doc had done his cyber homework well. "If it is the Captain Albert Cummings I found," he mused aloud, "Cummings was at one time in the same flying group as the three bodies dropped here. If that son-of-a-bitch is still in Alaska he might be lying somewhere out there right now. It's a true pity Midnight Poison didn't get him a week sooner." Doc jumped back onto his computer, bringing up the Midnight Poison screen once again. "Maybe she did get him."

***

"Mother of Jesus," Billings breathed back in Cincinnati. "That's pretty rank copy, Samuel. Couldn't you tone it down a bit? I mean it's not sexy, Sam, not to a healthy man. It would only appeal to a born pervert."

Samuel shook his head. "I think that is the type of man she is luring into her cave, Saul. 'This will draw them in like flies,' she wrote. Midnight ordered me not to edit one word of her copy. 'Like flies to honey,' I asked her, 'or flies to blood?' 'Either way will work,' she wrote back. 'To a fly, even shit is sweet. I repeat: Don't touch my copy!'" Samuel looked up at Billings.

"What is the name of the last client she accepted?" Billings asked.

"Bzit99 is the code name, Saul. I don't know his or her real name. That's your department." Samuel paused, letting the question hang.

"Right." Billings reached over Samuel's shoulder and hit a combination of letters and numbers. He stepped back into the room, away from Samuel. "When you press enter, Sammy, you are opening the door into this site's security room. It is something I have sworn to our clients I would never allow anyone else to do. In other words, Samuel, you will be accepting the responsibility of my company—soon to be yours. You will become far more than a stitch in my security blanket. You are sworn to secrecy." Billings looked down at the young writer. "It's your move, Samuel, think about it."

"Do other so-called secure sites treat their security with this same lockup?" Samuel asked haltingly.

"Some selectively, yes. There are those who disregard it blatantly. Especially in this business, but even Facebook has been accused of it. This office has been approached with generous offers to sell my client's information." Saul turned to his young protégée. "Saul Billings is a man of honor, Samuel. I will not take that step backward. And I certainly don't expect you to if you push the enter button." There was another pause. Samuel stared down at the keyboard. He spun the big chair slowly and looked up at Billings.

"You would trust me with this, Mr. Billings?"

"If you trust yourself, Mr. Bellefonte. There is no RFID chip that I know of monitoring your moves. You are on your own."

"RFID chip?"

"Radio frequency identification chip. A microchip implanted in your flesh. It can do good, I suppose. Some may think it to their advantage to have their medical records broadcast to the world. But an unscrupulous government or individual could also manipulate the RFID chip to control your brain waves, Samuel."

"I manipulate my own brain waves, Mr. Billings."

"Let's cut the misters, Sammy, and go straight to the truth."

Samuel spun his chair back to the keyboard and punched enter. A photograph and name, Captain Jason Blitzweimer, US Air Force, flashed up on the screen. Credit card number included. Saul Billings' hand gripped Samuel's shoulder. He looked at the big television monitor screen above them. It was rerunning the news clip under the transparent words in red: *Midnight Poison*. They both watched in silence.

"According to the media dispatch, Sammy," Billings said quietly, "Captain Jason Blitzweimer was the name of the naked body dropped through the ice of a Blood Red slough above the Arctic Circle in central Alaska."

"Can we trust the media?"

"No."

"Do we know who Midnight Poison is?" Samuel was staring at the TV replay. He had seen it weeks before, but not with names and numbers attached. Right now, Samuel was in a state of shock. He had personally emailed Blitzweimer and Midnight Poison. He felt he was definitely implicated in this bloody intrigue. The TV switched to a commercial about disposable baby diapers. Young Samuel Charles Bellefonte shuddered.

"Midnight Poison, Saul, do we also have that name and number to prove it?"

"We have names and numbers, Sammy, but right now they are only a mix for the rumor mill. Captain Blitzweimer seems to me more than a coincidence. Midnight Poison?" He shrugged. "Midnight Poison may be a media drum beating in the wilderness. Its sounds are large, but the rhythm means nothing: the lyrics—possibly Midnight Poison's profile put to music. As of now, we know nothing, Sammy. We are not about to join the dance. The FBI, the CIA, let them caper. In unscrupulous hands, the information we have could involve the innocent—including us." Billings thought a moment. "No, Samuel, not us—just including me. You had nothing to do with this."

"But I wrote them both, Saul. I communicated with them. I am a party to it."

"It? Let us not jump to conclusions, which is what we are doing. Don't jump until you know where you are going to land is my way of looking at it. Go back to work, Sammy. Let me sift through all this information. I don't want you to become more involved."

"Midnight Poison just changed her profile, Saul. I posted it. I am involved in that. What do I tell the client?" Samuel got up out of the voluminous leather chair belonging to his boss and walked to the door of the large office, a door with a doorknob and lock on it for privacy. "What do we tell the rest of your employees, Saul?"

"Nothing. If they ask, we tell them to keep working through their shift. And, Samuel, I will take it upon myself to remove

Midnight Poison's profile, picture, and every shadow of her information from our Sex, Fire & Ice site and Cum With Me. In minutes, no one will be able to find a trace of it. Not even the FBI."

Samuel nodded. "I hope you catch it in time, Saul." Sam headed back to his cubicle and his growing literary responsibility. His mind was aging rapidly.

Saul Billings was left drumming his fingers on the Formica top of his desk and thinking: *What was the address of that gallopingbanana site or banahbelt.com?* He kept that thought to himself, hoping Midnight Poison would eradicate it. *With all this publicity, if she is smart, she will.* He would check for that shadow as well.

***

In Fairbanks, Dr. Robert Singer pushed the print button to capture the new profile he had uncovered for Midnight Poison. The screen went blank. He tried to bring it back. There was nothing. Doc looked down at his notes and a printout of the previous profile for Midnight Poison. He had brought it up following Diana's cruel rape and death. Doc's determined search went deeper than that of Kerns and Slim's son Roy. The dossier he assembled on Midnight Poison led him nowhere until this break, this WikiLeak, sprung in the boat by an overzealous CIA informer. He started a search for Captain Blitzweimer, thinking as his computer was digging for information: *It's stretching my luck, but could there be a connection between this Captain Blitzweimer and the Captain Al, or Albert, accused of poor Diana's rape and murder? The violence matches, if nothing else. I'll give it a shot.*

***

CHAPTER 13

Rumors? Rumors.

Slim's ex-wife, Thelma, was glad to have Slim back in the house, even if it wasn't the house she used to live in with him. That house was up on Chena Ridge. She wasn't going back into that house until he invited her. She wasn't certain if she'd go then. She thought she would. Thelma wanted to. Slim didn't realize that. There were lots of things Slim didn't realize about his ex-wife, or his ex-marriage. The big thing he did realize: his drinking. He had overcome that. He was sure he had overcome that. He would never take a drink again. What he didn't realize was that he didn't realize a lot of other things. Like why didn't she just move back in with him when he dried out?

Thelma had her own house now, a house in town. She was and had been an independent woman. She was reluctant to leave it. When Slim finally screwed up the courage to knock on that door and stammer out an apology, she invited him in. That surprised him. It surprised him even more when she invited him into her bedroom. It has been said that action speaks louder than words. There were no words spoken for almost an hour. As he was leaving, Slim turned in the door and asked if he might come again.

"I'll think about it, Slim," Thelma said. There was a long pause—an awkward pause on Slim's part. "Call first," she said. "And thank you for the apology."

"It was long overdue," Slim said quietly. He closed the door and walked slowly to his state pickup. The motor was still running.

***

It was convenient for Slim to have a place in town. He would tell himself that the convenience was the important part of their relationship. The conversation was kept simple between them. There were no in-depth commitments. He always called first before he knocked on Thelma's door. She wanted him back for Roy, she told herself that, but not Slim. Slim's drinking was never mentioned either. He was sober. That she liked. It was convenient for her. They would sleep together and have a delightfully sexy time of it. She would make him coffee in the morning and he would be gone. Or he would make her coffee and be gone before she woke. That was as it used to be on the mornings he was sober. Having him there now, and sober, was good. Having him gone was nice, too. She missed him but knew he would be back and that it would be good again. He always called and asked permission. That was nice. That was good, too.

Thelma had almost had an affair during the three years they were absolutely separated. In Slims corner an affair was never considered. In his drinking days he missed her when he was hung over, but was suffering too much to realize it. He had his job, a job he loved. Hung over, he could do his job. Half drunk, he could do his job.

Slim had been the life of the party in those days, until something clicked. He never heard it click, that was his problem. When the switch clicked off, so did his memory. During those empty hours, or even days, he performed his job duties under cruise control. He took to making notes to remind him of what he had done when he slid back into the light. He never took notes about his forgotten home life. He angrily denied that. The anger was turned upon himself. He used that anger as a tool to keep the drink at bay. In time he needed it no longer. Thelma gave him visiting rights with their son. Slim tried to convince himself that was enough.

When drinking, Slim woke up on the floor of the kitchen more than once. Thelma started keeping score. When she presented him with the numbers, he rebelled. "My life is my life," he cried from the shower where he soaked his head and body in ice-cold water until he could think. When he reached the point of comprehensive thought it was too late for apologies. Slim would rather not make them anyways. Apologies, he felt when drinking, were a sign of weakness.

When he came home half drunk one day to find that Thelma had packed up and left him and taken his son with her—"their son," she pointed out in court—he blew up. The courtroom was the best place he could have blown up. The judge was a reliable witness. Thelma was given custody of Roy. She didn't ask for anything else. She had a job: vice president of the Fairbanks First Bank. She made more money than he did. "I don't need his money," she told the court.

"I don't need her money," Slim snapped back.

"I just want custody of our son," Thelma replied quietly. She was winning. She could afford to speak quietly.

"Keep him," Slim cried.

"Custody granted," the judge said.

Two of Slim's fellow officers locked arms with him and lead him from the courthouse.

"Case closed," the judge said.

"Thank you, Your Honor," Thelma said.

"You're welcome, Thelma. Court dismissed." And that was that.

Slim was given a month's suspension from the force. Two weeks later he quit drinking.

The intervening time, between then and now, is personal history and nobody's business. Slim was now courting his ex and she was receptive. Roy was happy, and that was that.

***

Slim sat at the kitchen table in his former wife's kitchen. This had been the first night in three years he, Thelma, and their son Roy had spent the night under one roof. Slim had made coffee for Thelma. She drank it in bed, the bed the two of them had slept in last night. Slim then made breakfast for himself and his son. They ate without saying a word. On leaving for school, Roy said, "I may have come up with a thing or two on the computer, Pop. Will I see you at the cabin tonight?"

"I'll be here, Roy. I'm hiding out."

"Don't blame you. Have a good day, Pop."

An hour later, Thelma left for the bank. She gave Slim a quick kiss and was gone. Slim opened up his office laptop and went to work. He got one call. Kerns' name flashed up on the screen of his iPhone. He answered it.

***

Kerns had spent the night in his camper with the heat on. Other than burning up his propane, the heater didn't do much to raise the temperature. He moved into Slim's log cabin sometime after midnight. The temperature in the house was above freezing. He cut some wood and lit a fire. Slim's land phone was ringing when Kerns got there. It was still ringing six hours later when he left. After getting the fire going, he switched Ma Bell to mute. The phone silently collected messages throughout the day. The first was from *The New York Times*. There were four messages from *The Times* before Kerns got there. *Thank God for modern technology*. Kerns had put the phone in bed and covered it with two pillows and a feather comforter to silence it. *How's that for modern muting technology?* Kerns then went to work with the computer, searching and asking questions. At 11:20, his cell phone went off. He was hoping for a call from Adriana. It had been a day or three. It seemed to Kerns like ten. A call from Adriana was not the case. He had wanted to call her but didn't want to break the mood they parted in. That had been a good, but fragile, mood. He wanted to ask her up to Slim's cabin. He would have it to himself tonight. But—

His cell rang again. Kerns grabbed it. Somconc was on the far end of the line but didn't answer right off. Finally a voice said in question, "Kerns?"

"Yeah, it's my phone. Who is this?"

"Actually, I am calling for Slim Dickerson. He told me to call this number and talk to a guy named Kerns if he wasn't there, or to his son, Roy."

"Well, this is Kerns. Roy isn't here and Slim isn't here. All you got is me."

"I see, well—this is John Winslow, Colonel William Cornwall's orderly, or gofer. I have news for Slim concerning Major Cooper's present location. Slim said that this information was important to him. It's about some case he is working on."

"It is important to him," Kerns answered. He grabbed a pencil and a sheet of paper. "Pass it on to me. I will forward it on to Slim."

"I would rather give this to Slim directly." Winslow paused and thought a moment. "Slim said you were a safe call."

"I am, Winslow. Go ahead."

"I will be in the colonel's office the rest of the day, where I don't dare receive a call from the trooper. Cornwall is paranoid. He keeps the place bugged. In fact, I bugged it for him. So I'll tell you what I know, Kerns—Kerns? Right?"

"Right, Kerns is the name and the person."

"Okay. First news first."

"Go ahead," Kerns said.

"The bug works both ways. I installed it so I could hear him, too. So, here goes, okay?"

"Okay. Go ahead," Kerns said again, a bit exasperated.

"First, Colonel Cornwall has, with a bit of help, hacked into the major's private email." Kerns was suddenly excited. The phone went silent.

"Go on," Kerns said.

"I was waiting for you to write it down."

"I take shorthand," Kerns lied.

"Good. It is old-fashioned, but it works."

"Right. Now get on with it, Winslow."

"Right. There is some weird connection, Kerns, between Major Cooper and this Midnight Poison thing we are seeing on the TV."

Kerns was writing furiously, trying to keep the cursive words decipherable so he could read them after the call. "Go on," Kerns mumbled. *Any connection between the major and Midnight Poison would be weird*, he thought, *and very interesting*.

"Second," the orderly continued, "as to the major's movements: He checked into the W—that's a hotel in Seattle. When the news broke about the body in the ice with a connection to this Poison person, he not only checked out of the W, he checked out of Seattle and flew to San Francisco. There he rented a car with no destination given to the rental people. It was open-ended. The major is no longer in the service of his country, but there is still a chip in his shoulder. Pass this on to Slim. I think he'll know what I mean."

"He will. Now, go on." Kerns' handwriting was now completely illegible. *Fuck it. I'll remember it. It's too much to write down anyway.*

"Shit, Kerns, I can't. The colonel just stepped out of the office and is headed this way." Winslow's voice changed to light-hearted small talk. "Love you, sweetheart. Talk to you later." The phone went dead.

Kerns looked at it in wonder. "Love you, sweetheart? Who does he think he's talking to?" Then it came to him: a cover for the colonel. Kerns brought up a blank page on his laptop and typed the conversation down as he remembered it. He had questions, which he also typed in.

1 - What is the name of the car rental company?
2 - Who is this guy Winslow?
3 - How did this colonel hack into the major's private email? Or did Winslow do it for him?
4 - Was the entire conversation a trap by the CIA to hook me?
Slim, you never mentioned the possibility of this call.

Kerns emailed the lot to Slim at his wife Thelma's email address. He got a return within five minutes. *Would you please come down here, Kerns?*

See you soon, Kerns replied and pushed send. Thinking that there might be something of importance in Slim's home phone messages, Kerns checked into them. Most calls were from TV stations and other news media seeking information on the falling bodies. There was one from Doc Singer: just two words—"Call back." Kerns made a mental note of it. The final call came from an unknown: "Thought we might talk—still thinking. May call back. Concerns M. P." No number listed.

"M. P." snapped a cord. "Midnight Poison? Might be more than interesting." Kerns was thinking aloud. "Blocked call. No number to call back. So be it."

Kerns banked the fire, got in his truck, and left the Ridge.

***

Major Almas A. Cooper III pulled off the interstate into a tiny town in western Utah. McDonald's had Wi-Fi. He brought his laptop in with him and over a double burger served with two inches of condiments, flipped it on. He checked his email. Captain Cummings had not answered his somewhat frantic communiqué sent from a McDonald's on the outskirts of San Francisco. The TV in this McDonald's was broadcasting in the mute mode. Midnight Poison blinked on and off over a rerun of old news about the naked falling bodies in Alaska. Cooper watched it with trepidation. Would his visage suddenly appear on the screen? At the present time and circumstances, he would not have been surprised. He looked about. There were no dark corners in McDonald's to hide from the glare of recognition. He thought of ducking into the men's room. Should he take his loaded burger and laptop with him?

The major had his back to the wall. Unlike Wild Bill, he would not be caught short. Nor was he headed for Deadwood. Dreading what might come up, he took a chance on opening his encrypted address. He drew a blank. Nothing was there. He typed in *Midnight Poison* and pushed search. After a longer than usual pause, a notice came up. *THIS SITE IS NO LONGER AVAILABLE*. This news did not placate the major. The fact that Poison had gone undercover only put him more on his guard. He bit into his giant double burger and swallowed the mouthful in two gulps. He took in another load of overcooked meat, fat, and roughage. With the exception of three Snickers, he hadn't eaten since leaving San Francisco. Should he take a chance on visiting his son in Colorado?

Where was he to go? The air force had been his only home for over thirty years. He no longer had a refuge. He searched his original email. That, too, was a blank page. Nothing. A sudden notice sprang up on the screen.

SOMEONE HAS COMPROMISED THIS ADDRESS.

The major closed his laptop, left the remainder of his meal, and fled to his rental car. He drove east on Route 80 for several miles before he pulled off onto a country road and parked. The major dozed off. Two hours later he was still parked in the same blank location. Two cars and a pickup truck had passed him where he sat. The three of them had slowed down, checking him out. Out-of-state cars parked on this little used county road were unusual. He was awakened by a knock on his window. A Utah State Patrol Officer was staring in at him. Cautiously, the major pushed the button that lowered the glass. The man who questioned him was wearing a uniform. Major Cooper was reassured by the uniform. He rolled up his window and followed the officer's patrol car.

***

CHAPTER 14

Paranoia

Captain Albert D. Cummings had received two emails from Major Cooper since he left Alaska. Deep in the heart of Texas, he felt reasonably safe. The news coverage of the Ice Murder, or Murder on the Rocks, as it was cleverly called by some in the media, didn't affect him at first. When a name and rank was attached to the iced-down body, Cummings was shocked. He knew the deceased well, had flown with him in formation for a number of years. Major Cooper had received an email from Blitzweimer following his wife's funeral. He was going to pay Cooper a visit, but never showed up.

When the names of the two other bodies came up, Captain Cummings became alarmed. Two were definitely dropped from a plane, the news said, and the third was found on a rocky mountainside above the Arctic Circle and presumably dropped as well. When the CIA leak connected the name Midnight Poison to all three bodies, it was too obvious to be ignored. Cummings started watching his back. All three dead men, Cummings, and the major had flown together in the second Gulf War. All had been involved in a sexual assault case in Baghdad. The five pilots were cleared of wrongdoing by the base commander and shipped out before there could be any personal reprisal.

That reprisal was now very much in the works. The fact that three of them had suffered the same fate resulting in bizarre deaths on the Arctic Circle seemed to be much more than a tragic coincidence. Captain Adriana O'Donovan, "the bitch from hell," under whatever name she used now, had to be the sick brain behind it. “We should have shot her where we left her,” he mumbled to himself. “I said as much at the time.”

Although only a woman Cummings thought, he knew from the experience of flying with her, O’Donovan was an extremely capable and determined aerial combatant. She had been decorated for blowing three enemy jet fighters out of the air in the space of fifteen minutes. He tried to push out of his mind the fact that his plane was damaged, and had Adriana not demolished the enemy fighters in such short order, he wouldn’t be here today. Captain Cummings was now definitely paranoid. *The major must be a bit worried*, he reasoned. Cooper’s orders had been to let her die of exposure in the desert. In the last email from Cooper, the major asked Cummings not to write back. “He knows,” Cummings muttered. “He knows.”

Cummings recalled the major finding the vile of perfume concealed in the floral arrangement surrounding his wife’s ashes. That was too close for Captain Cummings’s comfort. He was very pleased to have made it back to Texas. The major must have figured this out too. He and Cummings were the only two left of the five who had participated in the gang rape in Baghdad. *How in hell did that woman ever fight her way back from the desert? We should have put a bullet in her brain when we left her.*

Cummings wondered what the major thought about his precarious situation now. O’Donovan had to be somewhere in the Arctic where a million private planes filled the airways like mosquitoes. Having dropped off the vile of perfume at his wife’s funeral, Midnight Poison, aka Adriana O’Donovan, knew where Cooper was. The major would be easy pickings. However, with the media now blasting the Midnight Poison news from every TV set and shoddy magazine in supermarket waiting lines, O’Donovan would be laying low. That was definitely to the major’s and Captain Cummings’s advantage. “During this down time,” Cummings continued with his line of reasoning, “we must strike back!”

***

That night in a motel room in Dumas, Texas, Captain Cummings spent hours searching for Midnight Poison on the web. Except for ads for the legitimate perfume, everything had disappeared. Disregarding the major's request for email silence, Cummings tried to make contact. All attempts drew a blank. The major's site was an empty sheet—washed clean. Had the major retired? Or were his bones now embedded somewhere on the Arctic Coast? Location, unknown. Captain Cummings did not sleep well.

There were others keeping track of the major as well. The chip Almas Cooper carried in his shoulder was still broadcasting his location. Major Almas A. Cooper III would remain a marked man for the remainder of his life.

***

The silence of the moment roared in Major Cooper's deaf ears. *The witch was due for a promotion*, Cooper recalled bitterly. Her promotion had already been approved. She would have the rank of major, his equal. At least he and his comrades in arms had deprived her of that undo honor. They had gathered to celebrate her promotion. That was a laugh. They had celebrated, all right. They had toasted that promotion in more ways than one. She had paid dearly, but not dearly enough. *Bitch-witch*, the major thought as he followed the officer's patrol car to state police headquarters in Provo, Utah. *At least the man leading the way is an officer and a gentleman*, the major thought. *He wears his uniform proudly. I can use the office phone without fear.* The major needed to use a phone that was not compromised by Colonel Cornwell.

Major Cooper was definitely in a paranoid state. He knew Cornwell was not above chicanery unbefitting an officer of the US Air Force. O'Donovan was another one, but that bitch was out. She was no better than a civilian. She was a civilian. The fact that Cooper was now a civilian himself did not cross his mind. He was still wearing his uniform, proof of his position. He would pin the colonel's silver oak leaf clusters on his epaulets.

They would be there when he met with his son. Cooper followed the state patrol car into the police parking lot. The officer who had led him in got out and came back. He opened the door of Cooper's rental car. "Just follow me, Colonel. I'll get you a phone and an office space so you may have a bit of privacy."

Colonel? The major was a bit shocked before he realized he had already pinned the clusters to his uniform. *Colonel*, he thought proudly. *It's about time!* "Thank you, Officer. I appreciate it."

***

Slim prepared his press release before noon. It was carefully worded so as to not lay the blame for the leak directly on the CIA or the FBI. He pointed out that in all branches of law enforcement organizations, there was often a weak link. Or that there was sometimes a member of the organization who did not grasp the importance of the message, which may have been what happened this time. The reason for withholding the facts, such as they were, Slim noted, was a lack of definitive information concerning the victims. *If one cannot verify the information one has,* the detective pointed out in his dispatch, *it is best not to trust it and therefore not release it to the media. Until information concerning the deceased is verified and the next of kin notified, it is morally wrong to release it.* Following this statement, Slim listed standard clichés, dressed his report up, and emailed it to trooper headquarters, signing it officially:

Lieutenant Silas Leroy Dickerson, Chief of Detectives

***

Headquarters released Slim's report with no further comment. In the meantime, when a call came in for Slim, the dispatcher replied: "The Chief of Detectives is presently cruising the wilderness and is out of range. He cannot be reached by cell phone or radio." In reality Slim was with Kerns in the basement of Slim's ex-wife's home.

***

Colonel William Cornwell eagerly browsed through Major Cooper's personal email files. The colonel had downloaded the last one hundred transmissions to and from Cooper before the major's server discovered the illegitimate invasion and shut it down. Cornwell had all the information he needed and much he didn't need. He read it all eagerly. To his amazement he discovered Cooper's interest in Midnight Poison. There had been no direct email intercourse, but Midnight's site had been studied many times. He counted over thirty hits by Cooper. The tie-in with the media barrage on radio, TV, and in print was very intriguing: a secret side to Major Cooper. That information and the fact that the major was a silent suspect in an unproven sexual assault case in Baghdad five years previously added up.

Cornwell had no personal interest in the case involving Major Cooper, but the colonel was not one to remain in the dark for long. He feasted on this sort of supermarket gossip. He called in Corporal Winslow, his orderly, and ordered him to "discreetly" follow all of Cooper's moves.

In the meantime, Winslow had been trying to figure out how he could activate the tracer on Cooper without the colonel's knowledge. Now he had a free map. That was exactly what Cornwell wanted him to do. He could pass the information on to Slim without a hitch. It was late afternoon. "It will take a while to make the connection," Winslow explained to his commanding officer. "If I may take an early break for dinner, with your permission, Sir, I will come back and work on it through the night. There is better reception in the late hours as well, Colonel."

"Granted, Corporal. I will expect a report in the morning."

"It will be on your desk, Colonel." Winslow saluted and went to his quarters. He called Slim at Kerns' number and relayed the message. Kerns passed the phone over to Slim. "I should have the information by midnight, Slim," Winslow told him. "Should I call you at that hour?"

"At any hour, Johnny, and thanks. Another favor, if you can and will. I need to find the exact location of a Captain Albert Cummings. He is a pilot stationed in Texas and a close friend of Cooper's. Cummings was here in Alaska for Cooper's wife's funeral. He is wanted for questioning in a murder case and possibly connected to this one." Winslow and Slim also went over the information Johnny had left with Kerns that morning before they signed off. "Oh, and incidentally, Slim," Winslow, added, "your son called me on my cell. He said you had given him the number as you had given me his number in case of emergency. Roy is a smart young man. I gave him a few pointers to help with his Web search. He understands computers damn near as well as I do. Roy may have this information before I get it to you."

"Really?"

"Really, Slim. In any case, we are both on it. If this Cummings is a friend of Cooper's, I believe I can stretch the colonel's orders to cover Cummings. We should have the information you need by morning."

"Thanks, Johnny." Slim signed off. He turned to his friend. "Kerns, this guy is the Felix Pedro of this investigation. Johnny Winslow is the gold mine."

"Felix," Kerns pointed out, "the guy who discovered millions in gold here in Fairbanks was originally Felice, from Italy. He changed his name to Felix when he landed in New York City. What was he running from?"

"I don't know, Kerns, but many people on the run end up in Fairbanks."

"It caught up with Felix. I don't know when he was married, but his widow, Mary Doran, poisoned him here. Or so Gambiano, Pedro's partner at the time, surmised."

"Kerns, I can't bring up anything, but you give me a history lesson."

"Sorry about that."

"If I could remember any of it. Listening to you, I would be filled with useless information."

"Thank you, Slim. I think I'll take a trip to the Big I for a shot or two of Rye. By the way, what did you think about that last call you got on the answering service? The one including the Midnight Poison initials?"

"Could be something if he calls back." Slim shrugged. "Could be some kind of amateur detective too, or some kind of a nut. In any case, the dispatcher at the office is weeding out my calls. He'll put it through to me if it comes in again."

"And Doc?"

"His phone's been busy, or shut down. He's probably on the Internet."

"Okay, I'm off."

"Godspeed. Keep your phone charged up. The goldmine is going to call you back sometime around midnight. I believe he will have the address of Captain Albert Cummings. Kerns, call me with it please, no matter what time the call comes in."

"He wakes me and I wake you?"

"Right."

"I'm going to the Big I and then up on the ridge."

"Keep the home fires burning."

"I'll stoke them. I may screw up the courage to call Adriana. If I'm lucky, I'll drop by there on the way."

"Be careful. Remember Felix and his friend Mary—whatever her name was."

"Duran. Mary Duran. I'll keep the phone on, Slim." Kerns looked suddenly serious. "I'm going for the gold with Adriana, Slim. I think I love this lady with the wings." He headed up the stairs and out of the basement. Slim was left shaking his head.

Who am I to make negative assumptions? Look at the mess I made of my life. But at least I am in my wife's basement. Slim grinned and went back to work.

Slim thought of Kerns with trepidation. *There is something wrong here.* It was just one of Slim's hunches, the kind he worried about. He looked up Adriana O'Donovan again on his

Google browser. He had found nothing before. There was nothing there now. What was he worried about? But blank pages were what troubled him. Slim didn't like blank pages.

***

Kerns had been thinking about the acid and the patched carpet on the cabin floor of the Helio. If by any chance Adriana had dropped the bodies, a far-fetched assumption, and if all the bodies were a part of her flying squadron in Baghdad, and if the bodies were those who had sexually abused—no—raped her five years ago, was her revenge justified? At the Big I Kerns was shaking his head now. *This must be kept on a couch of silence*, he thought. Kerns would keep it there. He had a couple of Rye solos at Hap's bar. Hap asked no questions about his absence over the past two and a half days. Kerns offered no answers. He sat quietly building up the courage to call Adriana. Kerns had, while in Thelma's basement waiting on Slim, used his laptop to continue his search for the causes and effects of rape. He found that rape, or sexual assault, as they listed it ambiguously in the armed services, was a whole different "ball of wax," to coin a phrase. Kerns hated clichés, but they slipped out. In his writing, he could bleep them. In his thinking they were a wall of platitudes he couldn't climb over. So be it—another platitude.

Okay, Kerns reasoned, *Adriana was raped. That makes her no less of a woman, or person*, he thought. *Adriana has rectified the cause and effect.* Kerns had to rectify his thinking, had to put himself in her place. He found that impossible. *I am a man, for Christ's sake. I have never been raped; although men have been raped in prison and in the service, I have never been one of them. But Adriana,* he said in his mind, *I, although un-raped myself, understand your pain and frustration; at least I am trying to. In truth it is impossible to imagine, as impossible as it is for my mind to comprehend child molestation.*

Kerns recalled, with pain, the time his daughter, Salome, had been sexually attacked. She had been at a bar with friends and had to go back to her apartment to finish a report she was writing. It was a three-block walk and it was dark. She thought nothing of the darkness. She had walked that path in Alaska. To get to school she had walked many miles in winter darkness through the snow. Philadelphia was a city with streetlights, but the dark route through the alley was shorter. She saw no reason not to take it. A young man, a student also, knew of her habit. He left seconds before Salome and waited. She was attacked from behind and hurled to the ground.

Kerns was in Romania when he got her call. The following morning, he was in Philadelphia. He found Salome mentally bruised, but unbroken. There was no sign of a bruise on her body. The bruise was to her heart and her pride. A couple returning from the bar to their apartment fortunately had taken the same shortcut in the dark. Salome had cried out as she went down. The couple came running and crying out themselves. The rapist fled, leaving Kerns' daughter, her low-cut blouse ripped and her shorts about her knees.

She didn't go to the hospital. She had not been "penetrated"—a clinical term meaning she had not been *officially* raped. The couple saw her home. Struggling with her conscience, she called her father. She had recognized her assailant, she told him. On Kerns' advice, she reported the crime to the police. That afternoon, she and Kerns went to the station where they met with the prosecutor, Ms. Skinner, a pleasant looking lady of maybe thirty. Ms. Skinner's surprising advice was to drop the charges.

"Why?" Kerns cried out. "Isn't rape a crime? Worse than stealing her purse, but a crime just the same."

"It is a crime against the state, Mr. Kerns. Your daughter is only a witness," Skinner replied softly. "Tragically, it is not the same as stealing her purse. You and your daughter must prepare yourselves for that." The prosecutor took a deep breath. "Let me try to explain. The defense attorney will open his argument by pointing out that the clothes Salome was wearing were provocative. The tryst, most likely planned. The scanty blouse, torn by both of them in a fit of passion. Also, and most importantly," she said, "there was no proof of penetration. Your daughter, Mr.

Kerns, had bathed. She even douched to cleanse herself of the thought of penetration before reporting the crime."

"What of the two who witnessed the act?" Kerns cried out in frustration.

"It was in the dark, Mr. Kerns. What did they see? They interrupted an act of intercourse, the defense will say—sexual intercourse. Your daughter cried out in exotic joy, he will argue. The man, embarrassed, took to his heels. Your daughter, Mr. Kerns, the defense will say, was left arranging her scanty clothing."

"But my daughter is the victim!"

"The defense will never refer to Salome as a victim." She turned to the victim. "The defense will conclude his argument by saying you made up this story to protect your questionable reputation."

"Questionable?" Kerns stood and cried out in the sterile space where they were brought together. "My daughter's questionable reputation?" Salome, dressed modestly in jeans and a sweatshirt, was in quiet tears. Her father reached out and took her hand. "If he walks free after what he has done to my daughter, I will kill that son-of-a-bitch!"

"Mr. Kerns, it is best you retract that statement. Don't vocalize thoughts like that in front of anyone, especially me. This man has twice before been accused of rape, once with penetration proven. Neither case was settled or came to court. All charges were withdrawn. There are angry people out there—fathers, mothers, husbands—with the same wishes you have. If violent misfortune assails this man Salome has identified, you could be called up and charged on suspicion of possible criminal action."

"Just leave it there, Ms. Prosecutor. In truth the thought is there with my words and wishes." He turned to his daughter. "What are your wishes, Salome?"

"My wishes have nothing to do with it, Papa." She turned to the state's prosecuting attorney. "We will drop the charges, Ms. Skinner. We thank you for your very blunt, if truthful, scenario. It would make a great, if tragic, screenplay. Come on, Papa." And they left.

Once on the street, she turned to her father. "You didn't travel this far for nothing, Papa. You have given me strength, the strength I needed. I am a survivor, Papa. I don't care what people think. Fuck them! I am not changing schools, as some friends have suggested. I am going to stay here and finish my degree! But for your information, Papa, and my peace of mind, I am carrying an ice pick with me. If this happens again, there *will* be penetration."

***

The word, "rape"—"rapere" in Caesar's language, the language of the Emperor of Rome—means: to seize, steal, carry away. A man took the woman he wanted, raped her to prove his manhood, and carried her away to his cave, castle, or wherever. That was that. Carnal knowledge as in the use of force, or threat of the same, is the legal term or definition prescribed by the FBI. All definitions of rape describe a violent act destroying female pride and dignity. A male jury in a power-crazed, male-dominated court sanctions the laws. A court of fools in Shakespeare's time, Queen Elizabeth's time, was carefully worded by the bard. Under Lizzie's rein, Shakespeare danced before her, careful to hone his words to her satisfaction. In 400 BC Aristophanes, through his proxy, Lysistrata, a warrior for peace, used sexual satisfaction as her sword. The women of Greece went on strike, turning the tables on war's madness. Sexually deprived, the prancing male laid his sword aside for his penis. Unfortunately, that fragile organ didn't hold its edge for long. The warm, moist sheath of love was soon abandoned for the sword again.

Browsing the Internet for information on cases of sexual abuse in the military, Kerns found it to be entangled in red tape more so than the civilian counterpart. He knew that, through personal experience, the crime of rape was and is near impossible to bring to justice. *In the military, the commander, with a built-in conflict of interest, is given the power to decide which sexual assault cases to try. There is a bill right now in the US House and Senate, written and sponsored by women in both houses, that might change all that. As of today, the president has not signed it. We shall see.* "Another goddamned platitude," Kerns mumbled over his Rye.

In searching the Web, Kerns uncovered, among other things, a *New York Times* editorial, which said in part:

> *Broken Military Justice*
> *By THE EDITORIAL BOARD*
> *The abusive grilling last month of a female midshipman in a case involving three former United States Naval Academy football players provided further evidence that the military's handling of sexual assault complaints is seriously flawed.*
> *The woman, who has accused the three athletes of raping her at an alcohol-fueled "yoga and toga" party, was interrogated for about 30 hours over several days. Defense lawyers asked her questions that were irrelevant to the alleged crime and unlikely to be allowed in civilian courts, like whether she wore a bra.*
> *Her ordeal occurred during a preliminary hearing, known as an Article 32 proceeding, that helps determine whether cases are sent to courts-martial. According to military law experts, the harsh and degrading cross-examination was not unique.*

Kerns also discovered that an estimated seventy-one cases of sexual assaults per day took place in the military. But for fear of reprisal, almost none of them were reported. Of the estimated 26,000 cases of rape, sexual assaults, and unwanted sexual contact in the military last year, just 302 were prosecuted. If this bill was passed, that might change.

***

Adriana had given Kerns a sample of the biased military justice system, a commander's conflict of interest, and of the reprisals meted out to those who continued to press for justice.

Kerns didn't need to know more, but the figures kept assaulting his peace of mind.

Pushing his unwelcomed thoughts aside, Kerns stepped up to the bar where Hap poured him another drink. He decided to just "drop by" Adriana's hangar. If she wasn't there, he would try to reach her by phone at her Chena Hot Springs cabin. Despite the Alaskan darkness, it wasn't late. Kerns hoped she'd be receptive.

***

Slim was still struggling with blank pages when his phone rang. He checked the screen on his iPhone—blank, too. Then he remembered his phone was shut off. It was Thelma's landline. Slim waited for the answering service to come on. It was the dispatcher.

"Sorry to bother you, boss, but I think this is the long-distance call you were concerned about."

Slim thought a few moments before he answered the dispatcher. "Can you forward the call to this number?"

"It would be easier, Slim, to forward it to your cell phone. We have that set up already."

"Let me switch the cell on. Or just get the number and let me call him back."

"He won't give me a number. He's calling from a pay phone. I didn't think they had any of those things around anymore."

"Okay, hang on." Slim found the switch on his cell and flipped it on. After a few seconds, the screen lit up. "Hello. This is Slim. What can I do for you?"

"Is this Lieutenant Silas Leroy Dickerson?" a voice came back at him.

"Yeah. Do you want my mother's maiden name to verify it?" Slim answered tersely.

"No, no. I understand you are under pressure right now and I am sorry to bother you, but I do have information I believe you might be interested in, information about Midnight Poison. It is information I have sworn never to pass on to anyone, personal information, Detective. I need to trust you with it."

"Okay, you got it. Go on."

"This afternoon I got a call from the FBI to turn certain records over to them, including the personal information I have on Midnight Poison. I refused. Right now they are getting a court order demanding that I do so. I have sent my entire staff home until further notice. I have locked all doors to my offices. I need your advice."

"Who are you, and what kind of business are you in?"

"I have done nothing illegal, Detective. I was, and still am, a qualified professor of English and French literature. I am no longer working in those positions. I resigned my post with the University of Quebec, Canada, over a year ago."

"What are you looking for? A position at the University of Alaska?"

"I wish I was working there now."

"What's your name, and just what do you do that is not illegal?"

"My name is Saul. I have developed and own a number of sex sites originating in Cincinnati, Ohio."

"Saul what?"

"Billings. There, you have it. But then, the FBI has it, too."

"And the CIA and the E-I-E-I-O," Slim mumbled.

"What the hell is the E-I-E-I-O?"

"You are the English major. I don't know what the initials sound like in French. I think they have something to do with a pig farm in Ohio."

"Sounds like a branch of the CIA."

Slim broke down in laughter. "All right, Saul, whatever your last name is, you have passed inspection. Now, let us get serious. Once again, I ask you, what can I do for you, and more importantly, what can you do for this investigation?"

"I want to give this information to you before the FBI gets here. After I send it to you, I will absolutely eradicate it from my files, as I have already done back in the office. I have a copy on my laptop here with me in the bar I am calling from. With your permission, Detective Dickerson, I will send the files to you: Midnight Poison's name, credit card numbers, the works.

Do with it, as you will. I have a good feeling about you. I know you will do what is right."

"I appreciate this Saul, whatever your last name is—"

"Billings," Saul repeated.

"Billings, right. I don't know what your good feelings about me are or where they originated, but don't expect great things. Nothing may ever come of it."

"Great things are in the air, Detective Dickerson. What address shall I send this to?" Slim, without thinking, gave Saul his wife's email address.

"It's on the way, Detective. Following that, I am going to throw this laptop in the Ohio River. Have a good night." Billings signed off. Slim started mumbling to himself.

"Did I give him my wife's address?" Slim realized he had. "And what 'great things'?" He recalled bringing up Midnight Poison's profile on his ex-wife's email, too, the same one his son had brought up with Kerns on Chena Ridge. Had he saved it? He was afraid he had. "That will be the 'great thing.' It will be the end of our second marriage and I haven't even proposed yet."

***

All of the recent media attention hadn't helped Adriana either. The two times earlier that she lured one of her assailants into the web spun to bring them to justice, things moved smoothly. She dropped them into the icy lap of vengeance without a hitch. In the days that followed each drop, she felt relaxed. Her sleep was deep and dreamless. It was on an impulse she had dropped Blitzweimer where he would be found. *I wanted to put the fear of God into the hearts and brains of the other two, Cooper and Cummings*, she thought. All she knew was, her dark side had guided the plane to the target area. Once there, it pushed the eject button. That done, Adriana snapped back to herself. Spiritually relieved, as always following a successful drop, she set a course for home. In this case home was her Chena Hot Springs cabin.

***

Months earlier Alice came up with the crazy idea of the bombs-away displacement: "They did worse than drop you, Adriana. You drop them." Alice laughed at her own dark humor. A bit buzzed on wine, she had not been serious about dropping the victims off in space. She laughed at the thought. It was meant to be a joke. Adriana, however, caught a depth of justice in her laughter. They had been at the Hot Springs cabin sipping on a second good bottle of chilled Chardonnay. Adriana poured herself another glass and stepped out into the cool midnight sun. Her head spun with the thought her mechanic's dark humor had proffered. The drop made sense to Adriana. Her eyes filled with tears of righteous anger as she stepped into the deep shadows of the surrounding forest. Alice's joke was the perfect answer to her darker wishes. Adriana would give her victims time to think as they sat, naked, strapped, and helpless, in the open doorway of her Helio. She would rise above the silent clouds as they cried for mercy, as they had made her cry years before, strapped securely to that stainless cold steel table where there was no way out. They had given her little time to think and no freedom to move in her struggle to escape. And only animal horror served up at the conclusion.

Now, the tables turned. At five thousand feet the victim was in control. She would lock her plane in autopilot and step behind them. It would take no words from her to explain the truth. "On the way down, think about it. You have five thousand feet to fill your mind with love." It was all she would have to say. They would understand. They were now in the helpless position she had been put in five years in the past. Hands secured, legs hanging numb in the whipping cold, she would lift the plank they sat upon and whisper in their ear, "You chose to fly. May this flight take you into your midnight dream." With that, she would let them slide into the night. If they cried for mercy, she would act as they had acted five years in the past. "May every abused woman hear this cry," she called out after them, as they went screaming down and darkness lifted into light. "Be there no justice, the abused must make it on our own." Walking out of the darkened forest to her cabin, Adriana wondered at her harsh thinking: *Premeditated murder? But what else to do?* What they had done to her was worse than murder and, according to the military justice system, quite legal—if not legal, quite forgivable. *We, the abused, are made the guilty ones and made to suffer twice*. She felt a darkness closing in to force the issue.

Adriana argued her point successfully with Alice. Reluctantly her mechanic went along. Adriana had always been the stronger of the two. Alice was a follower. Adriana held the rank and she needed her mechanic to tie it all together. And together, on the Internet, they set up their deception. The lure was cast. With time and much patience, they got their first bite—and then their second. Adriana knew about the implant in her shoulder. She'd had it removed before moving to Alaska. Alice devised a strong electromagnetic scrambler positioned in the backseat of the car she drove the victims from the airport in. Once out of Fairbanks, Big Brother's heart was scrambled beyond repair.

***

Before takeoff with the final drop, Adriana had decided, with Alice's encouragement, and perhaps, her silent thoughts of Kerns and a fantasized life of peace, that she would do this no more. Jason Blitzweimer was to be and had been as of now the final drop. The two remaining rapists would live out their lives in a world of paranoia, wondering when their turn would come. Justice would be served. They would know the three who vanished before them had suffered the same naked fate awaiting them. The table was set. Adriana's dark side had dropped this one dead in the media's light. The result was to terrorize the two remaining. Cooper and Cummings would live the remainder of their lives in a terrifying irrational world of fear: a world of *paranoia*!

***

CHAPTER 15

Elusion and the Law

Adriana was not aware the two preceding drops had been discovered until the CIA leak became public and the blitz of rumor and half-truths flooded the nation's airways. It was like a drink of shattered glass slicing up the intestines of the mind. Blood-wet articles filled the supermarket magazines, drowning the sexual antics of unfaithful movie stars. Standing in crowded aisles, their baskets filled with beer, chips, and soda, the readers loved it. At home they soaked up the video blood with vengeance.

Alice, who had dreamed up the Midnight Poison website as a joke, now tried to convince her friend that the government, the FBI, the CIA, could and would track down all of Adriana's pertinent information. "He told me his site was secure," Adriana protested.

"Who is 'he'?" Alice cried in frustration. "We have no idea. Secure? This guy is some sick head taking advantage of thousands of other sick heads. Secure? Is Facebook secure? There are hackers all over the globe with a key to Facebook. These people thrive on useless information—not that your information is useless."

At the present time, Adriana knew her stolen identity would be worth a fortune on the open market. There would be many bidders. For what it was worth, Adriana had moved instantaneously to shut the site down. She found that the owner of the Sex, Fire & Ice site had already closed the door on Midnight Poison. Adriana's bipolar personage flipped out in a flood of dark anger. Her dual-personality disorder turned on and off as she struggled with her New England scruples and the overpowering dark hole of revenge. Alice watched over her friend closely in the days to come. "The manipulator of Sex, Fire & Ice and Cum With Me has obviously made the connection between Midnight Poison and Blitzweimer. What he does or has done with that information will determine our fate, Adriana." Alice was worried.

"In which case, Alice," Adriana replied, determined, "we leave it to fate. No harm is to befall anyone other than the guilty five." Adriana was adamant. "Your name is nowhere in the records, Alice. It was my credit card number that paid for it. I will answer for it one way or another. If it comes up, you are out of it, well out. If snared by an archaic law that still forgives rape, I can plead insanity."

"I dreamed up the site, Adriana—you manage it, but I am responsible."

"It was a dream as dark as the act that brought it on, Alice. Dreams are blameless. I took the fantasy into reality and therein lies the truth. I, in my darkness, to speak theatrically, did the dirty deeds, Alice. I devised the revenge I sought, which you thought a bit extreme. I didn't listen to you. I made the drops. I alone will take the blame, Alice."

"The man who owns the site has a perfect setup for blackmail. He has the records, and he's a man, Adriana!"

"He doesn't have all the records, Alice. And, Alice, I have learned not all men are untrustworthy. This man, whatever his name or intentions be, he doesn't have the emails sent from Blitzweimer to my address at bananabelt.com. I have deleted all messages sent to that address from Jason B. and his two predecessors. They all went into the trash. I then deleted the trash folder. There are no ghosts to haunt me, Alice. And I will not see you suffer for it."

"But—"

"No, Alice. This conversation stops here. It is what it is, and damn my dual personality. Damn the bipolar bitch. I have the strength to push her into a corner. I am my own master!"

***

Tech Sergeant Alice Baily, at Adriana's request, had been the crew chief servicing Adriana's planes in the second Gulf War. Major Cooper, Adriana O'Donovan's squadron commander at the time, had okayed the request. The two women became friends in the service. They thought alike on many issues. There was no rank between them. Alice's tour of duty was up shortly after Captain O'Donovan was unceremoniously mustered out. Alice was fully aware of the circumstances of her friend's situation. She followed Adriana to Alaska. Adriana depended on Alice now as she had then. Alice agreed to continue to be her ground crew. She had followed her captain's advice in the service and she would here in Alaska. Alice Baily hated the men who raped her friend and role model. Alice loved and believed in Adriana. She had dreamed up the mad revenge, never believing Adriana would carry it through to a reality.

In the confines of their small plywood office in the corner of the hangar that housed A-Plus Flying Service, Adriana walked over to the bookcase and picked up the bottle of Rye Kerns had left in her plane after coming back from Chena Hot Springs. She opened it and let the memories float out. "Alice," she said, inhaling the aroma, "to change the subject, I think I love this man."

"I'm afraid you do too, Adriana," Alice said, heaving a negative sigh.

"I wish he would call."

"Why don't you call him?"

"It's the man's place to call."

"Jesus Christ, Adriana, you are as stubborn as he is. Kerns is probably sitting down there with his cronies in that bar waiting for you to call. If men and women were truly equal, there would be no such stupid rules. You make me fucking angry, Adriana! I am going to go for a drive to clear my head of such nonsense." Alice pulled on her heavy parka. "I've got my own rats to kill, Adriana. You stay here waiting for the phone of fate to ring while you smell the memories." She repeated the line her mother used redundantly on the dry plains of Oklahoma. "I've got my own rats to kill." Slamming the door behind her, Alice left the office.

Adriana waved the open bottle of rye under her nose and let the memories subdue her. She lay back on the couch, tipped the bottle up, and drank. As the Rye in the bottle went down so did she. Adriana slipped into darkness.

***

Except for the short reprieve after each successful drop orchestrated by her bipolar person, Adriana hadn't slept well in the past five years. The fear of a dreaming replay of the worst night of her life kept her up until she would crash exhausted. She had slept well while Kerns was in her cabin at the Hot Springs. That rather amazed her. Hoping for him to call, she hadn't really slept at all since. She succumbed to the half a bottle of rye Kerns left in her plane and was now asleep and thrashing about in the cruel arms of that recurring dream. A dream set on a stainless-steel table in the officer's recreation room in the dry, hot winds of Baghdad.

Kerns was in for a rough reception.

***

He was a little buzzed when he left the Big I heading for Adriana's hangar. He was apprehensive but also buzz happy and hoping she would feel the same. He planned to take her to Slim's cabin on the ridge. He hadn't called ahead. As he pulled up at her A-Plus Flying Service and opened the door of his 4x4, Kerns heard Adriana screaming in the dark of the cavernous hangar. The sounds reverberated off the arched walls. Kerns beat on the small personnel door at the far end of the building, to no avail. He thought of calling 911, but Christ, they would be an hour getting there. There wasn't that much time. He hurled that thought aside and tried the wide roll-up entrance door of the hangar that would receive the Helio and larger planes. No luck. Locked and too heavy. It would only open if one had the box with the keyed numbers on it and the correct combination.

The screams inside were muffled now, as if someone was stifling them with a pillow or clothing. They died out as he raced back to his 4x4 and inserted a two-inch adjustable height trailer hitch with a 2 and $^{5}/_{16}$- inch ball connection into the female receiver beneath the tailgate of his truck. He adjusted it to the highest setting and the longest reach. He leaped behind the wheel and raced the truck to the rear personnel door. He spun the Ford around and, calculating roughly the area beneath the lock to the three-foot metal door, he mashed down on the gas. The large tow ball and heavy stainless-steel adjustable riser hit the door with the angry weight of Kerns' Ford 4x4 behind it. The lock snapped. The door swung open. Kerns pulled quickly forward. He set the brake and was through the ragged opening he had made in seconds.

Inside, except for a flickering night-light, it was dark as tar in a roofing barrel. He thought he remembered where Adriana's office was. He stumbled blindly through the dark in that direction.

"Adriana!" he cried out. "Adriana, are you all right?" He had a flashlight in the truck glove compartment. But he hadn't grabbed it. There was no time now. He tried to move quietly, but every step he made echoed through the bell-like building. He tried to cry out quietly. That was stupid. *Who can cry out quietly?* he thought. He yelled: "Adriana!" The words ricocheted like bullets back and forth across the huge dark room. "Captain Adriana O'Donovan," he cried, thinking foolishly her military title might dissuade her attacker. The cry was followed by echoing silence. Stumbling in the dark, he was about to call again when something steel and very well directed struck him horizontally between his ears at the back of his head.

Kerns dropped to the smooth concrete floor of the hangar. A warm, red, and wet stream flowed freely into his long thatch of salt-and-pepper hair. Kerns didn't feel it. Kerns didn't feel anything. When the high floodlights snapped on, Kerns remained in the dark.

Alice stood at the bank of switches beside the personnel door Kerns had opened with his truck. She called out, "What is it, Adriana? What happened?" Alice moved in at a run. "What have you done?"

"We got another one, Alice. Tie him up. We'll load him into the Helio and I'll take off and dump him." She headed back toward her office to get her winter flying gear. "When I'm in the air, clean up the mess. This one has trashed the place. There is a quart of hydrogen peroxide in the loo. That will dissolve the blood. There will be no sign of it within an hour."

Alice was kneeling at the body on the floor. "Adriana," she said quietly. "This is Kerns. You may have killed him. This is a lot of blood. If he isn't dead, he has suffered a major concussion. I'll call 911 for an ambulance."

"It's one of them, Alice." There was angry determination in Adriana's unusually harsh voice. Alice recognized it. She had heard that voice before, the voice of darkness.

"It's Kerns, Adriana," Alice said, almost to herself.

"It's one of those who raped me, Alice. He came to get me here. He's one of them. Now there is only one to go. Tie him up. It won't be long now. We'll have them all."

"It's Kerns, Adriana." Alice felt for his pulse. "I think he's still alive."

"No, Alice!" Adriana turned and stormed back to the scene, still brandishing the length of two-inch cheater pipe they used to tie down planes when parked out in the wind. "It's one of them. You have the list. Two of them were left. This piece of shit messing up the floor is one of the two. Now tie him up!" she ordered and headed once again for the office. Alice reached into her heavy parka for her cell phone. Nothing about Kerns had moved, except the blood pulsing through his hair onto the cold and concrete floor. Outside, his 4x4 still rumbled in the dark.

"Tie him up, Alice, goddamn it!" The cold words echoed in the seashell space like waves now on a distant shore. "I'll be back in a minute to help you load the body." She slammed the office door behind her.

Alice put her phone away.

***

Adriana, as Adriana #1, that is, as Kerns knew her, was aware of her dual personality, but once the darkness closed in, she lost touch with #1. Adriana, who had briefly studied psychoanalysis her first years at the university, felt she had her deep-seated problem under control through self-analysis. As an orphan child and a ward of the state of New Hampshire, she was moved from foster home to foster home. Adriana was sexually molested by a foster father from ages eleven through thirteen. In the eighth grade she was relocated with a married, childless couple in the tiny town of Dunbarton. She was moved to their farm several miles out of town. Her new foster parents were good people. Her foster mother taught high school English and French in an adjoining town. Her new foster father worked the farm. A stern, hardworking New Englander, he was honest and upright. Had he been asked about sexual abuse of children, he would have insisted there was no such thing. He couldn't even imagine it. Her new foster mother was not quite that naive. However, in the O'Donovan home, the subject was never discussed over the dinner table.

With the encouragement of her new parents, the young girl excelled in high school. In their home, Adriana blocked the horror of her first sexual experiences from her mind. It became a blank slot, a white out. It did not surface again until her tragic episode in the air force years later when both episodes struck down on her like the blow of a velvet hammer. Adriana knew it as her dark side: bipolar depression and guilt to be caged and kept there lurking in silence. She felt—mistakenly, she would learn later—that she could overcome or control this illness, this infection of the mind, and she was determined to do so on her own.

Long before the dark side groped her mind, heart, and body, Adriana graduated with honors from the University of New Hampshire, where she minored in psychology. Her major, inspired by her foster mother figure, was English literature. While at the university she started taking flying lessons, and with the support of her adopted parents she received her private pilot's license. Her foster father, although questioning her "insane desire to grow wings," was proud of Adriana. He loved her as a daughter. Adriana was their "pride and joy" in the true sense of parenthood. Adriana's love for them was strong and far-reaching. She insisted on adopting their name, as they had adopted her.

The elderly O'Donovan couple drove to Colorado for Adriana's graduation from the Air Force Academy. When Mr. O'Donovan saw his daughter's jet fly overhead, he cried with fear for her life and for joy that she had achieved her dream.

Mr. O'Donovan was very fond of saying, with great pride: "Although my daughter breaks the sound barrier in her jet, I will not be caught dead in an airplane." He was, however, caught dead in the car he and his wife were driving back in from Colorado Springs. His wife's head resting on his shoulder, the old man fell asleep at the wheel.

In their Will, the couple left everything they owned to their "loved and loving daughter, Adriana." The sale of the farm would later finance Adriana's A-Plus Flying Service in Alaska.

The shadow of her early rape at eleven raised in the dark, as she physically recovered from the horrors of the gang rape by fellow officers. She tried to deny it, to push it back into the past, out of mind, but in her time of anger and guilt as her assailants held her down on the cold metal table, that early shadow crept in with them. Adriana called upon her long ago studies in psychology to give her the knowledge and strength to repeal it. Now in Alaska she felt she was beginning to overcome the dragon, or at least banish the ghost. Then it flashed in the pan of her mind. Dragon was the name she had given the foster parent who soiled her body and spirit, who first filled her heart with guilt. Now she faced a desert filled with dragons spitting fire and brimstone.

Nothing would be done about the crimes they had committed. Justice Adriana sought was shut off by the very judges she called out to for help. To compensate, Adriana let her bleeding soul of guilt be led into another person—a personality she didn't know, a dark shadow she now depended upon to rid her of her viral dreams, to bring revenge into her heart and spirit:

to make her whole again. This second person, free of guilt, set her mind upon revenge in place of justice. In this second person, blind strength replaced the truth. The blood that ran was no longer hers. Yet in this second person there was emptiness when finished with the task at hand. Adriana had no control over her dual-personality disorder. After that vicious persona played out her role of vengeance, there was no guilt remaining in the emptiness at hand. The deed was done. The plane was empty, and for Adriana, rightly so.

Alice, although a silent partner in crime, lived with it, longing for the day it would be over --- the day the final drop was made and Adriana was released from the horrors of her past.

***

Entering her makeshift plywood office and living quarters, Adriana heard the door slam behind her. The door, banging in violent anger, opened her mind. She saw the empty bottle of rye lying on the couch. She heard the latch click in slow motion. In a haze she moved across the office floor and sunk upon the couch she had been sleeping on. Where was she going? Where the hell had she been? She looked down at the bloody iron pipe clutched in her hand. What the hell had she done? Her head was spinning—or was her body spinning here beneath it?

Bipolar—dual-personality disorder. The lines came back to her from the past, her classes in psychology. *Robert Louis Stevenson's* Strange Case of Dr. Jekyll and Mr. Hyde. *Welcome to the club, Adriana.* She dropped the cheater pipe with hair and blood matted to it. "What in Christ's name have you done now, Adriana?" She spoke her thoughts aloud as she stood. The empty bottle rolled out and broke on the floor. Unsteadily, she managed to cross back to the office door. She pushed it open. "Alice," she cried. "What's going on?"

"Thank God it's you again, Adriana." Alice got quickly to her feet. "We need to get an ambulance for Kerns. He has a pulse. It's weak."

"What happened to him?"

"I think he came to help you. It was the wrong time."

"Where is he?"

"He's that pile of flesh and blood over there on the concrete floor." Alice pulled out her phone again and this time dialed 911. "You sure you are okay now to go to him, Adriana?"

"I love him, Alice."

"Yeah, right. He looks like you love him." She looked down at the phone. It was still ringing 911. "Get the first-aid kit out of the Helio and get it over to him. I'll be right there." Then, yelling into the phone: "Are you alive in there, 911?"

"You've reached 911. What can we do for you? Do you need help?"

"We need a miracle, lady. Get an ambulance out here with medics. Get a full-fledged doctor. Fairbanks International Airport. Take the cargo entrance. Head north. I'll have some red lights flashing. Hurry! This is critical."

"Stay on the phone. I'll keep talking."

"Talk to someone else, someone with an ambulance" Alice cried. "I got other things to do besides pass the time. Get your ass in gear, lady."

"It's in gear, lady! They are already on the way. We have a unit stationed at the airport. They'll be there in minutes."

"Hangar seventeen. A-Plus Flying Service. Have them drive right in the hangar. I'll have the door open and the red light on above it—got it?

"Got it—red light above it."

***

When Adriana got to Kerns, the bleeding from the back of his skull was reduced to seepage. She had the first-aid kit from the Helio with her. After checking his pulse (she was amazed to find it pumping, if faintly), she wet a large swab with hydrogen peroxide and gently washed the area around the ugly wound. Adriana was badly shaken. Her hands trembled. *Could I have done this to you, Kerns? Christ, I am mad.* She heard the sounds of the hangar door rising. A layer of ice fog swept in, hugging the concrete floor, wrapping herself and Kerns in its icy vapors. In the near distance she heard the shrill cry of the paramedics' vehicle. Within a minute, two men gently lifted Kerns' body onto a wheeled stretcher. Adriana stood aside as they loaded Kerns into the ambulance. Then she got in with him.

"Are you going to be all right, Adriana?" It was Alice looking in, deeply concerned, as the medics started to close the rear door.

Adriana called back to her. "Alice, phone Hap," she cried. "At the Big I. Hap will know who to contact. A man named Slim." The emergency vehicle, sirens screeching, pulled out into the night. Alice pushed a button and the hangar door rolled down. She crossed to the personnel door and pulled it shut as best she could, then placed the call to Hap. She talked to him while taping the open twisted space around the door with gray duct tape.

"He'll be in intensive care at Saint Joe's," she said. "Adriana is with him. I am sure it is critical." Alice was breaking down. Hap could hear the tears. He asked no questions. "I'll meet you there," Alice sobbed. "It's not her fault. I love her. She didn't mean it." Alice pulled herself somewhat back together. "Slim," she cried, "Adriana said to call someone named Slim."

"I'll get in touch with him. You're Alice, right? Are you okay?"

"Right." Alice wiped the streaming tears on her sleeve. Blood from Kerns' wound smeared across her face. "I love her. I've got to be with her." Alice was sobbing again. "I'll lock up now and I'll be there." Alice shut down her phone.

What to do now? She hoped Adriana would not have a relapse. Alice hadn't studied psychology, but she had discussed Adriana's problems with her friend. She was aware of Adriana's unbalanced mental state. She also was aware Adriana had little control over it. Most often it would surface as she came out of her dream, as it had done tonight. Alice put the scenario together in her mind. Kerns had heard her screams, as Alice had the times the dream crawled into Adriana's brain, like a serpent out of hibernation. That was why Kerns had crashed through the door,

Alice figured—to save Adriana from her fate—but he'd walked into it instead. Alice dropped to the floor where the blood was coagulating. She had a bucket of warm water, hydrogen peroxide, and a box of painter's rags. Two large space heaters pulsed overhead. *The cops will be pissed off if I clean this up*, she thought. *But what should I do? Adriana's not to blame. Men—goddamn men. Why do they feel they have to prove themselves superior?*

She searched and found the length of black pipe Adriana used to even up the score. Alice washed it clean. *There are good men among the chaff*, she guessed. She liked Kerns, and she liked his friend, Curtis, who Adriana flew up into the wilderness to study birds. "Birds of darkness," Adriana called them. She said that was Kerns' term for them. Kerns was writing an article about those birds, Adriana said. *Adriana is one of those birds*, Alice thought. "Adriana is a bird of darkness."

With everything cleaned up, Alice flushed the bloody contents of the bucket down the toilet. She rinsed out the rags and hung them to dry. Looking in the mirror over the sink, she washed her face clean of tears and blood. Adriana had talked a lot about Kerns lately. "Adriana loves Kerns," she said softly. "Kerns will be better for her than me. I hope he lives, and I know he will. Think positive!" Alice had her thinking back together. She was the mechanic. Mechanics fix things. They pull things back together. Thinking of Kerns, she remembered that his truck was still running. She drove it into the hangar and shut it off. All was tidy and in place.

The mechanic headed for Saint Joseph's Hospital, where her work was needed.

***

CHAPTER 16

Coming Out

Slim stood by his wife's computer hoping for the expected Midnight Poison document to come through. He planned to forward it to his laptop and then delete it from Thelma's mail. That would be a hell of a lot easier than trying to explain it to her. Something was coming in. Slim's phone rang. It was Hap. Slim answered. Seconds later, leaving everything behind, Slim headed for the hospital. Early that evening, while still at the hospital, he got the call from Thelma. Her voice was anything but warm. She got right to the point. Thelma always did.

"Slim," she snapped. "You might as well pack up the things you have here. Wait until I leave tomorrow morning to come by and pick them up. After reading only a part of the filthy email addressed to you, but on my Yahoo account, I deleted it. I don't know what you have been up to the past three years, but I will tell you upfront: I would rather you were a drunk. How could you? How could you be taken in by this cheap skin trade porno shit? If your son ever found out about this—"

"Thelma, Thelma—wait a moment. You didn't delete it—did you?"

"I goddamned well did. I not only sent it to the trash, I deleted everything in the trash folder. No one can get it back now! I don't know anyone in their right mind who would want it."

"Thelma—"

"Don't 'Thelma' me. I don't want that filth in the same house as my son. If he ever saw something like that—"

"You deleted it?"

"If I could have flushed it down the toilet, I would have. It belongs in the sewer."

"The information I needed to close this case was in that email, Thelma. Midnight Poison—all her information: Who! What! Where and when! That was it. That document could have possibly closed this case that every lawman in the country is working on."

"What?"

"The Midnight Poison case. All the bodies dumped out of space. The connection and proof of it was on that email you flushed, Thelma. And that was the only copy in the country! Thelma, you know me better than that. I don't need that verbal trash." Slim had moved out of the hospital cafeteria, from where he had been sitting with Alice, Hap, and Adriana, into the relatively empty hallway. "Oh, Thelma."

"Slim? Slim, what have I done?"

Dr. Singer came running up the hallway from the emergency entrance. "Is your friend Kerns all right, Slim? I just heard. Oh, sorry, you're on the phone."

Slim gestured toward the cafeteria doorway. Doc looked in and saw Hap. "Sorry, Slim," he repeated and ran through the glass doors to Hap's table. "Thelma," Slim said softly into the phone, "what you have done has been done. There is no bringing it back. I am at the hospital. Kerns is in critical condition. That is where I am now. I will be here for a while before I come home, if I still have a home with you. I love you, Thelma."

"Slim, I'm so sorry." Slim knew she was in tears. "It's my Italian blood. I jump to conclusions without thinking things through. I'm sorry, Slim."

"So am I, Thelma. But you are more important to me. Just hang in there with your Italian blood. Keep it hot. I'll be home soon."

***

Kerns was in a coma for three days with the exception of one half hour of disturbed consciousness. Adriana never left his side. When he came around, his first words were to Adriana. "Are you all right?" he asked, thinking no time had passed. He remembered her screams and breaking the door open to her hangar. Now, looking around, he tried to figure out where he was. Adriana didn't dare throw her arms around him for fear of complicating his delicate condition. Surgeons had taken pieces of Kerns' broken skull out to relieve the pressure of blood building up between the skull and his brain. They had also cut a fresh piece of the skull out behind his left ear. At the present time a helmet was protecting the exposed brain tissue from any sudden movement and/or infection. She pressed the call button. The surgeon was there in minutes.

"What's going on?" Kerns said.

"There was an accident," Adriana said quietly. "You're in the hospital. You are going to be fine."

"We hope," said the doctor.

"We know," said Adriana.

The surgeon lifted Kerns' arm from beneath the light cover. "Can you move one of your fingers on this hand?" he asked, laying the arm back down in the open.

"I can move this one," Kerns said and gave him the finger. "No offence, Doc. I think I am going back to sleep now. Stay with me, Adriana." Kerns closed his eyes. His finger was still up.

The surgeon grinned. "He's going to be fine. I'm moving the time of the final surgery up to seven this evening. We'll put the pieces of the puzzle back together then. I think we can pull the tubes tomorrow. Your man is amazing, lady. Stick with him. The nurse will be in in a minute to check his vitals."

***

Slim had many questions for Adriana—and for Alice. Adriana didn't remember anything, so she was honest (to a point). In her emptiness she was evasive in her answers. Alice had walked in after the event had taken place, so she had seen nothing. Slim gave them the benefit of the doubt. The last words he had uttered to Kerns kept running through his head with troubling results. As a policeman, a detective, and an investigator, Slim depended largely upon his intuition. He never voiced that belief. People would think he was crazy. In secrecy Slim leaned heavily upon his sixth sense—he depended on it. He remembered his last conversation with Kerns as Kerns headed up the stairs from the basement of Slim's ex-wife's home in Fairbanks:

"I may screw up the courage to call Adriana," Kerns had said. "If I'm lucky, I'll drop by there on the way."

"Be careful. Remember Felix and his friend Mary—whatever her name was."

"Duran. Mary Duran. I'm going for the gold, Slim. I think I love this lady with the wings."

The lady with the wings seems to care a lot for him, Slim thought, *but there is something out of line here—another blank page*.

"Someone must have been hiding in the hangar," Alice had lied. "I think someone has been stalking Adriana," she told Slim. "Don't tell Adriana that," she said, suddenly on her guard. "Adriana has enough to worry about."

There was something offbeat in the way she said it that bothered Slim. He came back at her: "If there was someone stalking me, Alice, with a length of steel pipe, I would want to know about it. I think I would want a friend to tell me if she thought I was in danger." Alice shrugged.

"I'm not a detective, Officer. I wouldn't know," she said. "I think it best to leave some things in the dark." Kerns was sleeping the morning after his final surgery. Adriana had gone out for coffee after getting their promise not to leave Kerns' side. Alice and Slim both looked down at the patient. Tubes were running in and out of the man to keep life flowing. The surgeons had successfully replaced the bone fragments at the back of his head and the piece they had cut out behind his ear. The surgical team was pleased with his recovery so far. If all continued on this track, the tubes would be withdrawn later in the day.

***

"Why would Kerns have broken down the door if he didn't suspect something?" Slim asked, continuing his train of thought from the previous day. "Kerns has been on and off for three days, Alice. Perhaps we'll never know." The two of them were in the hospital cafeteria drinking brown water for coffee. "Do you think, Alice, I should keep a man here with an eye on both of them? For their safety?" Slim was fishing, and at the same time, serious. Maybe there was a stalker.

"I don't know what to think."

"Even when we don't know the direction of our thoughts, Alice, we still think. Kerns may be thinking now. You've been coming in here every two or three hours to check up on him—on them. When do you sleep?" Alice got up and went to the ladies' room without a word. *She needs time to think that one over*, Slim thought. *There is something here unknown. The unknown side of the scale always outweighs the known. A grain of stupidity outweighs a truckload of knowledge.* Slim took their cups up to the stainless counter and filled them both. He knew Alice drank hers black, or brown in this case. There was sugar on the table. He was sure, however, she didn't use it. He sat a while, stirring half a teaspoon into his. His brain was turning, too.

***

After the media rush of out-of-state reporters trying to wring information or false statements out of Slim, they gave up and only guessed at what the backwoods detective thought. Fortunately, they didn't mix Kerns' situation into the soup. They had not spotted a connection. Alice returned and sat across from Slim again.

"Officer," she said. "It might not be a bad idea to have someone standing by Kerns' room."

"Oh?"

"You brought it up."

Slim smiled. "Let's go check on them." Alice got up. Slim followed her. He had been hoping this Billings character would give him another call. Nothing came through from that direction. Thelma was still in agony because of destroying the email.

She had tried to get it back herself, to no avail. There was nothing in the trash folder. There was no sign of it on her iPhone. She brought up a number of deleted messages on the iPhone but nothing concerning Midnight Poison. Thelma didn't dare to turn it over to the email expert at the bank. She was afraid he might bring it up, and that man had a mouth that wouldn't stop talking. Thelma had given up.

***

The afternoon following his surgery, Kerns opened his eyes briefly. Slim and Alice had come and gone that morning. "Are you all right, Adriana?" he asked, his mind still racing on the same track it had been on the day before. "You were screaming—and then I thought someone was trying to strangle you."

Adriana turned to face him, her eyes filled with joy at the sound of his voice. "Kerns?" she said.

"Where are we?" he said.

"I don't know," she said hesitantly, not wanting to upset him, "but we are alive, Kerns, and together."

The walls of the room were a pale green, a military color concocted by some psychopath to erase a sense of hospital horror surrounding them—tubes and an array of needles, coffee cups, and TV screens tangled to the walls. The scene read "hospital."

"What the hell am I doing in here, Adriana?" His blood pressure indicator peaked.

Adriana pushed a button to summon nurses. Gun in hand, a man in uniform pushed through the door. Kerns sat up suddenly. The world began to spin. His mind blacked out. Adriana screamed. She moved forward with amazing speed, knocked the gun from the trooper's hand, and fled down the hospital hall toward the stairway. By the time Slim's planted guard had regained his weapon and made his way into the hall, Adriana was nowhere to be seen. Two nurses and an orderly ran past him into the room. Kerns had lapsed back into his coma.

***

CHAPTER 17

Back on Track

Slim, based on the information he received from John Winslow, Colonel Cornwell's orderly, had traced Major Almas Thomas Cooper III to and from the Air Force Academy in Colorado Springs. Cooper visited with his son only one afternoon. His son, Almas Armstrong Cooper IV, or A as the major called him, was shocked to see his father wearing the colonel's insignia.

Young Almas was due to graduate in the spring. His father arrived unexpectedly, but fortunately on a weekend. A had been trying unsuccessfully to reach the major via cell phone and email. All attempts made were rejected. His father's email address had been changed. Almas A. Cooper IV placed a call to Colonel Cornwell, his father's immediate commander. He didn't reach the colonel personally but spoke with his orderly, a Corporal Winslow. Winslow reported that the major had retired. He was in the States, he told the major's son. Winslow did not have the major's civilian address, email or otherwise.

"He is headed in your direction," the orderly said. "I am sure he will be in contact with you." The orderly paused. "Are there any other members of the family within reach? Anyone we might call? We are concerned here as well. The colonel will be pleased you called. We all thought a great deal of the major," Winslow lied. "He was an officer and gentleman." *A mundane phrase*, Winslow thought, *but officers loved it.*

"He still is," Almas replied tersely.

"Right, sir," Winslow said. "He still is, sir. Sir, is there anyone else in the family who might—"

Lieutenant Cooper signed off. He was worried. There was no one else in the family, except for Aunt Vita. Aunt Vita, he had learned while in Alaska, had very little respect for his father. The young lieutenant had not lost his respect for the major, but he feared there was a problem.

In Winslow's office, Colonel Cornwell's voice came over the intercom. "You handled that well, Corporal." The intercom clicked off. Winslow patted himself on the back. After he got off duty he would pass this information on to Slim. *This*, he thought with a grin, *is what it is like to be a double agent.*

***

When the major arrived at the academy later the same afternoon, his son was greatly relieved. Now he would know the truth. The truth, however, only hovered on the periphery of their conversation. A, on the surface, accepted his father's explanation of getting his promotion on the day of his retirement. The earlier rejection had been a mistake, he pointed out. The major had not planned to mention his retirement, but his son brought it up. "We all have to give up the good life at some point in our lives," Major Cooper explained. "After putting in many years, I was eligible for this retirement ages ago. The air force is my life, A, as it is yours. After your mother died, I had no family to live for, other than you. You, A, are on your own now. I have reached my pinnacle. It is time for me to 'kick back,' as you youngsters would say. My heels are in the air, A. I am a retired colonel now and in love with the remainder of my life. I expect you to continue using me as a role model, A. I may not have touched down in every country of the world, son, but I have split the air above each one of them and, I am proud to say, in the course of human events turned much of them to dust for the honor of my country."

Young Almas had heard "for the honor of my country" from his father many times. The rendition now was a bit desperate. His father didn't have to prove he was a hero. He was one. But was he a colonel? The orderly, Winslow, had not mentioned a promotion. The young airman recalled his father had, just a few months ago, been turned down for that same promotion. Was that really a mistake? Also, his mother, Velma, had hinted at some scandal the major was involved in that brought about the early termination of his tour of duty in Iraq. As a pilot, his father had never flown again.

Three of young Almas' fellow students gathered in front of A's quarters to listen to the colonel's stories. His comrades were eager listeners. For some reason, young Almas felt embarrassed, even uncomfortably humiliated, as his father ranted on. And that was it. His father was ranting. The major's uniform was wrinkled from miles on the road. His low quarter shoes were scuffed, unpolished. The major was always immaculate, uniform pressed, his face clean-shaven. Here and now, he wouldn't pass inspection.

"Major," his son asked, "where are you staying? It's Sunday. I have a pass. I can go back with you to your room."

"Room? Your father is a colonel now. I have booked a suite at the Hilton. Invite your friends. We'll drink and talk some more."

"We're students, Major—"

"Colonel, goddamnit."

"Colonel, sir." Young Almas saluted. "Forgive me, sir."

"Apology accepted. Invite your friends. We shall retire to my suite and celebrate."

"Colonel, sir. They all have studies to prepare. And we need time alone, you and me. We need time to talk." Almas' friends took the cue. Saluting, they bid their goodbyes, and backing off, melted into their respective hiding places. Almas heaved a hidden sigh of gratitude. "Come, Colonel," he said. "I'll ride with you. I can catch a cab back later. I can't stay out too late. We have a test tomorrow."

"Tomorrow's Sunday, asshole," Cooper shrieked, his voice breaking. Young Almas looked at the major, shocked. His father had never addressed him in such a way before. "Right, son. Asshole!" the old man continued, clarifying his statement. "A is for Asshole, as well as for Almas. Join the club. Come on. Get in the fucking car."

It was not to be a pleasant evening for the Coopers III and IV.

***

Alice found Adriana at the hangar, sitting bolt upright in her stiff oak office chair. She pressed a two-cup pot of coffee and held one out to Adriana. Neither of the women said a word. Alice didn't know how to start the conversation. Adriana couldn't for the longest time. Finally, she broke down with silent tears.

"I felt her coming on, Alice, the dark one. I saw the uniform and the gun. Kerns spoke and she took over. I was me enough to be terrified at what Ms. Dark could do. I had to get away and take her with me. This time I recognized her, Alice. Will I ever be able to defeat her? She is the bird of darkness. The bird of my darkness."

"Do you think you should get help?" Alice offered lamely.

"From who? Doctors will only dope me up—put my mind to sleep. No. I've got two to go: two of those sons-of-bitches to eliminate. Number one is that fucking major, and two, the arrogant asshole, Cummings, down in Texas. Maybe then the dark maiden will be satisfied. I gave Kerns Cummings's name when the news broke about the girl he raped and murdered here in Fairbanks. Foolishly I thought justice might be done in a civilian court." Hands shaking, Adriana sipped her coffee. "They located Cummings, Alice. This guy, Slim, we met at the hospital is deceptively sharp. He filed extradition papers. But Captain Asshole is protected by the US Armed Services. I doubt if they can pull that rotten tooth out of Texas."

"The major is a civilian now," Alice offered. "I have been keeping track of him, or I was—until he resigned his commission and fled the country for the forty-eight below."

"He resigned?"

"It was a forced resignation. It had something to do with his knowledge of Cummings."

"Two of a kind. Perhaps the major is with Cummings in Texas now."

"Adriana, we better call and find out how Kerns is doing."

"My God, Kerns," she cried. "I left him, Alice. I was afraid of her—afraid of what she might do in the dark. She is not very discriminating. I had to leave him. Alice, right now I am scared."

***

While Kerns recovered in Fairbanks and Cummings sweated out his possible extradition from Texas to the Far North, the self-made Colonel Almas A. Cooper III retired to a fairyland of his own construction. For his son, Almas Armstrong Cooper IV, the night together with the major was a tragedy. His father, he realized, was teetering on the brink of insanity. Assuming a false rank was a crime for a private first-class, let alone an officer.

A's father was in deep shit. At his mother's funeral, young Almas realized the major was acting strangely. He was no longer flying, which had been his first love in the service. He had received numerous decorations in his career for bravery and ability, but the war in Iraq had been his last tour of duty as a pilot. From there he had been shipped to Alaska and a desk job. The reason for his sudden and unexpected departure from Baghdad had been cloudy.

Young Almas had never gotten the whole story from the major at one sitting. The blame for his reposting, the major laid on his commanding general. "A brigadier who lacked in experience," the major pointed out to his son. "Even in the U S Air Force mistakes are made in promoting incompetent men to positions of power." The fact that the major did not receive his expected promotion rankled him even more. The major's wife had written their son that she was afraid of what the major might do if it didn't come through.

Aunt Vita's summation of what she thought of his father shook Young Almas' belief in the major even more. There was something Aunt Vita wasn't telling him. Her nephew didn't pry—out of respect for his aunt, or a fear that it might expose a weakness in his father's facade. The young cadet didn't know which. He wished now he had pushed for an answer.

His father's appearance at the academy, unannounced and disheveled as he was, shocked his son even further. He realized that his father, a hero he looked up to, was drunk and only masquerading as a colonel. When they arrived at the Hilton, the major went directly to the bar where he ordered a martini, giving the bartender instructions as to how to prepare it. His son slipped away to the men's room. Returning, he stopped by the desk. As he suspected, his father had made no reservations. There was no suite, as he had boasted to Almas' friends at the academy.

Young Almas reserved a room, paid for it, and picked up two plastic keys before returning to the bar. Four martinis later he led his broken father to the room, where the older man fell across the king-sized bed, passed out. Almas then went down to the rental car and picked up his father's overnight bag and toilet kit. He found another bag with a clean, pressed uniform in it and brought the two bags and toilet kit up to the rented room. The major hadn't moved.

Almas hung the fresh uniform in the open closet where his father could see it. That uniform still had the major's true rank attached to it. Almas left a note for his father, telling him that the keys to his rented car would be at the front desk. *I will call in the morning, Major.* His son concluded in the note: *Major, you need help. I am here for you. You do have family. I am that family. You can depend on me. I love you.*

The young man took his father's shoes and socks off. He polished the old man's shoes as he had as a boy. Almas had never referred to his father as "the old man." As he looked down at the major snoring, old and drunk, on the king-sized bed, he realized his father had no direction left. Almas sat on the edge of the bed, tears draining the sorrow from him. *What happened, Major?* he wondered. *What happened to you? I adored you. I looked up to you.* Thoughts rushed through the young man's head. *Were we ever father and son? No, we were major and little soldier. I was your orderly. I was your servant, your shoeshine boy. I was only a shadow of your future.* Almas stood and looked down at the man he had been led to believe in, the man stretched across the Hilton's king-sized bed in a stupor. *I wasn't your son. I was your goddamned image. What was my mother in this picture? Where was she? What was her rank? The two of us, we shined your shoes until we could see our image in the black heart of the polish. "Spit and polish, Son, that is what's important in this world,"* you said. *"You serve your country well, she will be your servant. Spit and polish, Son."*

"This is not a man of love," Almas said aloud. "This man is a false hero who loved to spend his life in danger for the thrill of it and nothing else. The thrill, now gone, he has nothing left. My old man is an empty bottle. No more elusions, Major!" Almas cried in sorrow. He took an extra blanket from the top shelf of the closet where the fresh uniform hung like a promise from the past. He spread the comforter over his father. "To keep you warm," he said, "until the cold takes over."

The major's son checked the note he had left. He pinned it to the uniform and called for a cab.

***

There was no answer the following morning when he called his father's room. "The colonel checked out at eight," a Hilton voice said. "And sir," the voice went on after a short pause, "the colonel left a folding bag in his room and a uniform. Will he be back for it?"

"I'll pick it up this evening. Thank you," Almas said. What more was there to say? There was no one to say it to. He pushed the "end" button on his cell and it was over.

***

Kerns' daughter, Salome, in a blinding winter storm in Philadelphia, had not been able to get to her father's side for three days. Uncle Hap—she had called him Uncle Hap since her mother died—kept her informed of her father's condition. Hap had called Salome after he got to Saint Joseph's Hospital and assessed the situation. He knew the worst thing he could do would be to call Kerns' daughter before he knew what was going on. The news wasn't good, but it was truthful. The situation was critical. There was a good chance Kerns would survive, Hap told her. There was an excellent brain surgeon in Fairbanks and that man was at Kerns' side. Salome managed to get to the airport where she waited for the first flight out. She finally arrived at Fairbanks International. At the hospital she spent hours at her father's side with Adriana and her Uncle Hap. Hap had a room made up for her on the floor above the bar of the Big I. From there she could take a cab and be at her father's side in minutes.

***

Kerns' recovery, after he truly came around to the living, was remarkable. Slim, Adriana, Hap, and Salome were with him. Kerns had a bad headache. He was dizzy, but the carousel came to a stop within the first hour. "Salome," he asked, "what in the fuck hit me?" It was his first question when he came out of his final surgery. Why he directed it to his daughter, he had no idea. Salome shrugged. Slim didn't know. Hap wouldn't guess.

"All I know, Kerns," Hap said, "is my business has gone to hell since you quit drinking. That is the only thing I know for sure." Kerns smiled.

"I hit you, Kerns," Adriana said. "Alice told me I hit you. With a two-inch pipe, I hit you. I didn't know it was you. I wasn't really myself. I'd had a bad dream and the lights were out."

"If they weren't out, they certainly went out for me," Kerns said.

"Your lights were out for three days, Kerns," Hap informed him.

"And nights," Slim added.

Kerns was studying Adriana. “Who the hell did you think I was, Adriana? The Grim Reaper? You were screaming. I heard you screaming. That is why I broke in. I guess it was in your dream. Under the circumstances I am sorry I interrupted it.”

“They say,” Hap interrupted, “not to wake a person when they are having a bad dream, Kerns. I hope you have learned your lesson.”

“This lady packs a wallop, Hap, in more ways than one. Did they put a steel plate in the back of my head?”

“No,” Slim said, “but your skull was a jigsaw puzzle, Kerns. It took three surgeons to figure it out.”

“Maybe it will cure my dyslexia. They didn’t put it together right the first time.”

“Spell Ticonderoga,” Hap said. “That’s an easy one. Just sound it out.”

“Fuck you, Hap.”

The brain surgeon and two nurses came into the room. “That’s all, folks. This guy has got to get some rest. It is amazing he is alive at all, let alone sitting up. All we could do was try to put the pieces back together as best we could and hope. The back of your shaved head is rough as the spring break up on the Chena River. I hope you never go bald. I know you won’t want to shave your head.”

The nurses laid Kerns back gently on the rack that supported him. Adriana stepped up and kissed him on the lips.

“Get in here with me, Adriana, and the rest of you can leave.”

“That woman gets in that bed with you, Kerns,” Slim said, “your brain will explode completely. Come on, let’s all get out of here and let this man regain his senses.”

“I’ve been resting for days, Slim. For Christ’s sake, at least let Adriana stay.”

“No!” the surgeon echoed Slim’s words. “Everybody out. In a few days, Mr. Kerns, you will be up and feel better. We have to make sure the fractures are healing and your brain has shrunk to the correct size before you exert yourself in any fashion. We must keep your blood pressure down, Mr. Kerns.”

"Okay," Kerns sighed. "Adriana, please stand by." Kerns' daughter reached out and took his hand. She gave it a warm squeeze of love and relief. "And Salome," he added, "I love you, too."

"Right, Papa, but . . ." she said, looking to Adriana, "I think you are in good hands. I have got to get back to school tomorrow. We'll talk before I leave. Adriana will be standing by."

"Right, Kerns. I'm truly afraid I love you, even if I did almost kill you." With that, led by Hap and Salome, Adriana followed the rest of the troop to the Big I to celebrate Kerns' recovery. Kerns, his brain swirling, was left alone with his healers. They were still putting the pieces together.

***

CHAPTER 18

On the Outside

Basic Military Training, Lackland AFB, Texas

Every enlisted person entering the US Air Force becomes a member of 737th Training Group. They must complete their basic training or boot camp with the group before moving on to develop the more specialized skills that will define their career path in the USAF. According to the Lackland website, the 737th has become known as the "Gateway to the Air Force."

Captain Albert D. Cummings had been called into the commanding general's office. He waited there for twenty minutes, thumbing through outdated magazines and recruiting blurbs. His picture was featured in a few of the blurbs. The captain liked that, but he never thought he would be relegated to training air force grunts, or recruiting them. Cummings was a combat fighter pilot. What the hell was he doing here? He waited in the reception hall for the general's staff to call him before his commanding officer. What the hell was going on? Cummings feared he knew what the hell was going on. And he was right.

In another half an hour, he was standing at attention in front of a member of the general's personal staff, some colonel, his chest blazing with strips of decorations. "The general is distressed," Colonel Zagoda said, after returning Cummings's salute. "The command has received a request for your extradition. It is a civilian request to return you to Fairbanks, Alaska. You are wanted for questioning in connection with a rape and murder case." The colonel took a turn back and forth in front of Cummings, patting his white-gloved hands behind his back as he did so. "To fill you in, Captain Cummings, the victim in the case, a young girl, a respected artist by the name of Diana Alderman, was found drowned in her car a mile from the Fairbanks International Airport in what they call the Chena River. They claim you were in Fairbanks at that time, Captain. We will need to verify this or you will need to establish your whereabouts as elsewhere. You were last seen, witnesses have said, at a local pub, in civilian clothes, escorting the artist to her car on the 'pretense'—their term not ours—of seeing the young lady home."

Cummings was still standing at attention before the strutting colonel. "At ease, Captain," Zagoda said. "I didn't mean to hold you at attention." Cummings relaxed slightly. The colonel went on. "You realize, of course, the seriousness of this action, Captain. We assume you were elsewhere at that time, but we do need proof of some sort. On your request for leave, you mentioned you would be visiting a Major Cooper, a member of the Air Force Drone Squadron at Fort Wainwright, Alaska, a short distance south of Fairbanks. Is this true?"

"I was there to attend his wife's funeral, sir. The major is a close friend of mine."

"I see. Can you tell me when exactly did you arrive in Fairbanks, and what was the date and time of your departure, Captain? That should clear this untidy little mess up neatly."

"I don't know if I have the receipt for my ticket, Colonel. I don't hang on to things like that, and I don't have a wife to do that menial task for me. I am a confirmed bachelor, and better for it. In any case, I don't know of a woman who would put up with me."

"Nor do I, Captain." Colonel Zagoda grinned at his own limp humor. "You are going to have to figure that one out yourself. Just check your credit card history and the ticket purchase will pop up loud and clear. With that record, listing your departure prior to the case in point, you will be exonerated. The US Air Force always stands behind our men in uniform. Good day, Captain." The captain returned the salute smartly. "Just remember, Captain. We at the 737th training facility of the US Air Force can't have a dark shadow over one of our best instructors. And, you, Captain Cummings, are one of our best." Zagoda checked the date on his gold-embossed wristwatch. "It's Friday afternoon, Captain. I'll expect to hear from you Monday morning. Have a good weekend."

Captain Cummings stood, watching quietly as the colonel made his way back into the general's office complex. Two young female cadets he worked with in boot camp training met him as he stepped out of the reception room. They smiled pleasantly and saluted. "Ladies," he replied, "it is always a pleasure." *Christ*, he thought. *They can't be over twenty. Succulent as California grape*s. He snapped his mind back to his problem. *Now, what was the name of that goddamn little blowjob artist in Fairbanks? I got to talk myself out of this one. Where the hell is Major Cooper when I need an alibi?*

***

Major Cooper was drifting southeast into Texas. Like the tumbleweeds gathered at the rusting metal posts along Highway 267, he was at the mercy of the winds in the Texas–Oklahoma panhandle. Tears built up behind his glasses, blurring his vision. Trying to keep the centerline of the highway on his left, he passed a few road signs. He had not read one in hours. The gas gauge on his rental car registered in the red. The major was in na-na land and headed nowhere. The car drifted off to the right into loose sand. Overcorrecting, Major Almas Cooper III jerked the rental vehicle back onto the pavement. The road was straight on. The gas tank dry, the car stuttered to a jerking stop. The left front tire was on the centerline. His fingers numb, the major's hands held tightly to the wheel.

Behind him a semi surged to a rubber-skidding stop as it pulled over onto the shoulder. The driver clicked his flashers on. He got out as he did so and rushed up to the driver's window of the stopped car. The door was locked. The uniformed man inside was stiff in position. He stared straight ahead, his hands still clutching the wheel. The truck driver knocked at the glass with no response. He ran back and got out his orange emergency cones and strung them from the major's bumper at an angle to the rear of his parked semi. The orange danger cones in place, the truck driver called 911. He reported the car locked in the middle of the road, with the motor dead and the driver comatose. He requested an ambulance and a tow truck to move the vehicle off the road. The semi driver then stood by the car, directing the sparse traffic around it. He watched for signs of life. He could see that the uniformed colonel was breathing, but nothing more.

The state patrol got there with tools to jimmy the car door. They got the major out and on a blanket. The state patrol officer applied pressure to the major's chest to get his heart pumping at a higher rate. Nothing brought the man back. He then searched and found the car rental agreement in the glove compartment and called in the information to headquarters, where a search was started. The emergency vehicle arrived. They loaded the major and headed for the hospital in Amarillo. The wrecker hooked onto the rental car and drove off in the same direction. The semi driver, with the officer's help, gathered up his bright orange emergency cones and got back to his job. The officer thanked him for his quick thinking and help. It was over. Everything was back to normal on Highway 267 headed into Texas.

***

Captain Albert D. Cummings was one of the 737th Training Group's prize instructors. As a pilot Cummings's record was impeccable, heroic even. He didn't boast about his many decorations for valor, but the air force saw to it that they were noted on base billboards and in the recruiting blurbs splashed up on television ads and in flyers passed out in high schools, junior colleges, and universities. Captain Cummings was billed as a USAF hero. He was looked up to by every enlisted person, male and female, entering the 737th. The astute Cummings saw to it that his record remained absolutely clean at the Lockland Air Force Base and surrounding territory.

The afternoon and evening of his interview with the general's liaison, Colonel Zagoda, Cummings spent hours on the Internet trying to locate Major Cooper. He desperately needed an alibi for his whereabouts the evening of the rape and murder in Alaska. It was now after midnight and he had nothing to show for it. Angrily, in 20-point bold font, he hammered out his vicious thoughts on the screen of his laptop:

JESUS CHRIST! SHE WAS JUST A FUCKING DRUNK. WHO CARES?

There was a hesitant knock upon the door of his posh lakeside condominium. Cummings was already pissed off. The knock didn't help his disposition. He crossed to the heavy front door and, without thinking, threw it open. Something hit him in the chest. He looked down in wonder and astonishment. It was a dart, the point embedded in his taut, trained flesh. Shocked and apparently helpless, for seconds he watched fluid in the vile forced through the hollow needle into his body.

"Don't touch it," a voice in the darkness said quietly. "It won't kill you, Cummings. It's built to only stun dumb animals like you." The door swung shut. It didn't close tight enough to latch. Cummings tried to kick loose the heavy towel-like obstruction keeping it open. His movements were already in slow motion when he turned back into the room. Before he could get to the pistol in his desk drawer, he collapsed. The door pushed open once again. In the cotton echo of his hearing, the captain heard muffled footsteps drawing near. An old leather satchel touched the floor beside him in the growing darkness.

***

In the flash of morning sunlight, Cummings's eyes flickered open. Naked from the waist down, he felt a throbbing, excruciating pain between his legs. He was well enough alive to feel and see. He drew his legs slowly up. He was naked in the light of dawn. Dried blood streaked down his thighs. He was on the floor. The rich Iranian rug beneath him was soiled with blood from an operation performed on him while under the stunning effects of the large animal tranquilizer. He forced himself to gaze down at his sexual ruination.

Captain Albert D. Cummings had been castrated. The veins and arteries leading to and from where his gonads once hung like Christmas ornaments were cauterized, the incision sewed up neatly. The needle, strung with a foot or two of extra filament, was thrust into his thigh. Captain Cummings pulled the needle out and struggled to his feet. There was no fresh blood. The incision had been made and closed professionally. There was only pain—excruciating pain. The surgeon had left no prescription drugs to elevate that.

In frantic hope, Cummings looked about for the missing contents of his shrunken scrotum. There was no trace. Nothing to be reconnected. No life to be revived. Cummings was a steer—a boar without his balls, an empty promise of consummation. The destruction was complete. He was now a plane without the wings to fly. In throbbing, unbearable agony, he hobbled to his desktop computer. He pushed the button, bringing the black screen back to life. His last typed words stood out strongly in the 20-point font:

JESUS CHRIST! SHE WAS JUST A FUCKING DRUNK. WHO CARES?

Beneath, in bold, as he had printed his callus thoughts, the reply read:

SOMEONE CARES,
CAPTAIN ASSHOLE,
SOMEONE CARES!

PS: If you are looking to reconnect your balls, check the garbage disposal.

***

In the San Antonio International Airport, a distinguished-looking gentleman checked his baggage through to Fairbanks, Alaska: a guitar case with guitar and a crumpled leather travel bag. He picked up his boarding pass, took his shoes off for a security inspection, and stopped in for a Bloody Mary made with Boodles Gin. His plane wasn't due to depart for almost an hour. He had time to enjoy his breakfast.

***

Captain Albert D. Cummings, the hero, called in sick on Monday morning. Five weeks later, to clear his name, he explained to Colonel Zagoda, he was flown by the US Air Force to Alaska. In civilian clothes he landed at Fort Wainwright, in the town of North Pole. It had been arranged for Cummings to be billeted in a private home in relative seclusion on Badger Road, south of Fairbanks. Cummings was provided with heavy winter gear and a 4-wheel-drive 2012 Toyota Land Cruiser. The Toyota was slightly scratched up and painted a not unusual off-white. It would draw little attention. Under the hood, the engine, transmission, and all electrical wiring, and heater were in excellent condition. The ten-ply winter-tread tires were new.

Cummings had mentioned to no one his sexual redirection. In the past weeks, while recuperating as well as could be expected from his unfortunate operation, an operation that left him totally impotent, he spent hours with the door locked cruising the Internet. He was acquainted now with every bush plane operation in the Yukon Territory as well as in the state of Alaska. Cummings felt he had found what he needed to know. All that was left for him to do now was act.

In the glove compartment of the 4x4 were a .45 army-issue automatic and a box of ammunition. Wrapped in plastic behind the back seat was a rifle with a large game tranquilizer in the breach. An additional supply of tranquilizers were standing by.

***

During his time of recovery from his operation, Captain Cummings had located his old commanding officer, Major Cooper. The major had suffered a stoppage of blood flow to the brain. The sudden stroke left him completely paralyzed, including his vocal cords. The major possessed no viable memory. He recognized no one. Not even Cummings when the captain visited him at the veteran's home where Cooper would reside for the remainder of his life. The major, he was told, would be tube-fed as long as he was unfortunate enough to live. Captain Cummings left the veteran's facility more determined than ever to carry out his plan of action. He was the only one left.

***

CHAPTER 19

The Last Revenge

Kerns was out of the hospital four weeks later and in the Big I for the first time, for the first drink since he suffered the blow administered by his beloved eleven weeks previously. Adriana was with him in the bar, as were Slim and Hap. They had just called Salome, giving her an update on her father's condition. With his first glass of Rye and soda, he was definitely on his feet and on the road to full recovery. Salome was definitely pleased, but anxious.

"Don't overdue the celebration," she warned her papa. "And keep Adriana in sight at all times. She is a dangerous woman."

"She's a lovely woman, Salome," her father answered.

"Most dangerous women are, Papa. Mind what I say."

While Kerns recovered on Chena Ridge, Adriana had learned of the fate of Major Almas A. Cooper III. Kerns wasn't certain of the connection between the major and Adriana. He knew Adriana knew Cummings and despised the man as she also despised Cooper. Kerns had honored his word to Adriana by not revealing his source of information to Slim. But her connection to Cummings was a matter that concerned him. Adriana had never even mentioned the name of Cummings following her five a.m. phone call the morning she gave him the information in the first place. Kerns decided Cummings had been a party to her rape in the military and thought it best not to bring the subject up.

The air force had denied Slim's request for Cummings's extradition. Captain Cummings would stay in Texas. He could die in Texas for all Kerns cared. Things were going well between him and Adriana. Kerns' plan was not to rock the canoe. They were in love—two people in love. Adriana was smiling and happy. At least she seemed to be. Kerns had no desire to sink that boat.

Adriana, on her part, struggled to keep her feelings concerning Cummings and the major under control. She and Alice discussed the darkness a time or two. Alice's strength and understanding were a saving grace in that direction. A week earlier Adriana and Alice had a long, in-depth conversation concerning Cummings. He was alive and in Texas and would not be deported to Alaska if the air force had anything to say about it, and they seemed to have that say. They were keeping Slim at bay. That was not all the ladies learned about Cummings. There had been an envelope addressed to Adriana and hand-delivered. That is, it was slid under the door of the A-Plus Flying Service hangar. No return address.

Adriana opened the envelope. Inside, on a sheet of plain paper, was a poem, or better stated, a clever little verse of four sentences, hand-scrawled. No name.

Spadones
Captain Cummings is guilty of murder and rape.
I have his gonads here on my plate.
As a Eunuch he's no longer virile.
Paranoid & impotent. Now that is his fate.

Alice read the verse Adriana showed her and thought a moment. "So, if this is indeed true, the ball-less bastard is still capable of destruction, Adriana. He is alive, paranoid, and angry—angrier now. So, what is he going to do in his new emptiness? His lack of potent manliness—of power?"

"Who do you suppose sent this delightful little piece of verse?" Adriana dropped her thoughts in the wind.

"This man, Cummings, is still alive, Adriana—dead between his legs, maybe, but still alive. Spadones? I don't know." She brought the word up on the screen of her laptop. "It goes back to the Bible, Adriana. This guy, Tertullian, in the second century thought Jesus Christ and St. Paul were spadones, or eunuchs. According to Tertullian, many monks and holy men of the time of Christ preformed the self-administered castration operation to ensure their vows of chastity."

"I'd say that practice is a bit extreme, Alice, but it would assure chastity." She grinned. "I doubt that Cummings was self-cut." Adriana didn't plan to bring religion into her thoughts, but: "What the hell is this all about, Alice?"

"Matthew 19:10 through 12, it says here," Alice went on: "Let anyone accept who can." Alice put the site to rest. "This Cummings may now be a eunuch, Adriana, but the son-of-a-bitch is still alive. That spadones is still alive, his gonads gone, perhaps, but his wish for power and revenge are feeding on his brain. And who sent you this note, Adriana?" Alice went on. "Who else knows the path Cummings took? Who, other than the two of us, wished him strong justice? And why was this other person involved?"

"Diana Alderman, the artist," Adriana said quietly, drumming her fingers on the desk. "The man who raped and murdered her was Cummings. Diana, the artist. That is the connection, Alice. And the person who performed the operation? Her friend and benefactor, Dr. Rob Singer."

"Doc? The guy we met the night Kerns went to the hospital?"

"Right. He's a friend of Hap's, too. It's got to be Doc, Alice. Hap said Doc delivered Diana. Her mother died shortly thereafter. Her father was already dead. Doc sort of adopted her—no paperwork. I know about foster children, Alice, and the different ways the bell can swing. Diana needed someone and Dr. Singer was there for her. She was a daughter to him. Hap said Doc spent the whole night looking for her the night she disappeared. He was the one who found her at the ice bridge."

"If this is the case, why didn't he just kill Cummings?"

"He's a doctor. He believes in the doctor's oath. He believes in saving lives, not taking them. From the little I know about Dr. Singer, Alice, he knew Cummings was a man who would never admit someone had taken his balls. Cummings is now like a violated woman who is afraid to report a rape because she's embarrassed and feels guilty—like I was—at first. Except in court with Cummings, the judge would reach down between his legs and recognize the loss. It cuts both ways, Alice, only this time the cut was made in the name of Right and Justice." Her fingers stopped drumming. "Singer—Dr. Rob Singer. The man is a doctor, not a lawman or a murderer."

"He had to have found Midnight Poison on the Internet," Alice spoke up. "And he had to place her in this building before he slid the note under our door."

Adriana reached for the paper with the verse on it and the envelope it came in. "Dr. Singer would never pass this information on, Alice." She dropped the paper in the shredder beside her desk. With a hum it was trash. "And Cummings, if he is not brought here in chains, will never dare return to Alaska. I am free of him as I am free of Cooper the Third. Both of them are screwed for life with no life in them. I think my dark friend may now be satisfied—gone forever. She accomplished what she came to do. And now, with Kerns in my corner, I am as free as ever I was and as ever I will be. Believe me, Alice, we are done with this charade, this travesty. If they haven't found me out by now, they never will."

"If that is truly so, Adriana, I am going to pack my bags and fly south to see my family. There is a plane leaving for Oklahoma in a little more than an hour. My carry-on will be packed in ten minutes." Alice jumped to her feet. She kissed her dear friend quickly. "You sure you are going to be okay, Adriana? You have a client coming by tomorrow—a cash deal, no paperwork. I checked her out. She is okay. You won't need me for a week or so?"

"Go."

"You go first," Alice said quietly. "I hate goodbyes. I'll call the front desk at the terminal and walk there. They will have my ticket waiting." She pulled Adriana from her desk chair. "Kerns is waiting for you."

"Thanks, Alice." Adriana grabbed her parka and headed for the door and Chena Ridge.

"One other thing, Adriana." Adriana stopped and turned back. "I did some early Christmas shopping. Your package will be waiting on your desk. Open it when you find it. Don't wait for the big day!"

"Okay, sister."

"It's important, Adriana! As they say in my home state, 'You might still have some rats to kill.' Now get out of here."

Adriana turned back for one last quick kiss of friendship. "I'll be fine, Alice." Adriana was smiling. "You go and have fun. Give my love to your family. One of these days I will meet them." Adriana turned and was gone.

Alice heaved a sigh. She had talked briefly with the sister of Adriana's new client. The woman was young and normal. She was coming to the office tomorrow to finalize everything for her brother, who would fly in later in the week. She pulled out Adriana's presents and arraigned them on the desk then called the Fairbanks International front desk and grabbed her carry-on. It was a ten-minute walk to the terminal. She made it in eight. Alice was relieved and happy. With Kerns' help, Alice honestly believed Adriana now had the darkness under control. It was safe for her to leave. *I don't know what she will think when she opens those presents and the instructions I left with them, but you never can tell*, she thought as she boarded her flight. "Perhaps she will run into a bear on her next landing," she said to herself. "Another rat to kill. It will come in handy."

***

With Kerns at the Big I, Adriana waved off the drink Hap was about to pour. "I got a client early tomorrow. Some crazy guy who wants to ski down the slopes of Mt. McKinley," she said. "I need to stay clean if I'm going to fly. I told him—actually I told his sister who made the contact—I'd give him a fly-by at dawn so he could check his fate. The sister paid in advance. The client doesn't get in until just before we take off in the morning. By the time we get there the sun will hit Denali like iced fire—or Mt. McKinley, as the sister calls the great mountain. I'm just going to take them for a look at it, a reconnaissance flight, so to speak. Hopefully he will change his mind. His plan is to deplane with a chute, which will take him down to the powder he wants to ski. His sister says he's made over a hundred jumps, many landings on skis. After he takes a look, we'll see where it goes from there."

"Who is this nut?" Hap asked. "He'll freeze before he hits the snow."

"We're warm in here," Kerns said. "He's a cheechako. Probably the closest he has ever come to this country is reading Robert Service."

"His sister says he's been here a few times, but not in Fairbanks. I told her I'd give him the fly-by, but not the jump. The jump this time of year is crazy. It's fifty below up there."

"In the spring, perhaps," Slim said.

"Skier of the impossible," Kerns said. "Nineteen seventy-two. A guy named Sylvain Saudan skied down the southwest face of Denali."

"Another historical fact," Slim stated, shaking his head. "Kerns' brain is working again, Adriana. I thought maybe you had knocked some sense out of him."

"It was the first time that mountain was conquered by a skier and a climber," Kerns said. "On the way up Sylvain must have carried his skis on his back."

"Extreme skiing. I think he took a helicopter," Hap said. "He studied the different slopes a few weeks before he took the plunge. He didn't do all of that on snowshoes."

"In any case, my client paid cash," Adriana said. "Or his sister paid in cash. She's going with us."

"She jumping, too?" Kerns asked.

"No. She said she wasn't crazy." Adriana stood to leave. Kerns got up with her. "I'll go alone, Kerns," she said. "I've got to get some sleep. I've been sleeping lately—whenever you let me. It's been nice. I'll stay at the hangar tonight." Kerns walked her to her car. He kissed her good night. It was a nice long, lingering kiss. "See you tomorrow afternoon, love," she said and paused. "Kerns, I'm going to tell you one other thing about this client. I didn't want to bring it up in there. Too many ears. This guy I am flying out with tomorrow has an eye problem."

"Is he blind? He's going to ski by Braille?"

"No," she laughed. "It's just that his eyes and skin are very sensitive to the sun."

"An albino?"

"No—well maybe something like that. His sister says he's very sensitive about his condition. She won't say much more about it. He wears very dark glasses and keeps his face covered much of the time, she said, especially when he is on the slopes. He loves to ski and wants to prove something. She asked me to treat him carefully."

"That mountain is not going to treat him carefully, Adriana. That mountain is not going to discriminate. Nature just does what she has to do—what has to be done."

"Kerns, I shouldn't have brought it up to you. I'm sorry. I guess it is just that, according to his sister, he doesn't want anyone to know he is 'different'—that he is unusual. Because of his looks and his strange eyes, he thinks people look at him as a freak of nature. In public he often wears a mask of some sort, she said. Tomorrow he will be wearing a ski mask."

"*Phantom of the Opera* on skis."

"Kerns. He only wants to be a normal human being."

"Sorry. Maybe he can do it, Adriana. Ski that mountain, I mean. I'm not knocking it. But he needs some time studying those slopes. He's got to be damn good and know his way down. The man is on a suicide run. Behind his dark glasses the truth may come to light. Good luck to him."

"Good luck to all of us, Kerns. I love you." Adriana drove away. Kerns followed her with his eyes. He was thinking: *Who the fuck would jump into the snow with only skies to take him down? How the hell would he jump with the skis on? There are some crazies out there. Blind man's bluff. Who is bluffing whom?* Kerns thoughts drifted to the three who had done worse coming down without skis and in the dark. With that chilling thought, Kerns turned back into the Big I for another Rye.

***

Driving to the airport and her bed in the office—a bed, thanks to Kerns, she hadn't slept in for some time—Adriana thought of Alice. Alice had flown to the States to visit her mother in Oklahoma. She would be gone through the holidays. Alice had left Adriana an early Christmas present. She made Adriana promise to open it before she flew another mission with a client. Alice called them missions as if they were still in the service. Adriana smiled thinking about her friend. *She's a great mechanic, but she's like a mother hen*, Adriana smiled at that thought. *Well, not exactly a mother hen.* "It's the slow season, Alice," she had told her. "I'll be fine. I have Kerns now. He is up and walking about—and very active in other ways, too." She grinned. Slim had given them the use of his cabin on Chena Ridge. It had been a beautiful eight weeks with him. Adriana felt confident. It would be a good flight tomorrow. Alice had serviced both planes. They were in the best of shape, as always, ready for anything they might come up against.

"All but the right rear passenger door on the Helio," Alice pointed out. "The lock's a little dicey, but it's not going to open into the wind."

"It will work, Alice. Don't worry." Adriana reran their conversation in her mind as she drove to the hangar. Adriana wasn't worried. She pulled her car into the reserved parking space and plugged the head bolt heater in. She would have a cup of tea before she settled in for the night, which is exactly what she did. She got a good night's sleep.

***

Adriana was up in the seven a.m. darkness. It would still be dark at ten. She had coffee and ran a takeoff check on her plane. The latch on the rear right-hand door was weak, as Alice had pointed out, but it would close enough to be almost airtight. If the need arose, a heavy bungee cord, the Alaskan fix, would hold it. All was in order. Her clients were to show up at 9:30. Adriana sat for her second cup of coffee and opened her Christmas presents from Alice. That was a surprise—a bulletproof Kevlar vest and a Colt .380 Mustang semi-automatic with shoulder holster and an extra six-shot clip loaded with Hydra Shok, hollow-point ammo—a killer. The Colt came equipped with a laser max sight enhancer, which flashed on when the safety flipped off. Alice had tied a tag to the trigger guard. On it she had printed in red: *Follow the red dot—pull when appropriate!* Also included was a Hooper high-performance gun-cleaning kit. *Alice always thinks of maintenance.* Adriana smiled. *What's all this about?* she wondered. There was an envelope with it. The typed note with the gifts explained: *Have a happy and safe holiday season*, and it went on:

> *Dear Adriana,*
>
> *I know you are satisfied with the fate of the major and his life controlled by tubes running to and from a dead brain. It is a life he deserves. I still have concerns, however, about the fate of Captain Albert D. Cummings. Together we came to the conclusion the note slid under the door is legitimate.*
>
> *PS: It could very well be from the guitar-playing Doc Singer, who lost his license to practice medicine by doing good deeds for many Alaskans. The doc was a close friend of Diana Alderman and that makes sense. I am sure he performed the operation on our friend Cummings.*
>
> *Cummings, although deprived of brains, the ones between his legs, is still alive—and pissed off, Adriana. I am certain he connects you with his surgery. We must be on the lookout for him. You must be ready to protect yourself, hence my gifts. You promised to open my gifts and have done so, as you are reading these instructions. Wear both the vest and little .380 when you are with a client or are alone at your cabin by the hot springs. This Cummings is a rattlesnake son-of-a-bitch! You won't be safe until he is dead! A second promise you must make to me, Adriana. Wear my gifts! I trust you will do so.*

Your Loving Friend, Alice
PS #2: Email me that you have received the "gifts" and are making the new promise.

Adriana poured another French Pressed coffee, got out her laptop, and proceeded to answer her friend.

Dear Alice,
Yes, my dear. I have received the "gifts." Good Lord. I had pretty much put all this shit out of my mind. I have even felt cleansed, almost pure, with the "darkness" in remission. Now, I am not so sure. Ha ha.
I am trying to live a normal life, Alice. How can I with this rope about my neck? The crimes I have committed to erase the "darkness" are evidently not enough to break the spell. I have considered opening my heart to Kerns concerning the airdrops. I have told him about the gang rape I suffered and my crawling out of that pit of guilt. I, right now, feel free, but Kerns doesn't know of the depths to which I have sunk to cleanse myself, Alice. Only you know that. I am feeling the guilt creep in again right now and bringing the darkness with it. Help me, Alice. I'll wear this goddamn vest and carry the little Mustang 9 mm. But these are not the kind of weapons I need.
LOVE YOU. Thank you for everything. I got to go.

Adriana pushed the send button.

She snugged up the shoulder holster and checked the loaded clip in the .380, plus the one round in the chamber for instant use. She flipped the safety twice to check the focused laser sight. It worked. The batteries were good. She locked the safety device. "I hope you are satisfied, Alice," she murmured. Adriana opened the door to the hangar and started the Helio. She pulled it out into the open, frigid air. Adriana was ready.

The Helio warmed up in the dark. The client had paid. If he didn't show that was his business. Adriana's business was to be ready. She was. She thought briefly of Kerns then cut him from her mind. With the gun and vest in place under her flight jacket she felt she was in the dark again. It was the first time in days she felt so empty.

***

An older model, off-white Toyota 4x4 pulled into the lot. Adriana recognized the sister as she got out. She plugged the head bolt heater in and crossed to the idling Helio.

"My brother will be here in a few moments," she called out above the noise of the plane. "He's always late. Forgive him. He will be here."

A cab pulled in. A man got out with a small backpack. In the dark, Adriana couldn't make him out, but the sister was familiar and encouraging. The brother wore a ski mask as it was mentioned he would. That wasn't unusual in this weather and definitely not unusual for her client. Adriana paid no attention to it. "We're ready to take off," Adriana told the sister. "The sun will be hitting Denali when we get there. You and your brother can have a good look at it and make your minds up. Your brother plans a dangerous move. He won't need that ski mask today, but he definitely will if he still plans to ski after this reconnaissance. The record low recorded on the high slopes of Mt. McKinley with the wind chill factored in was 118.1 degrees below zero. That was recorded November 30, 2003." The sister shivered noticeably.

"Will your brother have a helicopter ready for a rescue if things screw up when and if he makes the jump?"

"He'll make the jump, but Al won't do that on this trip. At your recommendation, today is just the look."

Adriana was relieved. "He won't be the first to do it anyway. A skier from Switzerland was the first. Has your brother studied the mountain?"

"That's what he's doing with you. It will take a few trips."

"I see."

The brother was rummaging about in the trunk of the cab, picking up, Adriana presumed, equipment, cameras, et cetera. She checked the gauges on the dash one last time. Everything was, as she had expected, in order. She felt the weight of the heavier passenger and his gear adjust in the rear seats of the plane as he buckled up. The client and his sister had not exchanged a word, Adriana noted. *Maybe his voice is strange, too*. The sister leaned forward and said unexpectedly, "Forgive me, Adriana, I'm going to wait for the second flight. Right now, suddenly, I have an upset stomach." She stepped across her brother's outstretched legs, opened the right rear door, and climbed down. She hailed the Fairbanks cab, which hadn't left as yet. "I'll take the cab," she cried above the noise of the plane. "I'll leave the 4x4 for your client—for Al—my brother."

Adriana shrugged. This was nothing unusual. A number of passengers backed out at the last moment. She called the tower for clearance. She got an okay and pushed the throttle forward. The Helio moved out. They were airborne in minutes. Denali's peak gleamed in the distance, a white diamond in the low morning sun. The client behind her was silent under his ski mask. *The awe of this view is enough to silence anyone*, Adriana thought. Contemplating his trip down Denali's steep, icy slopes on skies would be enough to quiet Sylvain Saudan. Adriana wouldn't break it for her client.

Adriana was thrilled, as always, by the magic of flight. It was warm inside the cockpit. Except for Kerns not being with her, it couldn't have been a more beautiful view on a more beautiful day. The darkness was now light. Her life had shaped up. The world was right-side up as well. In the air now and nearing her destination, she stretched back in her seat. Then she was reminded. What was she doing in this fucking corset? Adriana wanted freedom to move. Wearing this damn vest would take some getting used to. It was barely discernible beneath her shirt and flight jacket, but it wasn't looks she was after, it was comfort. Adriana had small breasts and often didn't wear a bra, but this paraphernalia was restricting and uncomfortable. She reached up under her flight jacket to loosen the Velcro shoulder straps. And open the ridged vest.

Adriana paused a moment, thinking about her client. How safe would he feel if he knew she was wearing a bulletproof vest? The .380 was a smaller problem. *Fly and bear it.* She had promised Alice. Adriana settled back into her seat to do just that. She couldn't very well pull the corset off now.

Her client had yet to speak a word. It was a relatively muffled quiet in the cockpit. The erythematic pattern of the throbbing engine fit in with her thinking, yet her thinking didn't fit in with easy conversation. *Al was what the sister called him*, she thought. Then she thought, *Al what? There are a million Als in this world.* It had been a cash deal. No paper asked for. Right now she felt uncomfortable. Albert D. Cummings? The rapist? Question mark indeed.

Alice always did the paperwork, but Alice wasn't here—hadn't been here. Adriana had been spending all her time with Kerns in Slim's cabin on Chena Ridge. That was sweet, but had she just let the business go to hell? There had been no business. She leaned back and called above the purring of the engine: "The earphones and a mike are right above you. If you want to speak, put them on. It will make it easier." He waved his hand—no problem.

Christ, she thought, *he's still got that ski mask on*. Well, that was the deal, ski mask and all. She studied the mask a moment in the rearview mirror. A green color, it was built of silk, or some artificial silk-like material. Dacron, perhaps. It was padded above the bridge of the nose and under the chin. The eyeholes were narrow slits. It was probably a new Massif piece of equipment. He had bubbled goggles strapped above it. Why the hell didn't he take it off? Who was going to see him up here?

Was she getting paranoid? She pushed Cummings out of her mind. Back to business. She wondered what area of North America's highest mountain this Al would like to study. As far as the topography around Denali was concerned, the West Buttress was the easiest access to climb. Not that it was an easy climb, and it would be a son-of-a-bitch to ski down. Even in the winter, snow would have blown from the protruding rock formations. Where the snow did cling for a time it was liable to let go suddenly and cause a small avalanche or whiteout. At lower elevations, where the snow gathered to greater depths, an avalanche could be truly disastrous. On the southwest face the slope was 50 percent or better. Any little thing could set off a major avalanche on the southwest slope. That was the face Sylvain had chosen after a great many hours of study. Sylvain's perception was: "You were on the sharp edge of death if you stayed relatively upright during the descent. If you fell on the way down, you were dead. If an avalanche crested, you rode the wave, or went under. Stay on top." Good advice.

As she flew on, Adriana thought about the mountain and of all the attempts to climb it, successful and otherwise. An Alaskan native by the name of Walter Harper was the first person to reach the summit. The man leading that monumental assault in 1913 was Hudson Stuck. The next attempt was made in 1932. Barbara Washburn, in 1947, was the first woman to reach the 20,320-foot south summit. The north summit was somewhat lower.

These thoughts were running through Adriana's head as she, her plane, and vision-impaired passenger pushed into the 20,000-foot elevation. On the edge of her thinking she felt the darkness closing in. Why? There was a sharp corner here she didn't understand; an emptiness she couldn't comprehend. *How do we move in ignorance?* In her mind Adriana reached out. There was nothing to touch.

She saw movement in the mirror of her mind, a terrible warning that came too late. As they swooped in on the snow-covered southwest face—unending white. The ski mask lifted and a face—not pallid albino, but well recognized—exposed itself. Captain Albert D. Cummings raised from the seat—the sister's brother? He was death at her backside. His sight was healthy and sharp, his face tanned by Texas sun. In Captain Cummings's hand was a large animal stun capsule. Holding it like a dagger, he lunged forward.

***

Instant darkness engulfed Adriana's thinking. All her military martial arts training snapped into focus. Popping her restraining seatbelt, she rose as the needle came down to snap off, lodged in the right shoulder of her protective Kevlar vest. At the same time Adriana drew the .380 Colt. Her thumb flipped the safety off. The laser beam vibrated on Cummings's chest as she fired point-blank three times. He dropped the now useless stun capsule as the sharp, heavy impact of the 9 mm Hydra Shok ammo slammed him back into his seat, stunned perhaps, but very much alive.

Adriana realized her adversary was armor-plated too, a knight of old encased in iron. He sprang forward once again, reaching for her gun. Adriana raised the muzzle. The laser dot came up beneath his chin to rest a split second between his eyes. She fired as her plane rolled out of control. The hollow-point Hydra Shok bullet grazed his forehead, opening up a vivid gash and knocking him unconscious as it did so. Adriana dropped the pistol and stretched for the controls. Her feet were on the roof of the cabin, but she now had the stick in one hand and managed to pull herself back into the seat. It was a sloppy position, but better than it had been. The plane was twisting in the air as it nosedived toward the deep loose snow of the southwest face.

At least I won't die for nothing, was the thought that raced through Adriana's brain. *I'll take this motherfucking spadones with me*. There was no going up. Going down was no choice. Going down she might gather enough speed in this thin atmosphere to pull out of the extreme dive she was in and closing fast with the white below.

Something changed. The white was moving. Mother Nature held the reins. The vibration of the Helio's engine, perhaps even a round from the .380, might have turned the tide and unleashed the delicate 20,000-ton weight of balanced snow. Once started, it rolled like an ocean wave beneath the plane. The Helio responded to Adriana's command. Her plane was pulling slowly out of the terrifying dive. The weight of Cummings's unrestrained body rolling about the cabin behind her seat was no help.

Trying desperately to keep control, Adriana put more pressure on the stick. The skis of her plane actually touched the top of the rolling avalanche beneath her. Looking back for an instant, she saw a second wave on her tail. She pushed the throttle forward. The engine responded, as she rode the crest of white into no man's land.

"Nose up! Nose up, baby," she cried. She felt and heard a dull crash on the tail of her ship. The weight of the heavy crest of snow behind was catching up. Ahead of her a great wall rose. The dead gray of solid rock showed through the white. Then Adriana was blind—flying blind. There was nothing dark here. She didn't dare to wing over sharply. At this slow speed the Helio would go into a slip. If her wing caught in the snow slide she would be tumbled, prop over tail, into oblivion. There was only white, wind, rock, and turmoil. "Full throttle," she cried. "Take an easy blind bank, full throttle, and hope for the best. It's all yours, baby," she spoke to her plane. "Pull me out of this one."

Suddenly the low-lying south sun was in her face. Adriana was sunblind but out of the snow tumbling beneath her. The Helio climbed into the freedom of space. She leaned forward and patted the dash. "Thanks," she said to her plane. "I'll kiss you when we get on the ground." Adriana buckled herself in.

"Nice flying, Major O'Donovan." She looked down. Between the seats the muzzle of her Pocketlite .380 looked hungrily up at her. Behind it was the bloody face of her rapist, Albert D. Cummings. It was a bloody grin he sported, but it was a grin of victory. "Thanks to your wild shot, you just knocked me out for a moment. I'm in pretty good shape, Major." He laughed a bitter laugh. "Perhaps you deserved the rank of major, Captain O'Donovan. Now get us leveled off and we'll put an end to this little charade."

Without time to think, Adriana pulled the stick full back. The plane stood almost directly on its tail, bringing the Helio to stalling speed. The air pressure on the faulty right rear door was drastically reduced. The latch relaxed. The lock, with no pressure against it, opened. She felt the cut of cold wind on her neck. Immediately she tipped the Helio sharply on her right side. The plane slipped rapidly back toward the rolling banks of snow beneath them. Cummings dropped the .380 and grabbed for support. He missed.

"You crazy bitch, you'll kill us both."

"That's the plan. You first, Cummings, and I will be the winner at five to one."

The abrupt angle and sharp descent slammed the captain's full bulk against the faulty rear door. With the weak latch, it couldn't take the sudden weight against it and flung wide into the wind. Cummings was deplaned, clawing at the air for a grip on nothing. He grabbed exactly what he deserved. Screaming, Captain Albert D. Cummings took flight. Adriana pushed the throttle full forward. With the wind now in Adriana's favor, the door slammed shut behind him.

Just feet above the riled power of nature that was eating Cummings, Adriana managed once again to right her ship. "You did it, baby," she spoke to her Helio. "Thanks again. And thank you, Alice, for fixing everything but that fucking door."

Without another word, Adriana set a course for Fairbanks and the light.

***

CHAPTER 20

In Conclusion

It was a Saturday morning. Slim was off duty, but on call. Roy was on the computer. Thelma was having her coffee in bed. It would be a day in her pajamas. She was looking forward to it. She still had not got over the fact that she had mistrusted Slim and deleted the information he was in need of, information he needed to close the case he had been working on for so long. Slim had forgiven her completely and, in the process, asked her to remarry him. Thelma had accepted. The three of them were a family again. Roy was overjoyed. He was going to give the bride away. Kerns would be the best man. Adriana would be the lady in waiting. Hap had purchased a $25 license on the Internet to perform marriage. He would officiate. The big day was tomorrow. The small, private ceremony would take place in the snow at the homestead on Chena Ridge.

Thelma came into the kitchen, the most used room in the house. Roy's laptop was open on the table. The room was empty. Thelma continued down to her office in the basement. Roy was sitting at her big Apple computer, staring at it intently. Slim was standing behind him also studying the large screen. They had not heard Thelma come down.

"What's going on?" she asked in the deep silence. Roy and Slim both jumped. "What am I interrupting, gentlemen?"

Slim spoke up hesitantly. "Roy, our computer genius here, thinks he can bring up the deleted document giving us the information on Midnight Poison, Thelma. If he can, it will be fantastic."

"Slim—sweetheart, we don't want the boy looking at that document." She crossed quickly to the computer. "You mustn't let him see it. It is blatant pornography in the worst taste. Let somebody in your office bring it back."

"You deleted the trash folder, Thelma. Someone in my office might know how to bring it back, but I don't know if I want them to know about it. We don't know what is in that file, Thelma." Slim's wife was wearing that Italian look. Slim didn't exactly know what the hell she was thinking. He did know that if there was a chance of bringing the file up he wanted to see it. "Roy won't have to read it, Thelma."

"Well, this boy is not to even see it!"

"How can I bring her up if I can't see her, Mom?" Roy had not stopped working the keyboard. He knew he now had the problem in hand. It was just a matter of time. "I've already seen what she looks like, Mom."

"When? How?" She turned on Slim. "You got him into this, Slim." A storm was gathering. Thelma was turning an angry shade of red. "Our boy! How could you lead him into this filth—his own father?"

"For God's sake, Mother—"

"Don't you 'mother' me, Roy!"

"Thelma—"

"And don't you 'Thelma' me, Slim!" Thelma actually stamped her bare foot on the concrete floor. "No boy of mine will be exposed to this filth! And that is that!"

"It's your Italian blood, Thelma. Don't get it riled up at a time like this."

Roy was still fingering the keyboard. "Mom," he said, his eyes riveted to the screen. "Jesus, Mom—"

"'Jesus'? Where did you learn that word, Roy?"

"In Sunday School, for Christ's sake. Now, Mom, stop it! I have been looking at porn sites since I was eleven."

"Eleven?" Both parents spoke the word at once. Both were shocked and staring now at their son.

"Well, maybe I was twelve. You and Pop never told me anything about sex, Mom. I had to look it up. You gave birth to a curious child, one with an inquiring mind. I looked it up." Both parents were speechless. Roy leaped from the chair in his excitement. He had succeeded. "Here it is, Pop. I got it. Here is the document you want."

The fantastic body of Midnight Poison stood headless on the screen. "It's a PDF file, Pop. Looks like about eight pages. You know how to move from page to page. I'm going to take Mom upstairs where she will be safe. Come on, Mom!" Roy grabbed his mother by the elbow and guided her from the basement. "Have fun, Pop," he called from the landing. "I'll take care of Mom. You guys are getting married again tomorrow! And that is final!"

Roy closed the door. Slim sat and stared at the screen.

***

It was almost an hour later when Slim came into the kitchen. He was visibly shaken. Thelma and Roy were at the table. They both watched him in silence. Thelma spoke first.

"I'm sorry, Slim. I lost it again. I hope you will let me blame it on my Italian blood." Slim said nothing. "Roy and I had a long talk, Slim. Our boy is a man, Slim. Kerns said it. Although I am sometimes deaf and blind, I know it now."

"We both do, Thelma."

"Pop, what happened? What did you find out?"

"More than I wanted to know, Roy. And more than I want anyone else to ever know. I re-deleted the file. Roy, I want you to go down there and clean that file completely. I don't want anyone to be able to bring it up again. Can you do that, Roy?"

"I can."

"Please do. Right now. Don't look at it! It is information you shouldn't be carrying with you. Not that I don't trust you, Roy, or that it is pornography. It is just that it is dangerous information to have in your possession. It is something I have suspected for some time, but I wish now I had no way to prove it. Justice has been done, but done outside the law. Justice isn't always legal, son."

"Okay, Pop, I won't look at it."

"Thank you, Roy."

The boy went down the stairs to do as he was instructed.

Thelma got up slowly and came to Slim. She had never seen him quite like this. She put her arms around him and held him to her. "It's that bad, Slim? Is it terribly upsetting information?"

"It's fucking awful, Thelma."

"I've never heard you use that word before."

"I've never needed to, Thelma. I am going to bury this information. There is only one person I must tell—then it is gone forever. We will never mention it again." He put his arms around her. "Kiss me, sweetheart. I need you. I'll never leave you."

"I won't leave you either." The kiss was deep with love and silent understanding. "This is forever, Slim."

"Forever, Thelma." Slim turned away and then back to her. "I have broken the law, Thelma."

"But, Slim, you have stood up for the truth, and for justice."

***

Adriana arrived back at the Fairbanks International Airport. She landed without incident and pulled her plane into the hangar. She shut it down and took a long, quiet hour to pull herself together. Her mind made up, she called Slim. When he arrived, Adriana showed him the bullet holes in the Helio and explained the action that had taken place. She had been too complacent with herself and her situation with Kerns to think everything would crumble beneath her. She had been dealing with the sister, a woman, and trusted her. Even at the mention of the brother's name, nothing clicked.

No one showed up to take possession of the Toyota. The vehicle had been left for Al. Captain Albert D. Cummings was the pilot slated to return. The cell number Adriana had for the sister was dead—out of order. Adriana was not surprised. She turned to Slim and leveled with him about Cummings. She gave him Cummings's approximate location on the southwest slope of Mt. McKinley—Denali, as it was now officially named. "He also has an active microchip implant. The military can locate him. Cummings killed Diana," she said to Slim. "He is a proven rapist and murderer. I am the living proof. Cummings came to Fairbanks this time to do me in, to dump me from my own plane onto the killing slopes of Denali."

"Why from a plane?" Slim questioned her.

"It's fashionable up here," Adriana replied. At the mention of Captain Albert D. Cummings, the dark started moving in. Adriana now knew if pushed too far, it would take over.

"I'm a backwoods cop, Adriana. Why did you call me out here? Why not call the FBI? You told me the story of Cummings. I appreciate that. But why me?" Slim could not meet her piercing stare. He turned and faced the bullet-ridden plane. "Why me, Adriana?"

"It's not safe to turn your back on me, Slim. I think you know that. You are a very perceptive man, a man Kerns looks up to. He didn't tell you who his informer was concerning Cummings, but you figured it out. Why do you still have your back turned to me?"

"A hunch." He turned back to Adriana. "I had to prove it true."

"You took a chance."

"Like an uncle of W. C. Fields. It's one of Kerns' favorite stories. Fields' uncle jumped out of an airplane into a hay mow."

"Did he make it?"

"No. But he might have."

Adriana burst out laughing and just as suddenly turned darkly quiet. "You know everything, don't you, Slim?"

"I'm afraid I do. Does he, Kerns, know everything about you, Adriana?"

"He knows a lot."

"Does the site *Sex, Fire & Ice* mean anything to you?"

"I used it to even a score."

"You used it as a lure."

"It worked. The law wouldn't. What I needed was justice. Those five men who raped me needed a good dose of justice, Detective. Maybe what has happened here will help to give rape victims strength to come forward. Do with your knowledge what you will, Slim. The story needs to be told."

"I have destroyed the file sent me by the owner of that site. He has destroyed that file, too. As long as you are here, Adriana, I will never bring it up or pass it on. It is between the two of us and a guy in Cincinnati by the name of—"

"No names, Slim. Am I arrested?"

"No."

"Tell Kerns I won't be able to make it tomorrow. Although by that time he will have figured it out. Don't tell him until tomorrow. And may you and your wife get it right this time, Slim. You are a good man. Kerns is a great man. I will miss him."

"Not as much as he will miss you, Adriana. Must you go?"

"It wouldn't work, Slim. There is still and always will be that bird of darkness circling within me. I am afraid of what she might do."

A 747 lifted off the Fairbanks runway, headed for Germany, L.A., France, or Timbuktu. "I got to pack, Slim. It's getting dark."

"Good luck, Adriana. You will be welcomed back here by all of us."

"Thank you, Slim, but it is not to be."

Slim nodded. Saying nothing, he got in his 4x4 and drove out. Adriana watched him out of sight, then fueled the Helio and took off. She was headed north.

***

After the wedding and no word from Adriana, Kerns called Alice in Oklahoma. He had found her phone number, in Adriana's handwriting, on the desk she and Alice shared. There was no note with it. Alice flew in the following day.

"She is a bird of the darkness, Kerns," Alice told him, "and in that darkness she will disappear. It is the only way she feels she can save the man she loves. When those sons-of-bitches in the military carded the wool, Kerns, it uncovered the dark. It opened a wound that had crusted over. The scab was broken by men she trusted, men she served her country with, Kerns. It was a wound that had healed in Adriana's high school days. Unmolested, it would have stayed that way for all her life. Now it is to dark to heal. There is no place to go, no evading it. Kerns, I loved her too. In my heart and sexually I loved her. My wish was my wish, not hers. Adriana never came to me as such, but that didn't mean my arms weren't open to her—and my heart. Where is she today? Where is which one of her today? I don't know, Kerns. She took both of her personalities with her when she left. The one that hurt you, Kerns, terrified her. Adriana loved you. She trusted you as she trusted me. The difference is—she loved you, Kerns."

"Did I do something wrong?" Kerns asked. Alice reached out and touched Kerns on his whiskered cheek.

"You did nothing wrong, Kerns. I love you, too, as a friend, and as a lover of my soul. Don't go into the darkness, Kerns. You won't find her. But you can tell her story. Do all women a favor, Kerns. Write Adriana's story so others will know her agony and her pain, so their minds and hearts can profit by it. You already have the title. Write it for her, for Adriana, so her life will not have been in vain. So all women will have the strength to speak out. Write the book, Kerns. Write the book. You have the title—*Birds of Darkness*. Write the book!"

***

Adriana's Helio Courier H295 was found intact on a snow-covered gravel bank of the Colville River. The gas tank had been drained. No trace of Adriana has ever been found.

THE END
Fairbanks Alaska 2016

***

Review Requested:

If you loved this book, would you please provide a review at Amazon.com?

CPSIA information can be obtained at www.ICGtesting.com
Printed in the USA
LVOW11s1653240416

485095LV00003B/215/P